Into the Wonder
Book 1

Children
of Pride

Into the Wonder, Book 1:
Children of Pride

Copyright © 2014 by Darrell J. Pursiful.

Published by Puggle Press

ISBN: 978-0615959887

For my cheerleaders,

Rebecca and Connie

Acknowledgements

Children of Pride began with a problem: how to keep my brilliant middle-schooler, who already reads at a high-school level, properly stocked with books that are appropriate for her stage of life and experience and yet don't talk down to her?

Friends who are teachers and librarians have been a constant and deeply appreciated source of guidance for my wife and me in facing this most wonderful problem. Some of their suggestions have been spot on. Others, maybe not so much—but thanks anyway for your help and encouragement!

Eventually, I started supplementing whatever treasures we could find at the library with little stories of my own—mainly Harry Potter fanfics (do I know my audience or what?). And since I have several friends who appreciate good teen/young adult fiction and share my (and Rebecca's) love of the fantasy genre(s), I usually asked one or two people to read behind me and help clean up my messes.

To make a long story short, somebody thought I might be on to something with my latest effort. It was suggested that I release it into the wild and see what happens. That's what you are currently holding in your hands or reading on your screen.

First of all, then, I must thank by daughter, Rebecca, for rekindling my own childhood love of fantasy fiction, and my wife, Connie, for putting up with all those extra hours I've spent on the computer the past year or so.

Thanks as well go to Jeremy Samples, Jennifer Becton, and Katie Brookins for reading *Children of Pride* and offering their encouragement and suggestions for improvement.

Dave Jones from ebooksbydave.com has been a treasure. I never could have gotten this project done as quickly or as easily without him in my corner. The cover illustration by Barclay Burns is all I hoped it would be. Thanks, guys, for making me look good!

Finally, a word of gratitude for Jo, Jack, Rick, Angie, Tollers, and all the other great writers of fantasy who have brightened my sweet girl's childhood, broadened her horizons, and, along the way, reawakened the kid in me.

Table of Contents

Chapter 1

Just Another Switch-Out

Danny slipped through the brush as silently as a gentle breeze, nearly invisible in the twilight. He breathed deep the crisp springtime air as he skipped over the tiny stream behind the house and crept up the slope of the hill to the chain-link fence at the edge of the property. His partner was already waiting for him. Danny pulled his Atlanta Braves ball cap down over his black, curly hair.

"Where've you been?" Bryn asked. She had that look again—the one that said, "What did I ever do to draw Danny Underhill as a partner?"

"There was a...Actually, I kind of..."

"Got distracted? What was it this time?"

"Squirrel," Danny said, shuffling his feet.

Bryn looked at him with both exasperation and endearment. "Well, at least you're here now."

"Anything to report?"

Bryn shook her head. "Pretty quiet. I thought I heard something in the woods a half-hour ago. It was just a bird."

"Are you sure?"

"Mostly sure," Bryn confessed. She turned back toward the back yard. "I swear," she sighed, "we should have switched her out a month ago."

"Mrs. Redmane said we had to be sure," Danny protested. "Given the circumstances..."

"I know, Danny," Bryn said. She smiled, and Danny's heart jumped just a little. Then again, Brynhilde Delling seemed to have that effect on everything with an Adam's apple. She tossed back her head in a way that made her golden hair seem to dance in the moonlight.

Crickets chirped. Somewhere, someone was grilling steaks. Danny realized he was hungry. The cafeteria food he had been eating for lunch the past few weeks never seemed to fill him up. Hopefully, all that would change tomorrow afternoon. He tried not to dwell on how much was riding on this assignment. He certainly couldn't afford to think about the news he had just received.

No, best not to dwell on how this entire mission might be the death of him. Let Bryn think he was late because he got distracted by a squirrel. He kept telling himself—and Bryn—that it was just another switch-out. He'd done this plenty of times. No biggie. He was even starting to believe it himself.

"Are you listening?" Bryn asked. Apparently, Danny wasn't.

"Uh," he said.

"I said I'll keep my distance till you call me. She knows you, after all."

"Sounds good," Danny said. "We don't want to spook her. Well, any more than is necessary, anyway." He gazed across the back yard toward the modest house. He pulled back as he got a little too close to the fence. Cold shivers spread in a wave up his arms and down his spine.

A light flicked on in the back bedroom. A young girl entered the room. Thin. Pale-skinned. A little on the tall side for her age—in fact, she was exactly the same height as Danny. Her long, straight hair that was not quite blonde and not quite brown hung loosely over her shoulders.

Behind her came another girl with caramel-colored skin and her hair in beaded braids. This second girl smiled at the first as they both plopped their backpacks on the bed.

"I just hope I don't have to get between her and her friend," Danny said. "That girl makes me nervous."

"What do you mean? She can't know anything."

"She doesn't like me," Danny said. "I'm not sure why." He wondered if she did know the truth about him. She didn't show up in any of the background checks, but background checks could be wrong. Things can get lost in the shuffle—otherwise they wouldn't be in this mess!

"You're imagining things," Bryn said. "It's not worth getting all worked up over some Jack kid."

"Yeah." Danny was not so sure. The truth was, he couldn't afford for anything to go wrong. Not now. He glanced at Bryn. She couldn't possibly know how much was on the line—what Danny was planning, and how much might be riding on the skinny girl in the back bedroom.

Focus! he told himself. *Only one more to go. You've got to get this right.*

"I'll talk to her in the park. It's usually pretty empty right after school. Then I'll take her to meet you at the ring."

"What about the other one?"

Danny sighed. "I'll play that by ear. If I have to, I'll arrange for her to go home early."

"Just don't give her anything too serious," Bryn said. "We need a clean ledger on this one. Nobody owes anything to anybody."

"I've done this before, you know," Danny said with a huff.

"I know you have," Bryn said. "You're in charge. I'm your backup."

"Right," Danny said. "But that means if anything goes wrong, it ain't your tail on the line, it's mine."

"And a fine, waggly tail it is," Bryn said, smiling. "You'll do fine. Like you say, this is just another switch-out. You're the expert. I'm just the placeholder until she makes her decision."

"About that: do you need anything else to pull it off?"

"Give me a heads-up tomorrow when you see what she's wearing. I can handle it from there."

"Are you sure? Honestly, Bryn. I'm asking a lot of you here. You've got to be perfect. What if somebody doesn't buy it? It could be a disaster! They'd call in the police, maybe even the

FBI." That would be a total disaster: guns, handcuffs...maybe even riding in a car! Danny shuddered at the thought. He found he had been drained of whatever optimism he had managed to gin up.

Then again, if Danny had to choose between the FBI and an angry Mrs. Redmane, he'd take the FBI any day of the week! *One last switch-out and I've fulfilled my contract,* he told himself. *One last switch-out and I'm free. Unless, of course, the whole thing blows up in my face.*

"Piece of cake," Bryn smiled, oblivious to Danny's concerns. "It could be fun. It's been a long time since I was a teenager."

"You've never been a teenager like her!" Danny scoffed.

"How different could it be?" Bryn pouted.

"Trust me, I've been living around them practically since Imbolc. They're not like us, Bryn."

"Then Taylor Smart's life is about to get very interesting," Bryn said with a twinkle in her eye.

"You can say that again!"

"Well, then, it looks like we're all set," Bryn said. "What do you say we stop by the drugstore and see if they've got any new teen music magazines. I'm still a little shaky on a couple of those boy bands you've told me about."

"All right," Danny said. "But just for a few minutes. I gotta study for a history test." He glanced at the light in the back bedroom window one last time.

He nodded to his partner. Then they both vanished silently into the gathering darkness.

"Somebody's out there," Jill Matthews said. She peered over Taylor's shoulders.

"You're seeing things," Taylor said as she drew the blinds of her bedroom. "There's nothing back there but woods. You must have seen a bird or maybe a deer."

"Right, 'cause the brilliant Taylor Smart has never been wrong about anything in her life."

4

Taylor just glared at her.

"Okay, that was cold. I'm sorry."

"Don't worry about it," Taylor said. She sat on her bed. Jill pulled up the desk chair and used the bed as a footstool.

"How long till you have to go home?"

Jill checked the time on her cell phone. "About an hour. Do you think we could do some geometry now? It was why I came over, you know."

"I thought it was for my mom's spaghetti," Taylor said. She leaned over to grab her backpack from the edge of the bed. She reached in for her math workbook.

"Well, that too."

"Okay. Geometry," Taylor said. "But admit it, you'd rather sit here and talk about Uncle Waldo."

"Taylor!" Jill threatened to throw her own workbook at her friend.

Uncle Waldo was Taylor and Jill's pet name for the creepy guy who had been hanging out in the park lately, a pasty-white old man who always dressed in black.

"I'm telling you," Jill said, "that guy is definitely up to something. He looks like a serial killer or something."

"Oh? And how many serial killers have you met lately?"

"You know what I mean."

"Jill, he's just a reject from a mental hospital somewhere. Sure, he's creepy, but he's perfectly harmless."

"Whatever," Jill said.

"Unless, of course, he's a foreign spy trying to steal Mom's spaghetti recipe."

Jill gave Taylor a sour look.

"Oooh! Or maybe he's an alien shapeshifter who's lost contact with the mother ship... Or a vicious monster on his way to a Cannibals Anonymous meeting!"

"That's enough, Taylor. I get your point."

"He could be the ghost of an evil mortician...or a zombie...or a Justin Bieber fan! But I shouldn't repeat myself..."

"Give it up, okay?" Jill said. She fumbled through her math worksheets. Taylor pulled back. She knew her friend could only take so much of her teasing.

"You've got to admit, though," Jill said. "He's a little strange."

"Yeah," Taylor said. "But not 'vicious criminal' strange. More like 'drools and talks to himself' strange. Or maybe 'dorky brother' strange." Taylor winked.

Jill grinned. "I'll be sure and tell William you're thinking of him."

Taylor stuck out her tongue.

"Which reminds me. You never said if you're going to Jared's party this Saturday."

Taylor sighed. "Probably not."

"Oh, come on! Do you know how long it took to convince my parents to let me go? 'Who are this Jared boy's parents?'" she imitated her mother. "'Where do they go to church? He doesn't get into any trouble at school, does he?' I swear, I'm surprised they didn't get the police to run a background check on him."

Taylor realized this was one of those times she probably ought to keep her mouth shut. Amazingly, she found it in her to do so. It didn't help.

"I don't suppose *your* parents gave *you* the third degree?" Jill said.

"My dad is his folks' accountant," Taylor said. "I think he's pretty sure they're not drug dealers or anything." She made a point of burying her face in her math book. "Look, if you want to go, just go. You already said your parents are okay with it."

"Barely. They'd feel better if they knew my best friend was going, too."

"I just haven't decided yet, okay?"

"But I don't want to go by myself!"

"Isn't William invited?"

"That's not what I meant," Jill said. "Come on. It'll be fun."

"Yeah, well." Taylor studied the floor. Then the walls. Anything to keep from making eye contact.

"Okay, so you're not the most sociable person in the world," Jill said. "It's really not that bad. Would it kill you to go eat some cake and ice cream?" She leaned in conspiratorially. "I notice the way you look at Jared at school, you know."

"Don't even start," Taylor said, her cheeks reddening. Jill started to giggle, but Taylor pressed on. "Besides, you know I...I don't like parties. I never know what to say. Nobody else is into the same things I am. I'm afraid people are talking about me. Laughing at me."

"What am I going to do with you?" Jill said, shaking her head. "This is Jared McCaughey we're talking about. You know the kids he hangs out with. He's not going to invite any of those glamour school rejects who are always cracking on you. Just say you're going, okay? I really want you to be there. Dad can drive us."

"We'll see."

There didn't seem any point to arguing, so Taylor held her piece, and she and Jill dove into their homework.

Chapter 2

The Man in Black

The next day started badly. Taylor got a text from Jill. She had woken up with a fever and a stomachache—probably the flu. She wouldn't be going to school today. Taylor would have to walk to school without her. That wasn't usually a problem except that, apart from lunch, the walk to and from school was the only time Taylor and Jill could properly make fun of their teachers and classmates. Some of them desperately needed making fun of.

Which led to Taylor's second problem. At breakfast her dad practically begged her not to get into any more trouble with Mrs. Markowitz, her English teacher. The old biddy had it in for Taylor ever since last September, when she complained, often and audibly, about the novels they were reading. It only got worse when they started a unit on "Technical Writing" last month. Although it fulfilled all the requirements of the assignment, Taylor's sample complaint letter to the Board of Education about the quality of teachers they were hiring might have hit a little too close to home. Now they had begun a unit on myths and fables—something Taylor actually enjoyed—but Mrs. Markowitz seemed determined to do her best to suck every last drop of wonder from the subject.

"Sometimes you've just got to let things go," her dad said. "Seventh grade won't last forever."

"Are you sure about that?" she scoffed.

"Positive. Come here." He opened his arms and invited Taylor to sit in his lap. Taylor didn't move. Sometime before Christmas, she had decided she was too grown up for such things. Her dad gave her a sad expression. He wasn't mad at her, she knew, he just didn't know quite what to do with her now that she was officially a teenager.

Mom came to his rescue. "All we're trying to say, honey, is that part of this is up to you. All of your teachers think very highly of you. They just wish you'd—"

"Apply myself? Take school more seriously?"

"Well, yes," Dad said, dropping his arms. "Taylor, right now, school is your job, and you need to start thinking of it that way."

"It would help if my 'job' weren't so boring!"

Dad sighed. "Every job in the world is boring some of the time. Do you think doing people's taxes is a nonstop thrill ride? Do you think Mom has a party every day as Mr. Caulfield's office manager?"

"No."

"I understand you haven't had the greatest year in school, but you still have to go. So, if there's no way around your problem, and no way over it or under it, you know what you have to do, right? You're just going to have to put your head down and go straight through the middle of it."

And with that pep talk, Taylor trudged off to another fun-filled day at Archibald Bulloch Middle School.

Uncle Waldo, the crazy old man in the black suit, was sitting on the park bench again, scaring away the pigeons. There was definitely something odd about that guy. Taylor had noticed him hanging out in the park for a couple of weeks now. All alone, never speaking to anyone except himself.

She picked up her pace the slightest bit. Not because she was scared of Uncle Waldo, of course, but because she really didn't want to walk to school with Jill's twin brother William, who was only a hundred yards behind her.

The real fun began when she got to school. Reggie Banks dropped a whole handful of sheet music in Chorus, so when Taylor finally got her copy, it had somebody's dirty shoe print all over it. As she and her classmates sang "'Tis the gift to be simple," she tickled herself with the thought some people were apparently more gifted than others.

Everybody was late for first period because a couple of eighth-graders got in a fight in the hallway.

The pizza in the cafeteria was greasier than usual—but still a better option than the overcooked-and-always-too-salty barbeque sandwiches.

And Jill wasn't around to help Taylor complain about any of it.

As might have been expected, third period was the worst. Mrs. Markowitz was in rare form. When the bell rang, she called Taylor up to her desk to discuss the homework assignment she had just returned.

"I give up," she began. She didn't even rise from her chair. "I've tried befriending you. I've tried encouraging you. I've tried having conferences with your parents. I've even tried threats. Nothing seems to get through to you."

It was all Taylor could do not to grin at the ridiculous shade of red of her English teacher's hair. The poor woman apparently didn't want anyone to know she was gray—probably had been for the last fifty years—but she never managed to buy the same brand of hair dye twice. Today, her hair was more violently red than usual. Actually, it was bordering on purple. That was appropriate, Taylor thought, as it pretty much matched the color the veins on her face were turning.

"This should have been a simple assignment for a bright girl like you. All you had to do was write a three-page summary of the major gods of Greek mythology."

"But that's what I did," Taylor protested. She held up her paper with the "C-" written across the top in very large, very angry red pen strokes. She resisted the urge to shove it in her teacher's face.

Mrs. Markowitz scoffed. "Two pages and only three lines onto the third page!"

"It's still three pages," Taylor said.

"In sixteen-point type?"

"Fourteen, and I don't remember you saying anything about font size when you gave the assignment."

"It is *assumed* that papers are to be printed in twelve-point type."

"Well, you know what they say about what happens when people assume."

Mrs. Markowitz seethed. Taylor's lips began to curl into a subtle grin. She absolutely hated her English teacher. Knowing she was getting under Mrs. Markowitz's skin was like a shark smelling blood in the water.

"Taylor, why must you always behave as if you're smarter than everyone else at this school—your teachers included?"

Taylor shrugged. An honest answer would not have been terribly diplomatic at that point. She congratulated herself on being able to hold her peace. Instead, she pushed on at her strongest angle of attack.

"Did I leave out any Greek gods that you consider to be 'major,' Mrs. Markowitz?"

"Of course not," she said. "You got all the Olympians and several others beside. But—"

"And I notice you haven't highlighted any spelling or grammar mistakes. So I take it you have no complaints in that area?"

"Miss Smart—"

"And you have to admit I gave you the three-page summary you asked for. The page numbers are all right there at the bottom. You never said we had to write three *whole* pages."

"Don't try to twist my words, Miss Smart. You know precisely what this assignment entailed. You could have done it properly in your sleep, yet—once again—it seems you've put more effort into intentionally misunderstanding my instructions than you have into completing your work. You'll be off to high school in another couple of years, and I can assure you that coasting along on your natural intelligence and hoping for a passing grade with the least amount of effort won't get you very far."

"With all due respect, Mrs. Markowitz, why shouldn't it? You only teach what's going to be on the state assessment tests anyway."

"That is not true!"

Then why couldn't we ever do anything different? I've already read just about everything there is about Greek mythology in the public library. But every time I brought up any of the really cool stuff in class, you shut me down."

"The 'cool stuff' as you call it is not suitable for a class full of impressionable twelve- and thirteen-year-olds."

"That's why I offered to write a summary of some other mythology. If the rest of the class needed the basics, then why not let me learn about the gods of the Egyptians or the Vikings? Anything but the same boring stuff I've already heard about since I first read *The Children's Homer*!

"Miss Smart, we are not going to rehash that conversation—"

"Of course we're not. Because the truth is, you only teach what the big shots in Atlanta tell you to. That's why everybody in the seventh grade is doing the exact same lessons in the exact same way at the exact same time. Oh, you may say you want your students to be creative and love learning. Heck, you might even think you mean it. But let's face it, Mrs. Markowitz, you just want us to score well on the test so you'll look like you've done your job."

"That is enough of that, Miss Smart!"

"I'm only following your exact words," Taylor mumbled.

"And I'm only giving you the grade your pitiful efforts deserve."

The two glared at each other for several tense seconds until students began to file into the classroom. "You'll be late for your next class," Mrs. Markowitz said. The conversation, it seemed, was over.

Taylor didn't mind the C-minus on her English paper, but she knew her parents were going to blow a gasket. Every report card, they had the same argument. "You're a smart girl," they would say. "Your teachers all say you're very bright. Would it hurt you to try a little bit harder?"

The truth was, Taylor thought it probably would. Simply put, school was boring. It didn't matter that she could usually get B's in every class while barely trying. She had figured out a long time ago that nobody was ever going to teach her the things she was most interested in. When Mr. Barfield explained geometry, she wanted to know how his proofs about different kinds of angles would work if the triangles were drawn on a sphere instead of a flat surface. "You'll get to that in college," he said. Well, she was interested in that now!

That's why she was so angry with Mrs. Markowitz. If she really was so far ahead of her classmates, what harm could there be in letting her study something that actually interested her? Instead, she had to write yet another brain-numbing report about stuff she had known since forever.

Taylor mostly quit caring about grades and schoolwork around the fourth grade. She had hoped her Greek mythology paper would be her crowning achievement: a paper written in one night with no prior research at all—just what was already in her head. She found it much more challenging—exciting, in fact—to wait until the last minute to finish her assignments, just to see if she could still land a good grade. And of course, she usually could.

A C-minus was not her definition of a good grade. She wondered how much trouble she was going to be in when she got home.

First, however, she had to get through fourth period. After Mrs. Markowitz's impromptu meeting, she was almost certain to be late. She weaved through the corridors, trying not to get crushed as she made her way to Mr. Barfield's room.

As Taylor navigated the halls, she tried to keep her head down, braced against any idiot classmates who weren't looking where they were going. Of course, some of them knew exactly where they were going but found ways to bump into her anyway. That came with the territory, Taylor supposed. Middle school was hard enough for a natural loner like her. It didn't help that she was also pale, scrawny, and asthmatic.

"You *did* get my invitation, right?" a girl called ahead of her. Taylor looked up in surprise, only to see it was Shelby Crowthers. Thankfully, she was talking to somebody else. "Dad has reserved a room at the country club for Saturday night. It's going to be the best birthday party ever! It'll be a hundred times better than Jared's lame party."

Shelby Crowthers was pretty, popular, and rich—all the things Taylor wasn't. Naturally, they hated each other. Taylor considered one of the high points of her year to be last September when she convinced her dad *not* to buy a car from Shelby's dad's car dealership—even though it boasted some of the best deals in central Georgia.

If only she could convince Mr. Crowthers to move to Australia.

Taylor wasn't in a mood for a fight, but Shelby was standing in front of Mr. Barfield's room, and the bell was going to ring any second. She didn't have a choice but to wait there for her to finish arranging her social calendar. She probably should have kept her mouth shut, but she just couldn't help herself.

"How inconsiderate of Jared to have a birthday the same week as yours," she mocked.

"Jared's party is fine with me," Shelby sniffed. "It'll just make it that more obvious who is who. The cool kids will be with me at the country club. The rest of you losers will just have to hope for the best."

"All I'm hoping for is that you would just go away."

"Dream on, honey. And are they ever going to do something about those eyes of yours?"

Taylor blushed. Shelby had said since third grade that Taylor's eyes were funny. They were too far apart, she said, and Taylor looked like she was part goldfish. Plus, they weren't a deep, pretty blue like Shelby's, but washed-out and pale.

She sighed, rolled her not-pretty eyes, and sidestepped Shelby to enter the classroom. Shelby and her best friend,

Jasmine, followed behind, along with Danny Underhill, Jared McCaughey, and the rest of the stragglers.

She took her usual seat in the back row and wished again that her best friend didn't have the flu. Even though Jill's brother William (never "Bill") was kind of a dork, she and Jill had been best friends since fourth grade. The two girls lived across the street from each other. Jill would understand about Mrs. Markowitz. She was always there to listen to Taylor gripe—and to smack some sense into her when necessary.

"C'mon, your life is pretty good," she could hear Jill say. "You're super-smart, and really good at music and stuff. Plus, you've got about the coolest parents ever."

The last part, which Jill never failed to point out, was the subject of ongoing debate between them. Jill insisted Taylor's parents were much cooler than her own. Taylor wished they weren't quite as strict and had a little bit more money. Though she had to admit she always knew her parents were in her corner, no matter what. They had fun family vacations every summer, and visits to Grandma Smart's house for Christmas were definitely the best.

But on top of everything was the fact that they had chosen her.

Nobody knew anything about her biological parents. Taylor figured they were probably unmarried teenagers who at least had the sense to know they had no business trying to raise a baby. Whatever the case, the Smarts were her parents now—not because they had to be, but because they wanted to be. And stern lectures about schoolwork aside, most days that was something for which Taylor was very grateful.

Taylor came up from her daydream enough to realize that her balding, ruddy-faced teacher was already well into his geometry lecture. He had written about half a dozen diagrams on the board and a whole list of things that looked like they were important. Taylor jotted them down, half-listening to whatever it was Mr. Barfield was rambling on about. She figured out what page she was supposed to be on and scrambled to open her textbook without anyone noticing she was coming late to the game.

After about thirty minutes, he gave them a set of problems to work. Taylor finished them all in about fifteen. Most of her classmates would be taking at least a few of them home for homework.

She counted down the minutes until the last bell. Without Jill there, she had no one to pass notes to or to help her make fun of Shelby behind her back. Mr. Barfield was bent over Tommy Morgan's desk, explaining basic geometry to the poor boy for what must have been the hundredth time.

She looked out the window. The sky was sunny and clear, but a stiff breeze blew through the trees. The school grounds-keeper was mowing the grass outside her window.

Across the street, a fat lady in neon pink sweat pants was walking her poodle. A funny-looking guy in a dark suit stood on the corner as if he was lost. Taylor realized it was Uncle Waldo. *What is he doing out there?* she thought. That alien undead Justin Bieber fan was really starting to creep her out.

She wondered if he was one of those guys her Dad always slammed the door on when they came by wanting to tell them about their religion, but those types always seemed to travel in pairs. No, Taylor couldn't imagine Uncle Waldo having any friends. And she definitely didn't want to join any religion that would have him as a member. It was almost spooky the way he always seemed to show up lately. She wasn't sure, but she thought she had even noticed him ducking around the corner of the restaurant when her folks went out for dinner last Sunday. Taylor's neck hairs tickled her collar.

The lady's dog nipped at Uncle Waldo, who bent down and yelled something. Fifi (or whatever its name was) twisted its leash around its human's legs, and she nearly fell over. Taylor couldn't help but giggle, and the spell of dread was broken. It was a perfect April afternoon, after all, and she couldn't wait to enjoy it.

"Taylor?" Danny Underhill whispered. Danny was about Taylor's height, his nose was a bit large, and currently there was a pimple on the inside thatch of his bushy eyebrow that was threatening to erupt. Taylor had been worried since February that Danny had a crush on her.

She glanced in his direction.

"Is this right?" He scooted a piece of paper her way. Taylor gave it a cursory glance and scooted it back to him with a nod.

Five minutes until the bell.

Jill always asked Taylor to look over their homework. As much as Taylor loved her, the girl couldn't do math to save her life. Taylor never minded helping out her few friends, but it was just fine with her that nobody else seemed to notice how smart she was.

Nobody except for Danny Underhill.

Danny was a transfer student from some place up north. His family moved to Macon shortly after her birthday in February—which seemed weird, but whatever. She didn't know much about him except that he seemed like a nice enough kid in a geeky, no-social-skills sort of way. But he was always looking for an excuse to start up a conversation with her. Taylor had spent the last two months trying not to encourage him.

"Thanks," he said.

"Don't mention it."

"Mr. Underhill? Miss Smart? Do you need my help?" Mr. Barfield said.

"N-no, Mr. Barfield," Danny said. "I think I've got it now."

"Losers," Shelby muttered.

"I'll have none of that!" Mr. Barfield said. He had pretty good hearing for an old guy.

Taylor noticed Jared McCaughey glancing at her from across the room. He smiled at her, and she immediately plunged her nose into her homework. Her face turned red, but she couldn't help but smile. If only *he* would ask her for help with his schoolwork!

The bell rang as Mr. Barfield reminded them about the test coming up tomorrow. If anybody heard him, they didn't let on. Rather, everybody bolted for the door like horses at the starting gate in the Kentucky Derby.

In a matter of minutes, she was at her locker. Directly across the hall, Danny fumbled with his combination.

"So, Taylor," a voice behind her called. It was Shelby again. Of course. "Do you have plans this weekend with your *boyfriend*?"

"Who—?" Taylor began, but Shelby's giggles signaled that something was up. Danny, still trying to get his locker open, turned several shades of pink all at once.

"I'd take him if I were you," Shelby said. "I mean, it's not like *you* can afford to be choosy! And is it just me, or have your ears gotten bigger since last year?"

Shelby was joined by her best friend, Jasmine Brown.

"What do you think, Dannyboy?" Jasmine said. "You want to ask her out?"

If anything, Danny turned ever redder. He finally got his locker open, but that only made things worse. Danny had one of the messiest lockers in school. As soon as the door flung open, a stack of textbooks and loose papers plopped to the floor.

"Cut it out, Shelby," Taylor said through gritted teeth.

"Hey, we're just trying to help," Shelby teased. "We know it's hard for *some* girls to get a boyfriend. If we can nudge things along..."

Taylor rounded on Shelby, and there was something different in her voice, an unexpected power or confidence. "I said, *Cut it out.*"

Her blue eyes turned icy cold. Shelby and Jasmine turned suddenly pale. Jasmine leaned on Shelby for support, as if her legs had turned to jelly. Both girls' mouths dropped open.

"C-come on, Jasmine."

They silently slinked away without another word.

Taylor stood there, dumbfounded. "That was interesting," she said to herself.

"Whoa," Danny sighed. "That's some kind of death-glare you've got. Think you could teach me?"

"I...uh...No."

She grabbed what she needed from her locker and joined the small clutch of kids streaming out the main entrance.

This wasn't the first time Taylor had been able to scare off somebody who was bothering her. Last winter, she did the same thing to Cassie White. Cassie was giving her a hard time in the girl's locker room after gym class. Taylor had a note from her doctor that excused her from activities whenever her asthma was acting up, and Cassie was teasing her about not being any good at sports. Taylor got so frustrated she felt like she could shoot laser beams out of her eyes. One look and Cassie choked up. She just walked away on the verge of tears.

And then there was the time she was home alone with her mom one afternoon and a vacuum-cleaner salesman showed up at their door. Mom was busy cooking supper, and Taylor learned the hard way that vacuum-cleaner salesmen didn't like to take "no" for an answer. Then she looked him square in the eye and said, "I told you, *We're not interested.*" The poor man dropped his clipboard as he retreated across the lawn.

"Death-glare," Danny called it.

Most kids had to wait for the bus or for their parents to pick them up in the carpool line. Taylor lived less than a mile from school, so she walked home. Usually, it was just her and Jill.

The quickest way home was through the park three or four blocks from the schoolhouse. On a nice day like today, she and Jill loved to watch the birds and the squirrels, maybe sit and talk on the swings.

Today, there were just a couple of moms with preschoolers.

Something distracted her, a movement in the trees. She couldn't put her finger on it, but something was wrong. She suddenly had goosebumps all over her arms despite the warm afternoon sun. She took in her surroundings, and though nothing seemed out of the ordinary, she couldn't shake the feeling that she was being watched.

Taylor pressed on. She made a point to steer as clear of the trees as she could. Whatever it was, it was hiding in those trees. Another hundred feet and she would be past the park and only a block from her house.

Then the stranger came into view from the other direction. He was tall, pale, with a sour expression on his face.

It was Uncle Waldo.

He scowled at Taylor and broke into a trot.

Taylor gasped and started to run, but he was too fast—faster than should have been possible. In an instant he had grabbed her by the arm and pulled her off the path and into the trees. She tried to scream, but he clamped his hand tightly across her mouth before she even knew what was happening. She tried to kick, but he was too strong.

He threw her onto the ground. As she looked up, the stranger was standing nearly on top of her. Something about him had changed, and not in a good way. He was still tall and dressed all in black, like undertakers always dressed in the old Westerns her Grandpa Miller liked to watch. But now she could see he was carrying an empty burlap sack in his hand. What most concerned Taylor, however, was the man's face.

His skin was mottled gray with splotches of pink, and his bushy unibrow made him look like he was wearing a fur-lined sun visor. His teeth were yellow and misshapen. There was a hard, brown wart on the end of his chin.

"Easy does it, *chica*. I don't want to hurt you," the man hissed.

He grinned a disgusting, toothy grin and reached toward her. Then he fell back, bowled over by dog that had appeared out of nowhere. It was lanky and medium sized with a tapering snout and short black fur. A Labrador retriever?

The dog chomped down on the strange man's right hand, the one that held the sack. He fell to the ground, roaring in anger and pain, but the dog didn't let go. It growled and shook its head back and forth. Taylor inched away and hid behind the nearest tree. Something in the back of her head told her to run, but she couldn't convince her body to cooperate.

Uncle Waldo threw off the dog, which yelped as it hit the ground. He rose to one knee, nursing his arm.

Somehow the dog disappeared, but in its place crouched Danny Underhill. "Back off!" he yelled. Uncle Waldo growled. Taylor's head swam.

"Oh...my..." she whispered.

Danny sprung forward, and this time Taylor saw him change. In midair, his face lengthened into a muzzle. His body shifted, compacted. His khakis and red polo shirt were overrun with sleek, black fur, and his hands and feet turned into paws. By the time he bowled into the stranger, he had turned back into a dog!

Uncle Waldo rolled on the ground, trying to regain his footing. The black Lab grabbed the tail of his coat in his teeth and held on tight. His eyes glowed like there was a fire inside his skull and his eyes were glass windows tinted yellow.

The stranger pulled himself out of his coat. The dog—could this really be Danny Underhill?—spat it out, growled, and bared his fangs. Uncle Waldo lifted his hands to shield himself from the next attack. And attack Danny did. He pounced on the stranger again. This time, the man with the sack took a bite to his throat and fell back bleeding. He shouted in fury, then threw the dog off him and scrambled away.

By this time, Taylor was hyperventilating. She sat on the ground at the base of her tree as Danny, who had once again turned into Danny, ran to her.

"Are you alright?" he asked.

Chapter 3

A Change of Plans

Taylor could do nothing but stare at Danny, trembling. She managed a nod. She hoped she wasn't having an asthma attack.

Her classmate reached into his pocket and pulled out a rock. He stared at it while intoning a name: "Brynhilde Delling. Brynhilde Delling. Brynhilde Delling." Then he breathed on it and spoke into it as if he were talking to someone.

"Bryn!" he said. "We've got trouble. A bag-man just tried to grab Taylor in the park!" Something flitted across Taylor's field of vision, like a sudden burst of light that vanished as soon as it appeared. Danny turned to Taylor. "Okay, be calm. Help is on the way."

"What...? What...?"

"Look," Danny said. "I realize this is all very sudden. This wasn't how it was supposed to.... What are you looking at?"

Taylor had finally begun to process what her eyes were telling her. Danny wasn't...Danny. He wore the same school clothes he had on all day, he had the same black curly hair, but his face was much older than any seventh-grader's, and he no longer looked entirely human. His nose was even longer than usual. His eyes had changed color: they weren't the familiar weird amber color she was used to. They had brightened all the way up to a *creepy* amber color that was almost yellow, and his ears—good grief!— his ears were pointed.

"Okay, Taylor," he said, extending a hand to her shoulder. She flinched, and he withdrew it. "I'm going to try to explain. We were sent to collect you. We wanted to take this easy, so—"

23

"Wait," Taylor said, "We? Who's 'we'?"

There was a sound of footsteps behind her. Taylor craned her neck around the tree to see a girl sprinting to meet them.

"Taylor, this is my partner, Bryn."

The first thing Taylor noticed about Bryn wasn't her expression of concern but rather how *perfect* she looked. Blonde hair, blue eyes, perfect skin, probably old enough to be in college. She wore the same kind of skirt and polo shirt Taylor had on, but on Bryn, the Bulloch Middle School dress code actually looked good. Taylor couldn't help but imagine how the idiot boys in her class would be falling over themselves trying to look cool in front of a girl like that. Something about her gave off a vibe that said she was good-looking and she knew it. There was confidence and grace in the way she moved, despite Danny's obvious panic.

But there was also definitely something odd about her—wild, dangerous, somehow powerful.

Then she noticed the tail.

Dangling below the hem of her skirt, plain as day, Bryn had a cow's tail that nervously swished back and forth.

"What...?"

"Hi, Taylor. Danny's told me all about you," Bryn smiled. She brushed back her hair, and Taylor noticed her ears were also pointed. Not as much as Danny's, but more than they should be. Her thoughts turned to elves in Christmas movies.

To Danny, Bryn said, "What do you mean, a bag-man? What's a bag-man doing here?"

"How should I know?" Danny said, obviously flustered. "If somebody else is after her..."

"Not cool," Bryn said. "How did he get so close?"

"He was shapeshifting," Danny said, looking at the ground. "I know; it was a rookie mistake."

"Will somebody PLEASE tell me what is going on?" Taylor shouted.

Danny took a breath, then looked her in the eye. "I'll try, but I'm afraid you're not going to believe me."

Taylor said nothing.

"A bag-man is...Well, do you remember when you were a kid, and your mom and dad told you the boogeyman came after bad little girls and boys? It's...well, something like that."

Taylor wasn't sure whether to laugh in his face or tell him to keep talking.

"And...Now, please hear us out, okay? Because you've got to believe neither of us want to hurt you."

"*Tell me*," Taylor said. Danny winced under the power of yet another Taylor Smart death-glare.

"Okay! Okay!" he said, as if he suddenly was the one afraid of Taylor and not the other way around. "You remember in English class the other day, when Mrs. Markowitz told us about faery tales? She said those old stories could be a lot scarier than the versions you see in the kiddie movies. Do you remember how she said sometimes in those old stories the Fair Folk would...um...kidnap a human child and replace it with one of their own children?"

"Look," Bryn piped in, "to make a long story short, there was a mistake—thirteen years ago. You were on the list, but the paperwork got lost somewhere."

"P-paperwork?"

"We're all really sorry," Danny said. "Mrs. Redmane nearly went through the roof when she found out about it."

"F-found out..."

"You're a changeling, alright?" Bryn blurted. "At least, you were supposed to be. That's why you always feel out of place. You don't belong Topside. You belong in the Wonder, with your own kind. But like I said, there was some kind of mix-up. We're here to fix it. We're supposed to...take you back."

Taylor opened her mouth, but somehow forgot how to speak. Her eyes darted left and right, looking for a way to escape.

"This was supposed to go down different," Danny said. "We were supposed to break it to you gentle-like. Give you time to let it sink in. That bag-man forced our hand."

"Sorry, kid," Bryn added. "Like Danny said, you deserved more warning than this. But we've got to get moving."

"You're...taking me away?" Things were only getting worse. Taylor was being kidnapped—by a part-time Labrador retriever and a girl with a tail! All those lessons in preschool on "stranger danger" never actually mentioned that as a possible scenario.

"It's for your own protection," Bryn said. "There's a bag-man on the loose, and who knows what else might come looking for you?"

"But...Why—?"

"We'll answer all your questions," Danny said. "Once you're safe." He glanced up at Bryn.

"Any ideas?" he said.

Bryn stood silently for about five seconds. "They'll expect you to take the direct route, so that's the one thing you can't do. There are only two people I know who would dare to cross Mrs. Redmane, and I'd rather not be on their bad side."

"We need to take her somewhere safe until we sort this out."

Bryn shifted her weight from one foot to the other. "Doesn't Moe Fountain live around here?"

Danny sighed. "Moe Fountain? Oh, can this possibly get any worse?"

"Just answer me, Danny."

"About a hundred and twenty, maybe a hundred and forty miles. But you don't underst—"

"What's your problem with Moe Fountain?" Bryn said. "And anyway, he's still our best shot. They won't cross him. You'd better take her."

"But what about my parents?" Taylor blurted.

"Fortunately, that part of our plan can still work," Bryn smiled. "Stand up, honey. Let me take a look at you."

Danny helped Taylor to her feet. She and Bryn were almost the same height and they had the same blue eyes—though Bryn's were darker with little flecks of green. But Taylor had darker hair, and she was only thirteen years old to Bryn's eighteen or twenty.

26

Only then did it sink in that she and Bryn were wearing the same outfit. They both had on a navy skirt, a powder-blue polo shirt, and a red Bulloch Middle School windbreaker tied around the waist. Bryn even had on the same blue socks and black walking shoes—although hers may have seen a little less wear than Taylor's.

"Let's see," Bryn said. A silvery mist formed around her, spreading from her back like butterfly wings and up over her head and down across the front of her body. Her hair began to darken. Her features glimmered and shifted until she might have been Taylor's older sister.

Taylor felt her jaw fall open.

"Nothing to be scared of, sweetie. I'm just applying a little bit of glamour."

"Glamour? Like that fashion magazine at my mom's beauty parlor?"

"Not even close," Danny grinned. "Glamour is like a magical aura Our Kind project. If you know how, you can use it to change your appearance. That's why I don't look like a geeky teenager anymore. This is my real face." He smiled as if that were something to be proud of.

"Whoa, Bryn, you're still too old," Danny said. Bryn sighed and closed her eyes. She seemed to de-age before Taylor's eyes. But there was still something not right. Sure, she looked younger, but somehow still overly mature. And there was something flirty, even sultry, about her expression. Taylor couldn't imagine herself ever looking like that. Then it hit her.

"Too much makeup," she said.

"Really?" Bryn said. "Are you sure?"

"She's sure, Bryn. You're supposed to be middle school kid, not a huldra on the prowl. Try to tone it down, huh? And while you're at it, your skirt is way to short."

Danny was right. Taylor's mom would kill her if she caught her dressed like that.

"And by oak, ash, and thorn, do something about that tail!"

"Oops! I almost forgot." Bryn's hem lengthened almost to her knees. At the same time, her tail retracted beneath her skirt like a fishing line being reeled in. She looked exactly like Taylor.

"Now, give me your backpack," Bryn said.

"I've got a math test tomorrow," Taylor said, still half in a daze.

"Ah, too bad for you, sweetie," Bryn said. "Math was never my best subject."

"All right," Danny said. "We'll stay in contact by seeing stone. Any trouble, we'll let the other one know."

Bryn nodded.

"Good luck, Bryn." To Taylor, Danny said, "Okay! Next stop: Moe Fountain's place."

He extended his hand. Taylor slowly reached out her own. Danny turned around, gently pulling Taylor's hand until it was draped over his shoulder.

"Hold on tight," he said. He brought Taylor's other hand up and made sure she clasped them around his neck. As soon as he did so, his neck began to thicken. It stretched out from his shoulders. At the same time, his head lengthened and darkened. His curly hair morphed into a shaggy black mane, and his entire body swelled, starting with his shoulders and reaching all the way to his feet.

Danny was now a horse! He was black as night, with the same eerie glowing eyes he had as a dog only a few minutes before.

He nickered and bolted away.

Taylor held on for dear life.

Chapter 4

Kidnapped by a Real Gentleman

Danny galloped through the park, down the street, and across an empty field at the edge of town in a matter of minutes. He weaved through the light traffic, hoping he could project enough glamour to keep the Topsiders from noticing a girl riding bareback through town on a magical horse!

Every few horse-lengths, he magically disappeared in a flash of superheated dust only to reappear almost instantly several yards ahead. Blinking, they called it. He zigged and zagged through traffic, around mailboxes and fire hydrants, and over fences. Any Topsiders lucky enough to think they saw something would convince themselves it was just their imagination.

The more often he blinked, the harder it would be for people to follow. But he was careful not to do it too often or too far at one time. Not only did it use up an awful lot of magic, the experience could be unpleasant for his rider. Handing a damaged changeling over to one of the most powerful fae in the Southeast was the last thing he wanted to do!

He had been afraid something like this would happen. The other side was looking for her, too. He could have kicked himself for letting the bag-man slip past him. All he could figure was he was one of the birds perched in the trees across the way from where Danny was waiting. He was on her before Danny could react. If he hadn't been there, who knows where the bag-man would have taken her?

This is it, he thought. *They've finally crossed Mrs. Redmane. From here on, all bets are off!*

Somebody else wanted Taylor Smart—somebody who wasn't afraid of Mrs. Redmane. Danny was certain the bag-man wasn't working alone. Bag-men weren't that smart—or that stupid!

His and Bryn's plan to get Taylor safely from Macon to Dunhoughkey had just been thrown out the window. Fortunately, Danny loved to improvise. The basic plan would still work. He only had to tweak it a little.

He lurched to a halt and put on his true shape as Taylor slid off his shoulders. He had made it to the ring in record time. The wind had picked up, however, and heavy gray clouds were swirling overhead.

Then the real trouble began. Taylor started to gasp for air. She leaned over and rested her hands on her knobby knees.

"Taylor, are you all right?" Danny asked. He felt about as frantic as she was starting to look.

She nodded as she coughed. "Inhaler," she whispered. She reached around, looking for something. Then a look of dread crossed her face.

"What's wrong?"

"Backpack..." Taylor gasped. But Bryn had her backpack! That meant Bryn had whatever it was Taylor was looking for.

"Taylor?" Danny said. "Is there anything I can do to help?" She looked up at him only to cough in his face. He tentatively placed a hand on her shoulder. This time she didn't pull away.

She finally managed a gulp of air, a loud, wheezy gasp that sounded like it burned her lungs all the way down. She coughed a few more times, then managed another raspy breath.

She exhaled hard and slow.

"Taylor?" Danny said again. "Are you okay?"

She only glared at him.

"Taylor?"

She settled herself. Her voice was weak, but it was boiling over with anger. "No," she said, "I'm NOT okay." She coughed again. "I've just had an asthma attack. I've been kidnapped by some kind of...I don't know what!" She took another long, shallow breath. Her eyes were bloodshot and filled with tears.

"Sorry, I didn't realize..."

"Bryn has my inhaler."

"Yeah, maybe we didn't think that through properly..." *I'm a complete idiot*, Danny thought.

Taylor seemed to be getting better. She looked around. There were trees all over the place and no signs of human presence. Leaves rustled in the wind. In front of them was a ring of mushrooms about twenty feet across.

"Wh-where are we?"

"Macon's back that way about three or four miles." Danny pointed. A narrow path led toward a cultivated field a few hundred feet in the distance. "But we need to go this way." He pointed toward the mushrooms. "Are you hungry? I'd offer you something, but you need to understand first."

"Huh? Understand?"

"Yeah, there's this thing about faery food. Eating it is...kind of a commitment."

Taylor looked at him like he was crazy. Danny imagined food was the last thing on her mind. She still looked awfully shaken up. He bet her stomach was in knots.

"You ready to move?" he asked.

"Hold on." Taylor was still bent over, waiting for her head to stop swimming. She took two or three more breaths.

"Take your time."

She threw her head back and took a long wheezing breath. At the same time, she stumbled forward.

"Taylor!" Danny called.

She stopped herself and stooped over.

SLAM!

Danny never even noticed the fallen branch by Taylor's feet, but in an instant she had grabbed it and swung her whole body around. His face throbbed when the branch made contact. He fell back with a groan.

He sat on the ground, his vision blurry, for a few seconds. When he could finally see straight, he pulled himself up. He looked around. There was no sign of Taylor on the footpath, but he already knew she was pretty smart. Maybe she was hiding somewhere, hoping he'd give up looking for her.

"Taylor!"

She didn't answer, although he didn't expect her to. If the bag-man's friends were around, he hoped they would take their time getting there.

Danny slipped his backpack off his shoulder and shifted to dog form. He picked up her scent almost immediately. He bounded through the woods until he found the tree she had chosen for a hiding place. He sat on his haunches at the base of it, staring up at her and wagging his tail. He tried his best to tone down the glow in his eyes.

Taylor sighed. She looked like she was at the point of tears.

"I want to go home!"

"Woof!"

"I'm serious!"

Danny once again transformed. "I am, too," he said. He tried to smile, but that was harder than it sounded with a cheek already beginning to swell. He gingerly set his fingertips to his face and pulled them away streaked with blood.

"I'll take you home if that's what you want," he lied. "But first we have to go see Moe. And we've got to go now. Please?"

Danny could tell Taylor was considering her options. Scream for help? Land on him and bowl him over? Rip his head off with her bare hands?

"It might not look like it, Taylor, but you can trust me. I promise."

"Why are you doing this?" Taylor thundered. The floodgates opened and she started bawling. "Who are you, anyway? *What* are you? Will someone please tell me what's going on?"

"Taylor," he said. "I never hurt you. I never even tried to tie you up."

She sighed. "Yeah, I'm being kidnapped by a real gentleman."

"The truth is we need to get moving. I have to keep you safe. I can't do that here."

They looked each other in the eye. Finally, she gave in.

"Okay, I'm coming down."

Danny took his time guiding her back to the ring.

"Now, when we enter the ring, you'll need to hold on tight. It can be a little weird if you're not used to it."

"The ring?"

"The ring," Danny said, gesturing to the ring of mushrooms once again in front of them. He retrieved his backpack and tried to explain. "It's kind of like a gateway into the Wonder. Only we won't be going all the way in, not yet anyway. Not until we know what's going on. We'll be harder to track if we just slide around the edges.

The expression on Taylor's face told him she didn't have a clue what he was talking about.

"I guess I should back up," Danny said. "The Wonder is where we...I mean Our Kind...live. It goes by lots of different names Topside. For us, it's just the Wonder..."

Judging from her expression, Danny's explanation didn't help much.

"Just hang on," he said.

He gestured with his hands like a conductor calling for a dramatic crescendo. Suddenly a whirlwind spun around the ring, a shimmering wall of gold and silver lights.

Danny turned his back on Taylor so she could once again grab hold. It was obvious she was having second thoughts.

"You can trust me," Danny said.

She sighed and locked her arms around his neck. When he was sure he had a secure hold on her, he stepped into the sparkling whirlwind and vanished.

Chapter 5

The Fair Folk

Entering the ring felt something like jumping onto a moving sidewalk that had been thrown into overdrive. A swirl of sights and sounds assaulted Taylor. It was too much to take in. One second, she was soaring high above the countryside. Next, she was barreling through the woods at breakneck speed. All the while, wind rushed past her ears, a sucking sound as if someone had opened a door and let all the air out of the world.

Lights flashed before her eyes in a hundred different colors. Taylor felt as if she was on a runaway roller coaster, sliding and twisting in every direction at once.

As suddenly as it began, it was over. Danny sprawled forward with a grunt, and Taylor went flying over his head and onto the grass. She rolled a couple of times and stopped spread-eagle on her back.

Danny barked a curse. "Idiot!" he yelled. At whom, Taylor wasn't sure. She sat up. The grass stains on her skirt were going to be murder to get out.

Danny was livid. "Of all the...I ought to...Arrgh!" He coughed and heaved like he had swigged a giant gulp of antifreeze.

"What's wrong?" Taylor asked.

"What's wrong? I'll show you what's wrong! Look!" They had landed beside another ring of mushrooms. This one, however, had seen better days. Most of the fungi were wilted almost completely away. Only a slight discoloration of the grass showed where a healthy ring once grew.

"Some Jack decided he didn't like one of our rings!" Danny said. "Probably soaked the ground in chemical fertilizer. Well, I'll show him!" He marched away, his eyes blazing yellow just as they had been in his horse and dog forms.

They were in a wooded patch at the far end of somebody's property. Danny stalked out of the trees into a vast yard cluttered with farm implements and old, rusty car parts. He rubbed his hands together and muttered under his breath. There was a large vegetable garden, several outbuildings, and beyond them a modest wooden house.

"Stay back!" he spat.

Taylor stood at the edge of the woods trembling. She had never seen anyone this angry before. Danny became a horse. He galloped straight into the vegetable patch, trampled down as much of it as he could, then turned and kicked down part of wooden fence beside it. He took on human form, stormed into a tool shed, and returned with a container of gasoline, which he splashed in every direction.

He threw down the gas can. He held up his hand, and a tiny ball of fire appeared in his palm. Taylor gasped and crouched behind the nearest tree.

"Who's there?" someone yelled.

In half a heartbeat, Danny vanished into thin air with only a subtle flash of light to mark the place where he used to stand.

A man stormed out the back door, red-faced. He cursed the neighbor kids at the top of his lungs as he ran to inspect the damage.

"Come on," Danny whispered. Taylor hadn't even noticed him reappearing behind her. He yanked her by the arm and led her away.

"We'll have to walk the rest of the way," Danny said. At the back of the property, he hopped over an old wooden fence and then helped Taylor climb over after him. They started walking through the woods.

"As soon as this mission is over, that stupid Jack is definitely getting the jellyfish treatment!"

For a second, Taylor thought about running back to the house, but with her luck, the man would accuse her of having something to do with the mess. Danny stomped on for several minutes, cursing and grumbling. He finally seemed to calm down enough to talk.

"I'm sorry you had to see that," Danny said. His eyes were back to normal. "I thought we could make it all the way to Moe's. Those stupid deathlings have slowed us down by breaking the ring. No respect..."

More than ever, Taylor wanted someone to tell her what was going on. The only thing that made sense was that Danny had somehow slipped her some kind of drug. None of this could be real, could it?

Her head spun. For the longest time, she was afraid she was going to be sick. Her head buzzed with the weird sensation that she was watching herself from the outside. She was in a forest, or at least in a place wilder and more overgrown than the park back home, or even the patch of woodland from which they had first vanished.

The path they followed eventually led them to a potholed country road. Trees draped in Spanish moss seemed to wrap around them. The sounds of nature—birds, frogs, insects—were everywhere.

At last, Taylor dared to speak. "Wh-where are we?"

"About two miles outside of Grubb, South Carolina," Danny said. He started hiking down the road.

South Carolina? Taylor thought. *That's got to be over a hundred miles from home!*

She didn't seem to have any choice but to follow her kidnapper. As they trudged along, the sun beat down on them whenever it broke through the shade the forest provided. Two miles outside of Grubb, South Carolina a lot more humid than Macon, Georgia.

As her stomach settled, Taylor's brain finally started to get in gear. In her mind, she walked through everything that had happened—the attack in the park, Danny, Bryn, faery tales, and changelings.

They had been on the road about ten minutes and still had not seen a single car. Taylor swatted at a mosquito on her arm.

None of this made any sense. Maybe she was right, and Danny had drugged her. Maybe she was having some kind of seizure. This had to be a dream. Sure, it was a very lifelike dream complete with nausea and asthma attacks, but still just a dream. Right? Until somebody woke her up, there wasn't much she could do but go with it.

"So...what's all this stuff about faeries?" she said.

"I'd rather you not use that word," Danny said. "It's not really politically correct."

"But didn't you say something about 'faery food'?"

"That's different," Danny said. "That's a thing, not a person."

"I don't get it."

"It's not really a bad word, so to speak," Danny mused. "It's just a little forward, you know?"

Taylor stared at him.

"Let me see. How can I explain this? Okay, take Mrs. Markowitz, your English teacher. Have you ever called her by her first name?"

"I would love to call that grouch 'Elizabeth' to her face just once!" Taylor grinned.

"But you never have. Why not?"

"She'd have me in detention till I'm twenty!"

"Why would she do that, though? It's her name, right?"

"But you just don't call your teachers by their first names. It sounds disrespectful."

"I'm kind of surprised you noticed that. Good for you," Danny said. Taylor resisted the urge to slap him. "But that's the way we feel about being called 'faeries.' It's okay to talk about faery food, faery castles, that sort of thing..."

"But not, uh, faery *faeries*?"

"Now you're getting it."

Taylor wasn't sure about that, but she didn't see much point in arguing.

"Anyways," Danny said, "there's better ways of saying it. A while back, some of us wanted to say 'eldritch Americans,' but it never caught on. 'The Fair Folk' or 'Our Kind' is better. Most just say 'fae,' or else refer to each other according to their kindred."

Taylor stared at him blankly.

"You see, Our Kind comes in a lot of different tribes or families: kindreds. I guess you could say they're like Topsider ethnic groups. For example, I'm a pooka. Bryn is a huldra. That sort of thing."

"O-o-o-kay."

"I know this is hard to take in all at once."

You can say that again! Taylor thought.

"But," she began, "...and I don't mean to be rude or anything... Faeries don't exist!"

"We get that a lot," Danny shrugged. "And 'eldritch Americans' or 'fae,' if you don't mind."

"All right, 'fae.' But...people like you...are supposed to be tiny! And have little butterfly wings!"

Danny smiled—then winced. His cheek was starting to turn purple. Taylor had given him a serious bruise with that tree branch!

"One thing you gotta to know about Our Kind, Taylor: Between the shapeshifting, the size-shifting, glamours, and all the other spells and whatnot, powerful fae can pretty much look however they want. And as for the tiny bodies and the wings and all, that's what we want you to think! It makes us look like a joke, you see? Something nobody would take seriously. Get enough people believing that Our Kind are nothing but faery godmothers, or tiny women in mini-dresses, or jolly toymakers who live at the North Pole..."

"Or the tooth faery...."

"*Never* let one of Our Kind anywhere near your teeth!" Danny said, suddenly serious.

"Okay," Taylor agreed, startled at Danny's abruptness. "Good advice. Thanks."

"But yeah, we started all those stories ourselves to throw Topsiders off the trail. Been doing it for centuries."

"Topsiders?"

"Mortals. Deathlings. Folks like you. Well, folks like your parents, or the kids you go to school with. Basically anybody who's non-eldritch."

"Oh, Muggles."

"What?"

"Never mind.... And you kidnap Topsider children?" her voice took on an accusatory tone.

"It's not what you think," Danny protested. "There are lots of reasons we do switch-outs."

"*Such as?*"

Danny shuddered. Taylor wasn't trying to give him a death-glare, but she was having a hard time controlling her emotions.

"S-sometimes we take a child to rescue it from abusive or neglectful parents, then we magic a piece of wood or something to put in its place."

"But my parents aren't abusive! They're great!" As soon as she said it, Taylor thought about her biological parents—the ones she never knew, the ones who put her up for adoption. Could her real mom have been some kid strung out on drugs or something? Is that why she gave her up?

"Sometimes a baby with strong magical potential is born Topside. Nobody really knows why. Maybe they have some eldritch blood a few generations back. Maybe it's just a fluke. Either way, a little bit of magic is fine, and kids like that can grow up to be great: Mozart, Walt Disney, Michael Jordan. But too much magic and they have a hard time fitting in Topside. Things usually end badly for them.... You ever heard of Janis Joplin? It's better in the long run if we...you know...." Danny let that all sink in as they walked along the road, faces forward.

Taylor swallowed.

"Of course, there are other reasons to do a switch-out. Some of us think it helps both groups to mix up the gene pool a little bit, so they'll do a true swap—take a kid from a Topsider family and leave one of ours in its place. Some just take a liking to a Topsider kid and figure, What's the harm in switching it out?"

"That's terrible!"

"Don't look at me like that, I ain't never said I approved of it! The Fair Folk are just like Topsiders, Taylor. We can be some of the friendliest, most helpful folk you'd ever want to meet. But we can also be cruel, selfish, petty, and destructive. You've got to take the good with the bad."

They came to a fork in the road. The main road curved gently to the right, but a side road made an abrupt left turn. Danny pointed them toward the side road. "Not too much farther," he said.

The sun was still fairly high in the sky. Between the hiking and the humidity, Taylor had pretty much sweat through her school clothes. She thought it must have been close to five o'clock, but she didn't have a watch, and her phone— the brand-new cell phone she got for her birthday nearly three months ago!—was in her backpack a hundred miles away.

"This is a lot to take in," she sighed. "Faeries—fae, Your Kind, whatever—are real. But...but...where do you come from?"

"Indiana, but I kind of move around a lot. Why?"

Taylor glared at him.

"Oh! Sorry, I thought you meant.... Yeah. Actually there's a lot of different opinions on that. Some say we're descendants of Adam and his first wife, Lilith."

"Adam had a wife before Eve? I don't remember that from Sunday school!"

"I guess that story didn't make the final cut," Danny said. "And who knows if it's true or not? Others say we're older than Adam, creatures made of smokeless fire while Adam was made from dust. Of course, Topsiders used to have all kinds of funny ideas about us, that we're the spirits of the dead, or even fallen angels—As if! But like I said, there's a lot of different opinions.

Some say we're the minor gods and nature spirits people used to worship."

"Gods? You mean like Zeus or Poseidon?"

"I said '*minor* gods.' The kind whose names are mostly forgotten. Nymphs and satyrs, animal totems, ancestral spirits, guardians of rivers or rocks or trees. That sort of thing. Leastwise, that's what the Gentry say. Of course, they *would* say something like that."

"The Gentry?"

"Well, they're called daoine sídhe if you want to get technical. That's Gaelic for 'People of the Mounds.' They're the ruling class. And trust me, they'd love it for people to worship them!"

"*Deen-yeh shee*," Taylor practiced pronouncing the unusual term. When Danny nodded his approval, she asked, "But what do *you* think?"

Danny shrugged. "Doesn't really matter, does it? We're here. As far as I know, we've always been around. But if you look at it scientifically, we've got to be close cousins of Topsiders, though."

"Why?"

"Because fae and Topsiders intermarry. They can have kids together."

"They..."

"Yeah. Like I said, sometimes we do a switch-out to bring new blood into both populations. And Our Kind and Topsiders are always falling in love with each other, at least if you believe the old stories."

Taylor gulped as she remembered the way Danny had treated her ever since he showed up in her life in February. Her face turned pink. "Listen, Danny," she started, "I appreciate you being nice to me in school and all, but..."

"What? Oh, no!" Now it was Danny's turn to blush. "Oh, crud, did you think—? Honestly, I was just trying to be your friend, Taylor! Just part of my job. I mean, I'm two hundred and three years old, for Pete's sake!"

"Two hundred...but you don't even look as old as my dad!" She took a breath. "Well, then," she said, trying to compose herself and hoping she wasn't blushing, "as long as that's cleared up..."

"Hey," Danny said, "there's where we're headed." He pointed to a run-down building set off from the road by a gravel parking lot in which sat a single battered old pickup truck. A sign over the door read, "Carl's Catfish House."

"Now, Mr. Fountain can be a little intimidating," Danny said. "He's a cymbee. They say he came over from Africa in colonial times. And he's got very traditional ideas about showing proper respect."

"Thanks for the warning," Taylor said. "And we're going to see this guy because...?"

"Because both sides are afraid of him."

"Oh, this just keeps getting better," Taylor muttered. "What exactly do you mean by 'both s—'"

"Later," Danny said. "Just trust me on this."

As if I have a choice!

They approached the front door of Carl's Catfish House. From the parking lot, Taylor could already smell the aroma of frying catfish and hushpuppies. She realized it was close to suppertime. Her stomach was still queasy, but she wondered if a little food would help.

A chime rang when Danny opened the door. He guided Taylor to a tiny booth in the back of the cramped—but mostly empty—dining area.

The place was definitely nothing special: plain tile floors, chipped and cracked Formica-topped tables, an old-fashioned lunch counter with revolving stools upholstered with red vinyl. A couple of older African American men sat in the booth closest to the door, arguing about local politics.

Taylor nudged Danny. "Are those two regular humans? Don't you think you'd better...." But as soon as she looked at him, she realized Danny was back in his geeky teenager form.

"H-how...?"

"I've been wearing this husk since we got to the road," he whispered. "You mean you just now noticed? See? I told you you had some magic in you. You'd have to if you can see through glamour like that. Go ahead, look at me again, real close."

As Taylor slid into the booth, she concentrated on Danny's face. If she squinted just right, his appearance flipped from normal (well, mostly normal) teenager to adult pointy-eared, long-nosed, cheek-puffed-up-and-turning-every-color-in-the-rainbow goblin-thingy. It was sort of like when you shut one eye to see and then switch to the other: the view slightly changes. She decided she preferred the human form, though. At least it was what she was used to.

"What'll it be, darlin's?" The woman who appeared at their table to take their order looked to be in her forties or fifties, but Taylor wasn't prepared to take anything at face value any more. She tried to squint and see if the woman was using glamour on her. If she was, Taylor couldn't see through it."

"Whatever you want," Danny said. "My treat."

"Uh, just a Coke, I guess. And maybe some French fries?"

"A Coke for me, too," Danny said.

"Sure thing, sugar, and if you decide to try the catfish, you can just tell me later." She walked away.

"So...shouldn't you try to call this Moe guy?" Taylor said.

"Oh, he knows we're here," Danny said. Taylor must have looked confused, because Danny continued, "He probably had us on his radar since we got to the fork in the road. If it happens in this valley, he knows about it, and maybe even before it happens."

Even as Danny was talking, Taylor heard shuffling footsteps approaching from behind. She turned her head to see a man approaching their table. She gazed up—way up. He was a giant of a man—easily six feet tall and maybe closer to seven. His wooly hair was white, and his chocolate-brown face was wrinkled but not unhandsome. He wore nice clothes: black dress pants held up with suspenders and a long-sleeved turquoise shirt with a button-down collar.

44

"Danny Underhill," the man said. "Still getting into trouble, I see."

"I suppose." Danny touched the side of his face. "Mr. Fountain, I'd like you to meet Taylor Smart."

Taylor squinted. After two or three tries, Moe Fountain's face flipped the same as Danny's. One second, he was just as she had seen him at first. His un-glamourized form was mostly the same, but his coloring was different. Now there was a subtle hint of green in his skin and especially his hair. His ears didn't look pointy like Danny's but—Taylor started—his eyes had slit pupils like a snake's!

"P-pleased to meet you, Mr. Fountain," Taylor said at once, remembering her manners.

Moe Fountain nodded to her. "The pleasure is mine, Miss Smart." His voice was genial but powerful, as if there were a little rumble of thunder behind every syllable. Darth Vader could take voice lessons from this guy! He slid into the seat next to Danny. "If I had known you were coming, Danny, I'd have put some crawfish on to boil for you and your friend."

"About that: I...uh...ran into a bit of a problem. We'd appreciate it if we could spend a day or two at your place?"

Moe Fountain studied Taylor with his snaky eyes. He looked at her the same way Mrs. Markowitz did when she handed back her C-minus English paper, only with those creepy eyes, it looked a hundred times more threatening. Taylor rubbed her own eyes to get him back to his normal human appearance.

"You want to tell me what this is about, young man?"

"Not here, sir. If you don't mind."

The waitress boxed up their food. Mr. Fountain insisted on upgrading their order to a catfish basket ("Gonna be a long night," he said), and in a few minutes they were leaving Carl's Catfish House and headed further down the road. They hadn't gone a hundred feet, however, when Mr. Fountain turned onto a narrow footpath leading into the woods. There were no Topsiders in sight.

"Well?" he said, looking down upon Danny.

Danny swallowed. "I was doing a switch-out over in Georgia," he began. "Taylor here was supposed to be picked up when she was a baby, but obviously somebody messed up. Mrs. Redmane sent my partner, Bryn, and me to fix it."

"That's your story, huh?" Something in Mr. Fountain's expression made Taylor think he didn't quite believe that was all there was to it.

He gave Taylor another long stare, then turned back to Danny. "What do you know about her, Danny. She got talent? Half-blood? Or just a pet some Gentryman decided to get for his own kid to play with?"

Taylor felt a surge of resentment as she once again realized that she was in the process of being kidnapped—and talked about as if she wasn't even there.

"I'm not sure," Danny said. He blushed beneath Taylor's angry glare. "But she's not a pet, that's for sure. She's going to get to choose." He was very emphatic about that last sentence, and looked directly into Taylor's eyes as he said it.

"I only know we were supposed to pick her up. You know how Mrs. Redmane is about tidying up loose ends. Quality control. Standard operating procedures, right? Since she's so much older than most switch-outs, Mrs. Redmane said she—Taylor, that is—would have to make the final decision herself. But she was very definite she wanted us to bring her to the Summer Court."

"Which raises a very interesting question," Moe said. "Why haven't you taken the young lady to the Summer Court?"

"See, we were about to, but that's when things went a little crazy."

"I'm listening." There was impatience in his voice. Taylor had a feeling he knew more than he was telling.

They reached the bottom of the valley. There, they found a creek maybe a stone's throw across. As they walked, Danny explained how he pretended to be a student in Taylor's class until they were sure she was really the girl they were after, then how, on the very day he and Bryn had intended to make contact,

46

the bag-man showed up and almost beat them to her. He told how Bryn had taken Taylor's place while the two of them came looking for Moe.

"We couldn't think of anything else to do. Under the circumstances, they might have expected us to go straight to the Summer Court."

"That's how I'd have played it," Mr. Fountain said appreciatively. "A bag-man's a pretty low-level threat, but he can get you off your game. Make you nervous. Nervous people make mistakes. They get in a hurry."

"Yes, sir."

He led them onward. "I can't believe they actually had the nerve to cross Anya Redmane," he finally said. "The girl must be someone special to make her worth the risk." He gazed deep into Taylor's eyes. Now Taylor was certain he knew more than he was saying.

"I sure don't want to be in their shoes, whoever they are," Danny said.

"Mr. Underhill, you know who it is just as surely as I do," Mr. Fountain said. Danny let the comment pass. Taylor studied both their faces trying to pick up on what was not being said.

They followed the creek upstream until they reached its source in a natural spring. From beneath a rocky outcropping, water gushed forth from the earth with bubbly effervescence, filling a pond nearly as big as Taylor's back yard.

Mr. Fountain stood on the edge of the pond. For the first time, Taylor noticed he was barefooted. He wiggled his toes, and Taylor saw that he had webbed feet, like a frog or a duck or something.

"I'll be happy to carry your supper for you, Miss Smart," he offered. Taylor handed over the Styrofoam box with the catfish, hushpuppies, and fries. Moe turned back to the pond and waded in until the water reached his knees. Danny waded in after him. Very reluctantly, Taylor stepped into the water. It was cool on her tired feet, but it made her socks feel squishy inside her shoes.

"Follow me," Mr. Fountain said. The water was up nearly to his waist. He bent over and vanished into the spring. The last thing Taylor saw of him were his greenish webbed feet flapping upward as he dove deep.

"Uh..." Taylor said, "I'm not exactly a great swimmer."

"Just take my hand," Danny said. "Get ready to take a deep breath."

"Actually...that's the part I'm not so good at."

The cool water swirled around her legs. Danny gently led her deeper, but she stopped when it reached her waist and refused to go any farther.

"It'll just take a second," he said. "I promise."

She looked him in the eye. Through the glamour, she could see the same look of concern he had been wearing all afternoon.

"All right," she said. She took a breath and scrunched up her face. The next second, she was plunging deep into the water.

Chapter 6

Five Questions

Taylor came up gasping for air. Fortunately, the experience didn't trigger another asthma attack.

It took a second for Taylor to realize they hadn't simply surfaced after a deep dive into the spring. They were still in the forest, but something was different. Behind the gathering clouds, the sky had an odd greenish tint—more turquoise than blue. The air was warm, and the breeze carried the subtle scents of flowers and spices.

Most obviously, a house stood at the edge of the water that hadn't been there before. It was a single-story log cabin with a big front porch with rocking chairs and an old-fashioned wooden swing. Danny guided Taylor out of the spring and onto a path of rough-hewn stones leading directly from the water's edge to house.

"This way, if you please," Moe Fountain said. Taylor and Danny were drenched, but their host was completely dry even though he was wearing the same dress pants and shirt he had on before. He stood on the porch and motioned toward the front door.

He led them through the door into what looked like the den of an ordinary house. Taylor stood dripping on the carpet as she took it all in. There were several overstuffed leather chairs, a huge bookshelf, a sofa and an enormous coffee table carved from a single piece of driftwood, and an antique globe on a brass stand. Several African ceremonial masks were mounted on the walls along with flint-tipped spears, vicious-looking curved bronze knives, and shields made of animal hide stretched over wooden frames. Oil lamps bathed the room in bluish-white light.

Other than the weird lighting, Taylor's mom would have called the room a "man cave." All it needed was a big-screen TV. Instead, a large mirror hung over the mantle of a fireplace—which had been bricked over. Nobody was going to build a fire in it anytime soon.

"Can I get you anything?" Mr. Fountain said.

"A towel?" Taylor said, shivering.

"Of course," he said, as if only then noticing that his guests were leaving a puddle all over his floor. "Danny, why don't you take the guest room that way," he gestured right, "and Miss Smart, you'll find some dry clothes in my daughter's old room over there to the left. I hope you can find something that fits."

"Thank you, sir," Danny said. "We'll be right back."

The whole house was decorated in dark wood paneling or antique wallpaper with aquatic themes. The hallway back to Mr. Fountain's daughter's old room had wallpaper with blue and purple scenes of fish and snakes. The bedroom itself was adorned in green water lilies.

Taylor found plenty of towels in the connecting private bathroom. When she opened the closet, however, she had to stop and wonder when Mr. Fountain's daughter last visited. There were plenty of clothes, and some of them even looked like they might fit. But all of them looked like they came from the costume department of a Civil War movie.

She couldn't quite figure out how any of the garments worked. The underwear was worst of all, but she took her best guesses and got dressed as quickly as she could.

She picked out a simple green and black ankle-length dress with lace around the collar and the hems of the sleeves. It was only slightly too big, but Taylor figured that was partly because she was only wearing bloomers and not the corset, hoop, and petticoats that were supposed to go under it. The only shoes she could find were loose and clunky—she wondered if Moe

50

Fountain's daughter had webbed feet like her dad. She pulled on a pair of black stockings before she realized she would need garters to hold them up. She decided she could just go barefoot.

She returned to the main room, the hem of her skirt dragging on the floor behind her. Mr. Fountain sat in a chair in front of the not-quite-fireplace. He had set the carryout box on the coffee table along with a plastic fork and a paper napkin. Danny was apparently still in the guest room.

"Have a seat," Mr. Fountain said. "I'll pick up your wet things later and have them washed and dried. But right now you must be hungry."

Taylor sat down.

"I expect you have about a million questions."

She picked up a French fry with her fingers and ate half of it. Her eyes never left Mr. Fountain's.

"Well?" he said.

"Who am I?"

"Direct. I appreciate that," her host chuckled. "I'll bet you live up to your name, too. Am I right, Miss Smart? How old were you when first learned to read? Four? Five?"

"Three I think...but I thought you were going to answer *my* questions." There was a soft rumble of thunder at her outburst. It took Taylor a second to realize it was coming from Mr. Fountain. *Show respect!* she told herself. She finished her French fry and dug into a catfish filet with her fork.

"In due time," Mr. Fountain said. "But first Danny and I need to answer some of the questions you don't know you should be asking. Ah, here comes Mr. Underhill now."

Danny entered the room in a bright red and green dashiki and blue jeans several sizes too big for him with the cuffs rolled up. He had apparently taken the time to treat his swollen face; his cheek was covered in a cloth bandage, and he smelled of some kind of ointment. He sat down in a chair across from Taylor and Mr. Fountain so that the three of them formed a triangle.

"But you do know who I am? Why this Redmane lady is after me?" she persisted.

"I have a strong suspicion."

Danny glanced in Moe Fountain's direction, his eyebrows arched.

"As I was explaining to Miss Smart," he turned to Danny, "we need to start at the beginning."

"All right," Taylor said. "The beginning. Then I'd like to revise my question."

"Go on."

"Who is Anya Redmane?"

"Very good," Moe smiled. "I knew from the moment I met you that you'd be a bright young lady. 'Who is Anya Redmane?' That is the question, isn't it? Danny, would you like to handle this one?"

"Well, uh," he cleared his throat, "Mrs. Redmane is one of Our Kind, obviously. Daoine sídhe, in fact. She's from a very old, very powerful family. She's been the Chief Matron of the Summer Court since before I was born. She's got all kinds of connections. She's practically run it for the last forty years or so—ever since her husband faded."

"Our Kind don't actually die as a rule," Mr. Fountain explained. "Oh, most of the things that will kill a Topsider will kill one of us just as easily. But we don't get sick or die of old age. When we get tired of the world, we simply...fade."

Danny continued. "They say Mrs. Redmane's husband— Bright was his name, Vergosus Bright—they say he wasn't so much tired of the world as tired of her," he grinned. "B-but I wouldn't repeat that where she can hear you!"

Taylor leaned forward in her seat. She popped half of a hushpuppy in her mouth. The food was clearing her head and settling her rumbling stomach. She gulped down the morsel so she could ask her next question.

"All right, then what's the Summer Court?"

"The daoine sídhe are more sociable than most of Our Kind," Danny explained. "They love to get together to throw parties, trade news—mostly to make sure nobody threatens their power. The Summer Court is a gathering of Fair Folk. I guess you could say it's part social club, part ruling council, part intramural sports league, and part political party. Mrs. Redmane and the other powerful sídhe run things, but other kindreds can join, too: pookas, hulderfolk, pretty much anybody that wants to, really."

Taylor sat back. She felt like she was on the verge of understanding something really important. The wheels in her brain were starting to turn.

"You said the Summer Court is like a political party, right? That must mean there are different opinions about...about whatever it is Your Kind like to argue about. So there must be others who disagree with the Summer Court?" She turned to Mr. Fountain. "And before, Danny said he was taking me to you because 'both sides' were afraid of you." Danny's face turned beet-red, both his real one and the geeky teenage version. "So, who are they?"

Mr. Fountain leaned back, crossed his legs, and grinned from ear to ear. "She really is quite impressive," he told Danny.

"Yeah."

"Suppose I field this one, eh?" Moe uncrossed his legs and leaned in toward Taylor.

"The sídhe love to lead. Unfortunately for them, none of Our Kind is particularly good at following. So any fae chiefdom that grows to an appreciable size is likely to be quite divided. To the north and west of us is the great Chiefdom of Arradherry. It's one of the largest on this continent. It has held itself together for the past several centuries by sharing power among four Seasonal Courts, of which the Summer has long taken the lead.

"The Summer Court is beautiful and civilized, the best of fae society, at least in their own minds. As a rule, they're more kindly disposed toward Topsiders. They certainly don't cross them unless they think they've got a good reason. Its members are genial, polite, and passionate."

"I don't think I like where this is going," Taylor said.

"And then there is the Winter Court," Mr. Fountain continued.

"Bingo."

"How shall I explain this? If the Summer Court is warm and bright—albeit hotheaded—then the Winter Court equally lives up to its name. Its members are cold, dark, harsh, and cruel. They thrive on secrecy and silence."

"Uncle Waldo? I mean, the bag-man?"

"...was almost certainly sent by the Winter Court to rob Anya Redmane of her prize," Mr. Fountain said.

Taylor took a deep breath. She suddenly wasn't hungry any more.

"So let me see if I've got this straight." Her voice shook as much with rage as with terror. "There are two groups of super-powerful magical beings who basically hate each other. Of these two, even the good guys think it's just peachy to go around kidnapping people. And for some reason, I'm the 'kid' both of them are trying to 'nap.' Is that about it?"

"I'd say that's an apt summary," Mr. Fountain said. "I believe you need to ask two more questions, and then perhaps we'll be done."

"Two more? Are you serious? I could ask a thousand more. A million more!"

Moe Fountain's snaky eyes began to smolder. "No," he rumbled. "You should be thankful I took you in at all. I don't much care for uninvited visitors, and especially not visitors who stand to cause me trouble." Danny shuddered and hung his head. "Even so, Danny has been good to my daughter in the past. I owe him a favor. Two questions will do the trick, I think... if you choose them wisely."

"All right," Taylor whispered. She looked at Danny—she could see he wanted to say something, maybe coach her on what to ask, but he didn't dare open his mouth—then back at Mr. Fountain.

"Who runs the Winter Court? Why are they so mad at Mrs. Redmane?"

54

"The Hellebore family has pulled the strings of the Winter Court since before the Revolutionary War," Moe said. "Currently, that means Mara Hellebore and her husband, Crom Cornstack. Crom is the Court's Primus—you might call him the Chieftain. Maybe even the King if you're feeling generous. And, of course, Mara is Chief Matron of the Winter Court. Those two may be angry with the Redmanes for any number of reasons, although I suspect that these days it mostly has to do with Aulberic and Shanna."

Danny shook his head. "Those were some rough times!" he said. Taylor looked at him, inviting him with her eyes to say more.

"See, like Mr. Fountain said, the Redmanes and the Hellebores ain't never got along. But somehow, their kids met. And...well, they sort of decided they liked each other."

"You're kidding!"

"No, that's what they say. Aulberic Redmane fell for Shanna Hellebore, and apparently the feeling was mutual. Of course, none of the parents was happy about the situation. Both sides laid down the law: the two were forbidden to see each other ever again."

"Okay. How long until they ran away together?"

"About five or six m—Whoa! She *is* impressive, Mr. Fountain!"

"That's what I'm telling you!" He smiled.

"Yeah, about five or six months later the two of them eloped. They lived on the run for over a year, both courts on their tails. It must have been torture! But I guess they figured at least they had each other. They finally got caught, though. It must have been about the first of August about fourteen years ago."

"Lammas Day," Mr. Fountain said. "The day the Summer Court's power begins to wane and the Winter Court's begins to increase. The Spring and Autumn Courts usually follow the lead of the other two Courts, you see. Lammas Day is thus a day of balance, when the scales could tip either way."

"The Summers got there about five minutes too late," Danny continued. "The Winters were already in control of the situation. They killed Aulberic in front of his own mother. Apparently it was pretty gruesome. Then they sent Shanna packing back to the Hellebores' palace. Rumor is, they threw her in a dungeon and she's been a prisoner in her own home ever since.

"Mrs. Redmane is never going to forgive Crom and Mara for what they did to her son; you can take that to the bank. And the Hellebores blame the Redmanes for turning their daughter against them. That's the way it's been since before you were born. Neither side misses a chance to make trouble for the other."

"Wow," Taylor said. "Then what happened—?"

"I'm sorry, Miss Smart. You've used up your two questions."

"What?"

"'Who runs the Winter Court?'" Mr. Fountain said, holding up a finger. "'Why are they so mad at Mrs. Redmane?'" He held up two fingers.

Taylor wanted to explode, but she didn't dare.

"I don't know about you, but I'm ready for bed," Mr. Fountain announced. "You two stay up as long as you please." He chuckled to himself as he strolled out of sight.

Taylor watched him go. She wondered what he suspected about her. More than that, she was frustrated he wouldn't just come out and tell her.

"I'd better check in with Bryn," Danny announced. He pulled his magic rock out of his pocket. It was small and smooth, reddish in color, about the size of a cell phone. He held it in front of him like he did back in the park and whispered Bryn's name three times. The air around him seemed to ripple like hot pavement on a scorching summer day. Taylor noticed a tiny hole in the middle of his rock that Danny studied intently.

"Bryn?" he said. "Danny here. What's the story?"

"Pretty much the same," a voice echoed. Taylor hitched up her skirt and hopped over to Danny's seat. He reached out and touched her arm and stared down into the hole in the rock. Immediately, her surroundings shimmered and shifted. She was still in Moe Fountain's living room, but she also saw shadows and glimpses of someplace else. And she could see what Danny saw: a gauzy form floating in front of them, a greenish-tinged ghostly figure that looked like Taylor—though it had spoken in Bryn's voice. She sat on the ghost of Taylor's bed with her legs tucked beneath her. She was also holding a small rock in her hand.

"That's me!" Taylor said.

"That's Bryn," Danny said. "This is a seeing stone. It lets you see into the Wonder. Our Kind use it to communicate over long distances. So, Bryn...you were saying?"

"They haven't made any further moves, Danny, but ever since sundown, there's been a troll camped out just past the back fence."

"A troll?" Taylor gasped. The fact that she could be surprised by anything at this point was itself surprising. Did she really say a troll?

"Hey, sweetie!" Bryn called. "Don't you worry. He's not getting near the house, though. I was able to put protective spells up as soon as I got home. All he can do is lean against the fence and grumble. By the way, you're going to a party Saturday night."

"I *what*?"

"Yeah, there's this boy named William. He came by before supper. Wanted you to know Jill is feeling better—it wasn't the flu after all, just a twenty-four-hour virus. He came to pick up her homework. Seems like a sweet kid." Bryn smiled. "I think he likes you."

"No."

"Cool, huh? Anyway, he wanted to make sure you knew about the party at the house of some other boy named Jared something or other?"

The world started spinning again, and this time it had nothing to do with ring-travel.

"Uh, Bryn?' Taylor said. "I hate to break it to you, but I got a C-minus on an English paper today. There's no way my parents are going to let...well, you...go to a party on Saturday. Least of all a boy-girl party!"

"Don't worry about it," Bryn smiled. "I already cleared it with Mom and Dad. They're cool with it."

"They are?" Taylor was dumbstruck. "Wait a minute, did you just refer to *my* parents as 'Mom and Dad'?"

"What else would I call them? Gotta stay in character, you know. But anyway, they didn't mind about the C-minus. Everybody brings home a bad grade every now and then, right? I don't mean to brag, but I can be pretty persuasive when I want to be. So, who are the boys you like? Anybody you want me to break the ice with for you?"

"Bryn," Danny moaned, "we're talking about thirteen-year-olds here! Just...tone it down, okay?"

Bryn pouted. "Oh, there's so cute at that age. All you have to do is smile at them and they practically melt!"

"Well, then, no smiling until I can bring Taylor home!"

"You're no fun!"

"Anyway," Danny said, trying to change the subject, "it sounds like you've got the troll situation covered. And you're sure Taylor's folks don't suspect nothing?"

"No, everything's under control. I just have to ace that math test tomorrow, do a little shopping at the mall—"

"Shopping at the mall?"

"Well, I have to have *something* to wear to the party!"

"My life is over," Taylor muttered.

"Uh, listen, Bryn," Danny said, "Unless you have something else to report, I'm just going to sign off now, okay?"

"Okay, Danny. Toodles!"

Taylor fell back into the chair Moe Fountain had been sitting in. There was a long, awkward silence.

"Faeries are out to get me," she said.

"Eldritch Americans."

Taylor glowered. Danny flinched.

"*Eldritch Americans* are out to get me. There's a troll in my back yard..."

"Actually, Bryn said it was just past the—right, shutting up now."

"And some...*cowgirl*...is doing a better job of living my life than I ever could."

There was another long silence.

"Long day?"

Taylor sighed. "My brain has turned to mush. I feel like a vegetable."

"You're a long way from being a vegetable," Danny said. "Trust me: I once spent three weeks as a turnip...." He stopped when he noticed Taylor staring at him. "I got better."

Taylor slumped down in the chair and closed her eyes. She imagined swirling pictures of fae gangsters putting out contracts on each other and mowing each other down with magic wands instead of machine guns.

She pictured a troop of Christmas elves in curly-toed shoes and jingle-bell hats playing out the balcony scene from *Romeo and Juliet*. Then the gangster faeries burst in and strung up Romeo, played by a pointy-eared Leonardo DiCaprio, and lynched him on a tree out behind Carl's Catfish House.

She looked up at Danny. He looked as sad as anybody she had ever seen. He knew it was his fault she was in this mess. For once, Taylor found it hard to blame him. She just kept going over what he and Moe Fountain had told her.

Nothing made any sense. Unless...

She lurched upward, wide-awake.

"Danny?" she said.

"Yeah?"

"The Redmanes and the Hellebores basically hate each other's guts."

"Right."

"But Aulberic and Shanna fell in love anyway and ran off together."

"Uh huh."

"But then Shanna's folks killed Aulberic and locked her up in a dungeon somewhere."

"Right."

"And that was in August. What year was that again?"

He told her.

Taylor counted off months on her fingers. Six months between August and February. She started trembling.

"Danny?" she said, her voice cracking.

"Yes, Taylor?"

"What if Aulberic and Shanna had a kid?"

Chapter 7

Summer and Winter

"A kid?" Danny nearly fell out of his seat. "You mean, like, a *baby*?"

"Well, that's the way Topsiders do it," Taylor said. "I don't know about Your Kind."

Danny frowned. This switch-out was getting more interesting by the minute. Danny was pretty sure that wasn't a good thing. "It's possible. It's definitely possible. Wait a minute. Are you thinking...?"

"That's exactly what I'm thinking! If Shanna were already pregnant when her parents killed Aulberic, she'd have had the baby after they locked her up. And from everything you and Mr. Fountain have told me, there's no way the Hellebores would have let her keep the child. It would have just rubbed salt in the wounds about how Shanna disobeyed them to marry Aulberic. No way they'd let a Redmane baby be brought up in their own home!"

"They'd leave it Topside," Danny said. He felt his eyes beginning to glow with emotion and quickly shut them.

"That would be the worst. Cut off from the Wonder, it would grow up weak and sickly. Probably have health problems its whole life. Worst case, it might not even live past high school."

"She'd never fit in," Taylor said, her lower lip trembling. "She'd know she was different but never understand why."

"And if Mrs. Redmane ever found out..." Danny said.

"Oh, crap!" Taylor gasped. She sprung to her feet. Danny did the same.

61

"She would order a switch-out," he whispered.

"She would order a switch-out," Taylor echoed. She began to pace the room, which couldn't have been easy in her over-long Civil War dress. Danny paced with her. Taylor was sharp—so sharp she could be dangerous! He felt the whole mission was about to go up in smoke. *Focus,* he told himself. *Let's see what happens next.*

"There was never any paperwork mix-up, was there?" she said, her voice cracking. She held back tears as she continued, words spilling from her mouth as soon as the thoughts came into her head. "That was just a cover story she used to put you and Bryn on my case. She knew exactly who I was, but she couldn't let you two know—she couldn't let anybody know until she had me where she wanted me. She wanted you to collect me so she could...so she could..."

"Nothing good," Danny said. "Use you for leverage? Try to turn you against Shanna? Make you suffer just for the fun of it?"

She stopped square in front of Danny and slapped her hands on both his shoulders.

"Anya Redmane is my grandmother!" she said.

"Yeah," Danny said. "It looks that way." Taylor suddenly looked very small, very vulnerable.

Just another switch-out my eye!

He hated to admit it, but he had gotten close to Taylor over the past few months. She was like the little sister he never had. In that instant he realized he had broken one of the basic rules of switching: he let it get personal.

"But...None of this makes sense!" he said. He had to tell her the rest. She had to understand what she was up against. "She said you would get to choose whether to stay in the Wonder or go back."

"She lied. There's no way she's going to let me go home."

Danny shook his head. "Not possible. Our Kind keep their word. Mrs. Redmane would rather die than make a promise she didn't intend to keep."

"Are you sure?" Taylor asked. "Are you absolutely sure? Tell me her exact words, Danny."

"Mrs. Redmane said there was a teenage girl we needed to switch out." Danny bowed his head and scrunched his eyes shut. "She said she was upset that the paperwork had not been filed and she was going to have a long talk with the person responsible. But she said to bring the girl—you—to see her."

"And?"

"Bryn asked her about switching out somebody so old. It happens sometimes, especially when a Topsider shows really powerful magical potential. But it's rare. We asked what would happen if you didn't want to stay in the Wonder.... She said, 'Just bring her to me and let me worry about that. I will explain the young lady's options. I insist that she make the final decision herself.'"

Taylor sighed. "I still don't believe her."

"You've got to understand how important Our Kind take oaths and promises, Taylor. For Mrs. Redmane to go back on her word...I'm not even sure it's possible!" He didn't say it, but he hoped Taylor would realize that meant he couldn't go back on his word, either.

And for good or ill, he had promised to deliver Taylor to the Summer Court.

"Danny, now that we know my story, do you seriously believe Anya Redmane is going to let me just go home to Macon, Georgia after we've had a little chat?"

He closed his eyes again. *This girl is going to be the death of me*, he thought. If she really was the daughter of Shanna Hellebore.... "I don't know," Danny admitted.

"Well, I do," Taylor said. She slumped into the nearest chair. "I'm already a prisoner—I just haven't made it to the jail yet." She glared at Danny, who shrunk into his seat like it was made of quicksand.

"We'll figure something out," Danny said in almost a whisper. "Maybe make contact with the Winter Court..."

"What good would that do?" Taylor bellowed. "They're the ones who abandoned me in the first place!"

"Okay, not my best idea," Danny protested. "But there's got to be something we can do."

Taylor yawned. Her face looked pale, even more than usual. There were bags under her eyes. "You look beat." And Danny was finding it more and more difficult to look Taylor in the eye.

"I am," Taylor sighed. "What time is it?"

Danny glanced at the mantle clock above Taylor's head. "Eight-thirty."

"Is that all? I thought it had to be at least midnight."

"Why don't you just go to bed, okay? Maybe things will look different in the morning."

"I doubt it," she said. But she did look beat. This must have been the worst day of her entire life.

She stumbled off to her borrowed bedroom leaving Danny to sit alone in the silence. He sunk back into his chair, leaned back his head, and closed his eyes.

Shanna is her mother!

This made things even more complicated than they already were. How could he possibly turn Taylor over to Mrs. Redmane? More than most, Danny knew what the Chief Matron of the Summer Court could be like when she was angry.

He learned more than he ever wanted to about Mrs. Redmane the first time he ever met her. It was years ago, and Danny had been called before the Triad.

She called his name like it was a curse word. As he stood before the dais on which the three Matrons sat, he was sure he wouldn't live to see another day.

"Dandan Underhill," she said. Her eyes shot daggers into him. She wasn't trying to conjure with his name, but her voice gave him the willies anyway. It was all he could do to keep from shaking apart beneath her gaze.

"You do not deny that you were responsible for the pumpkins?"

"Yes, ma'am—I mean, no, ma'am."

"And the trampoline?"

Danny sighed and nodded.

"And the goat?"

"Actually, ma'am, I...uh...*was* the goat."

The Matrons murmured among themselves. One of them, the youngest, eyed Danny with an expression of alarm and revulsion.

"You...*were*...the goat," Mrs. Redmane said.

"I'm afraid so, ma'am. And I'm really sorry for what happened to Mr. Bright."

"Sorry or not," Mrs. Redmane said, "my brother-in-law was intended to become the next Primus of the Summer Court. This little prank of yours has cost him his reputation."

"If you just give it time, ma'am, I'm sure things will settle down—"

"Settle down? He's the laughingstock of the entire Wonder! They're telling jokes about him as far away as Xian Jing! 'What did Ambicatus Bright say to the goatherd?' No one is ever going to let him live this down. His career is over, do you understand, Mr. Underhill?"

Anya Redmane's powerful presence rippled through the courtroom in waves of frustration and disapproval. Even the other Matrons flinched.

"Yes, ma'am," Danny squeaked.

"You may have singlehandedly set in motion the end of a dynasty that has ruled the Summer Court for centuries. It will take years—decades—to undo the damage you have caused."

"If...if there's any way I can make it up to you..."

"The Triad has considered how you might best make amends."

Danny couldn't bear to look Mrs. Redmane in the eye. Instead, he glanced up at the other two Matrons. They didn't seem any happier than the Chief Matron.

"We're told you're a rather skilled switcher—when you're not destroying the fabric of fae society with your ridiculous pranks, that is. Suppose we strike a deal."

"Yes, ma'am?"

"The house of Fairchild has already started maneuvering to put one of their own in place of my departed husband. Other families may do the same. It would be good for us to build up our retinue."

"Y-you want me to supply you with changelings?"

"In prison, you're simply a drain on our resources. We would rather make use of your skills. My cousin Martha has already drawn up a contract." She motioned toward her fellow Matron, who produced a roll of parchment from an ornate box on the judges' table.

"You do know how to read, don't you, Mr. Underhill?"

"For the most part."

"It's a fairly standard contract. We agree to reduce your term of imprisonment to the time you've already served and to supply you a basic standard of living within the Summer Court. In return, you will provide us with ninety-nine changelings over the course of not more than forty years. Do you understand?"

Danny understood fine. He was being made an indentured servant to pay for his crime.

"I'm sure I don't have to explain to you that we expect only the highest quality switches."

Danny let his eyelids fall and slowly expelled a breath. "J-just write me out a list, Mrs. Redmane. I'll bring in anybody you want."

Chapter 8

The Song of the World Tree

Long ago when the world was young, the First People lived in harmony under the shade of the great World Tree.

One day, the World Tree began to sing a beautiful, ancient song that stirred the hearts of all who heard it. The birds flocked to rest in its branches, and around its roots flowers grew in the rich, black earth. No one among the First People, however, could understand the song or tell what the World Tree sang.

The sages who guarded the ancient wisdom scratched their beards, for the World Tree's song sounded to them like the long-forgotten language of their ancestors.

The earnest women who knew the secrets of herbs and berries shook their heads, for the World Tree's song seemed to them as the babbling of children.

The brave hunters who could track wild animals from one end of the world to the other threw their hands in the air, for the World Tree's song was as elusive to them as a shadow or a morning breeze.

Everyone asked, "What does this song mean?" But no one could understand what the World Tree sang.

There was at that time a certain young maiden who listened to the song and held it in her heart. She stole away every night to sleep beneath the World Tree, and every morning she arose singing the words she did not understand.

For nine days, the World Tree sang. For nine days, the First People wondered. For nine days, the young maiden drank deeply of the tones and chords of the song she did not understand.

And on the tenth day, she announced to her mother and father, "The World Tree has spoken at last, and I can now understand its words!"

The maiden's father spread word to the other brave hunters. Her mother spread word to the other earnest women. And the young maiden herself approached the sages and bid them hear what the World Tree was singing.

Under the shade of the World Tree's branches, the young maiden interpreted the song.

"There is coming a time," she said, "when the whole world will be filled with people. Our little village will grow to become many, and villages will grow into cities, and cities will grow into kingdoms with mighty castles. In those days, the earth will be filled with noise and smoke and fire. People in that time will break oaths. They will sell their labor for pieces of metal. The wisdom of the sages will be forgotten. The secret knowledge of the earnest women will be lost. The skills of the brave hunters will count for nothing."

Most of the First People did not believe the young maiden. They laughed her to scorn because she was so young. She obviously didn't know what she was saying!

But the few who knew her best sensed in their hearts that she was right and wept for the world that was about to pass away.

Her words caused great conflict among the First People, however. Those who didn't believe her demanded that she keep silent and never speak such words again. Those who believed her prophecy insisted the sages do something to prevent the tragedy from occurring.

Soon the conflict became so great that no one was willing to listen to his or her neighbor.

It was then that the oldest and wisest of the sages called a meeting of all the families of the First People.

"We cannot go on as we are," she said. "The young maiden's prophecy has made us two people. We are no longer one. Therefore, let us separate before angry words give rise to angry deeds."

And although the First People were heartbroken by these words, they recognized the wisdom they contained.

The very next day, those who believed the young maiden's words withdrew from the village, determined to preserve the wisdom, secrets, and skills of the First People against the changing world.

The young maiden's father led them deep into the woods, where he spoke magic words and opened for them a door into a new and better world where they could be safe and secure in their ancient ways. And they called their new home the Wonder.

The young maiden grew up, and at the appointed time she married a keen and crafty hunter. And when they had children, they were so beautiful that she kept them hidden within the Wonder, where they had children of their own, and on until the world changed just as the World Tree said it would.

Chapter 9

Five Answers

In her dream, Taylor was eleven years old again. It was late April, and she was on her fifth-grade trip to Stone Mountain Park.

Stone Mountain was nothing but a big lump of granite five miles around. It rose over 800 feet in the air, and Mrs. Fletcher said it was solid rock for miles underground. When it was still a working quarry, it produced granite for buildings and monuments in nearly every state.

A hundred years ago, somebody started work on an enormous stone carving of three Confederate war heroes on the north face. Later they converted the whole area into a tourist spot with shops, a Civil War museum, miniature golf, a petting zoo, and lots of other attractions. It had been one of Taylor's favorite family outings for years.

Taylor, her friend Jill, and a few other fifth-graders were in the Marketplace Gift Shop by the miniature golf and the train station.

"Just get the snow globe," Jill said.

"No, I'd rather have a box of fudge. Let's go back to the candy store. We've got time."

"We're supposed to stay together." Jill glanced over her shoulder at Mrs. Fletcher, who hovered over three other girls by the tee-shirt racks.

Taylor shook her head. "I'll just be a second. Are you coming or not?" She didn't wait for her friend to answer. With one eye on her teacher, she ducked outside and sprinted across the pavement to the Candy Kitchen.

Jill followed. "Taylor! It's almost time to go!"

Taylor paid no attention. She knew exactly what she wanted and marched directly to it: a small box of chocolate walnut fudge that she still had just enough money to buy.

Jill caught up to her in the line. She kept peeking out the window to see if they had been missed.

"C'mon, Jill. Loosen up a little."

"Mrs. Fletcher said—"

"In another couple of weeks, Mrs. Fletcher will be history. Or do you want to stay in elementary school forever?"

Taylor set her candy on the counter and pulled a wad of loose bills out of her purse. The cashier bagged her purchase. She felt very adult, managing the transaction, saying "please" and "thank you," and handling the change the cashier gave back.

"Oh no," Jill said.

"What is it this t—uh oh."

Mrs. Fletcher stood in the middle of the road with her hands on her hips, looking this way and that. Three other girls from Taylor's class circled around her.

"She doesn't look happy, Taylor."

"When has Mrs. Fletcher ever looked happy?"

Taylor put her fudge in her purse. "Okay, here's the plan: we wait till Mrs. Fletcher is looking the other way, then we run around the corner."

"Toward the Dippin' Dots?"

"Right. There's a path that runs along behind these buildings. We double back and wait for her to find us in the gift shop. We'll say she left without us."

"You call that a plan?"

"Just trust me."

Taylor hunched toward the door, trying to obscure her face. She wished she and Jill weren't wearing the class tee shirts everyone else had on. It made them easier to spot in a crowd. But with a little luck...

"Now!" she said. The two girls burst out of the store and rounded the corner as fast as they could. They hung another sharp right and rushed down the path behind the shops.

This was a grassy area littered with trees and—thankfully—deserted.

Jill ran ahead. As much as Taylor wanted to run faster, she knew she had to pace herself or she'd run out of breath.

Jill was a good twenty feet ahead of Taylor when the strange little man walked onto the path.

"Look out!" Taylor shouted, certain the two would run into each other.

But the man kept walking, and Jill barreled right past him without slowing down.

"Come on!" Jill called. She spun around, breathing heavily. Taylor had stopped in her tracks.

"Wait, what was that?"

The man ducked behind a tree, studying Taylor. He couldn't have been more than four feet tall, with ruddy cheeks, pointed ears, and dressed all in green. He smiled and put his finger to his lips in a shushing gesture.

"What're you waiting for?" Jill called. "Something's giving me the shivers. Did I run into a spider web or something?"

"You don't see him?"

"See who?"

And as quickly as he appeared, the strange creature was gone.

"Taylor!"

It took another second for Taylor to come to her senses. She hurried to catch up with Jill. The two spun around the corner and wove through the lines outside the Funnel Cake Gourmet.

"Fletcher!" Jill said. Sure enough, their teacher was wandering in their direction.

"Quick!" Taylor said. She yanked Jill inside the nearest door. Guest Services. Perfect! She strode to the counter, trying to hide her grin. Mrs. Fletcher walked through the door just in time

73

to hear Taylor's tearful story about being left behind at the gift shop and needing to find her teacher!

The scene changed.

It was her sixth birthday. Her mom was driving her home from kindergarten.

"Mommy?" she said.

"Yes, Doodlebug?"

"Explain again why my first mommy didn't keep me?"

Taylor's mom sighed. "Your first mommy wasn't able to take care of you, honey. But she must have loved you a whole lot, because she made sure somebody would always be there for you."

"You and Daddy?"

"That's right. Daddy and I wanted a baby so badly, but the doctor said we couldn't. When we found out we could have you to take care of, it was the happiest day of our lives. We've loved you since we first met you."

"And you're going to keep me, right?"

"Oh, Doodlebug, of course we're going to keep you! We would never give you up! Why would you even think such a thing?"

"The other kids say I'm weird." Taylor crossed her arms.

"Well, *I* say they're just jealous," her mom said. "Miss Perkins says you're the best reader in her class, and you've got such a wonderful imagination—always telling such creative stories. That's nothing to be ashamed of, Taylor. You are a special little girl. If some people can't see that, well, that's their problem."

They rode in silence for only a minute before her mom added, "You know, I bet your first mommy and daddy are thinking of you today. If they could see you now, I know they'd be very proud. Just like Daddy and I are.

"Yeah?"

"And don't you ever forget it."

She woke up with her head still swimming.

She remembered that day at Stone Mountain, how she and Jill avoided getting in trouble with Mrs. Fletcher. She had mostly convinced herself the tiny man she saw (a leprechaun, maybe?) had been a figment of her imagination—it had all happened so fast, and he disappeared so suddenly. Now she wasn't sure.

Had she always lived with elves and faeries just around the corner?

She looked around the darkened room. She was on the bed Moe Fountain had offered her, still wearing her black and green dress. She hadn't even bothered to find pajamas or get under the covers. Yesterday's school clothes were cleaned and neatly folded on the foot of the bed.

Stone Mountain and the little heart to heart with her mom were just a dream. Yesterday, sadly, was not. This was all really happening. That meant Taylor had to get her wits together and decide what to do next.

The first item of business was a long, warm shower. The brass fixtures and marble tile in the bathroom made it feel like she was in a luxury hotel. Even the soap smelled better than anything she had ever had Topside.

Once she dried off, she put on her school clothes. After all, she didn't know how far Moe Fountain's hospitality could be pressed. Her own clothes were clean and dry, so she might as well wear them. Something told her she didn't want to owe the cymbee any favors.

Mr. Fountain and Danny were sitting on rocking chairs on the front porch. It was still dark outside.

As soon as she heard them, her mood turned sour—even sourer than it was already. She wondered how long they had been up talking about her. She stalked across the living room as quietly as she could.

"Well, you've got guts, kid," Mr. Fountain was saying, "I'll give you that."

"So, you think it'll be all right?"

"Just keep playing dumb. It's what you do best, after all."

75

Danny started to say something, but then he noticed Taylor approaching. Like her, Danny had put on the same clothes he wore yesterday. His backpack lay at his feet. His face was nearly healed. Only a little bit of discoloration showed the place where Taylor had decked him with the tree branch.

Moe Fountain wore denim coveralls and a red flannel shirt. He was sipping from a steaming mug of coffee as if this were just an ordinary day. For him, perhaps it was. Taylor wondered if she would ever have an ordinary day again.

"Good morning," Mr. Fountain said. "Have a seat on the swing. Danny says you two had a productive conversation last night." She took the seat her host had indicated. Mr. Fountain and Danny scooted their chairs to see her clearly.

"I guess you could call it that."

"Well, let's see. Suppose I ask the questions this morning?"

Taylor wasn't in a mood for games. It didn't look like she had a choice.

"Okay. I asked you five questions last night. I'll let you ask me five questions today. Deal?"

Mr. Fountain smiled. He looked at her with kindness—or at least a decent approximation of it. Taylor didn't hear any rumble of thunder in his voice or see sparks flash in his inhuman eyes.

"My thought exactly," he said. "You answer my five questions, and then we're even."

"Then let's get started, shall we?" she said.

"When were you born?"

"February second, thirteen years ago. Since that's almost exactly six months after Lammas Day, I'm guessing Groundhog Day is also some kind of transition period. Summer and Winter are evenly matched. Am I right?"

She kept her voice low and even. In fact, she surprised herself how composed she managed to stay. It was as if the emotion that usually came out in her death-glares had settled in her chest. Instead of flaring uncontrollably, it was a constantly burning fire inside her.

"We usually say Candlemas or Imbolc instead of Groundhog Day," Mr. Fountain said, "but you are quite right. And is there any further significance to this date?"

"Danny said last night that was about six months after the time when Aulberic Redmane was captured and killed. That means it's possible that Shanna Hellebore was three months pregnant when her own family killed her husband and took her prisoner. I doubt anybody knew that at the time, though, except for her."

"I see." Mr. Fountain took a sip of his coffee. "What happened next?"

Taylor bit her lip. "Mom and Dad say all they know is that I was left at a hospital. Of course, nobody knew I was...different. They only knew my birth parents abandoned me. I went into the foster care system, but it wasn't long before the Smarts, my foster parents, decided to adopt me.

"They never met my birth parents—nobody did. I guess the Hellebores didn't want to do a regular switch-out. That's what you call it, right? A switch-out? That might tip off the Redmanes that I existed. But I've heard of cases of newborns getting left at hospitals or police stations, places like that. That's why they have Safe Haven laws. They figure it's better for a mom to give up her baby that way than leave it to die somewhere. So I guess the Hellebores must have used back channels, left me somewhere and...and just walked away. Maybe they kept track of me over the years, maybe they didn't."

"Very good," Mr. Fountain said. "Now, tell me, Miss Smart, why does Anya Redmane want to switch you out?"

"Because she hates me," Taylor said, fighting back fury. "She hates what I represent: the death of her son, the fact that he disobeyed her to be with Shanna, the fact that I'm something she has in common with Mara Hellebore—and always will for as long as I live.

"If I may say so, Mr. Fountain, a better question would have been, 'Why did Anya Redmane want to switch me out *now?*'"

Danny let out a desperate whine. He looked imploringly into Taylor's eyes with a look that said, *Please don't make him angry!*

"Go on," Moe said.

"I don't have a clear answer to that one, but I think you do. Did she even suspect that Shanna was pregnant? If so, she'd have had her flunkies—no offense, Danny—looking for me from the start. And from the little I've seen since yesterday afternoon, I have a hard time believing it would take you people thirteen years to find me."

The words tumbled forth. Everything she had pondered the night before seemed to come together, like the pieces of a puzzle falling into place. Letting it all come out was somehow energizing. Her anger grew, but with it a sense of eerie calm. Moe Fountain continued to indulge her rambling thoughts.

"So the other possibility is she only recently discovered that I exist. But what happened to tip her off? That doesn't sound like the kind of thing you find out by accident. Danny told me last night she promised to have a long talk with the person responsible for me not having the necessary paperwork for a switch-out. That sounds to me like somebody spilled the beans, somebody close to the Hellebores. If that's so, then somebody from the Winter Court is in deep trouble—as if I care.

"Now, when we first met, you said you had a strong suspicion about who I was. I've been wondering how that could be, Mr. Fountain. Danny says you pretty much know about anything that happens in your valley. So, I'm curious if any other Fair Folk have passed through here in the last few months and what stories they may have told. Or maybe you have other sources of information. I don't know for sure, and it doesn't really matter. You know who tipped off...my grandmother. That's not a question, Mr. Fountain. It's a fact."

Danny shrunk into his seat as if bracing against the storm that was about to break. Moe Fountain, however, only grinned.

"Mr. Underhill, Miss Smart is a real find, don't you think? I don't think I've ever experienced such presence in a sídhe girl that young, have you?"

Danny shook his head. All the color had drained from his face. His warm, amber eyes had faded to pale canary yellow. Only then did Taylor realize what had happened. The whole time she was laying out her theory she was giving both of them the "death-glare." Only Mr. Fountain was able to give back as good as he got. He gave off a completely different vibe than Taylor: more primal, more powerful in some way, but he was definitely answering her "death-glare" with his own kind of fae magic—and poor Danny was stuck in the middle, taking it from both sides!

"Can you imagine what she'll be like once she buys in?"

Danny squeaked and shook his head. Taylor made a note of the phrase, "once she buys in."

"You're quite right, of course," Moe Fountain said. "I do have several trustworthy sources of inside information, and I have known for a while that the situation between the Redmanes and the Hellebores has, shall we say, changed in recent months. Neither side admits it openly, each for their own reasons, but the Hellebores have in fact suffered a rather significant...setback."

"I'm waiting," Taylor said.

"Well, if the rumors I hear are true—and I have no reason to doubt them—then Shanna Hellebore managed to escape from her prison shortly after Christmas."

Taylor gasped. "My...my mom..."

"Unfortunately, this only resulted in her capture by those loyal to her mother-in-law."

"What?"

"That's why I wondered about you when we first met. You favor your mother in some ways, and given what I knew about her recent abduction, a sudden order to switch out a girl of your age seemed somewhat fishy to me. Now that we have had a chance to talk, I find myself even more convinced of what I only suspected yesterday.

"Miss Smart, I'm afraid your mother—your biological mother—is in the custody of the Summer Court. I suspect that she is the one who pointed Anya Redmane in your direction, although against her will, I'm quite sure."

Taylor hugged herself tight. Her death-glare seemed to drain out of her like water through a sieve. She felt small, weak, and alone.

"M-my mom...," she said. "My mom...is..."

"I believe I'm entitled to one last question," Mr. Fountain said. Taylor couldn't even bring herself to glare at him. She just sat there with her head in her hands.

"M-Mr. Fountain, do we have to—?" Danny said.

"Of course we do, Mr. Underhill," he said. "The last question is the most important question of all. It is the question on which everything else depends, and I insist upon my right to ask it. Miss Smart now knows the whole story—what she is, the circumstances of her birth, the enmity between her grand-parents, why she is such a valued prize for both the Summer and the Winter Courts."

He leaned forward in his rocking chair.

"So, Miss Smart, I have one more thing to ask."

Taylor looked up, tears in her eyes.

"What are you going to do about it?"

The question hung in the air like a suffocating fog. All the times she wondered about her biological parents and why they would give her up, she never imagined anything like this! She had long fantasized about searching for her birth mother when she was older, just so she could know the truth. Now, the truth left a bitter taste in her stomach.

My mom is still alive, she thought. *She's in trouble...My grandmother is using us both...*

"Miss Smart?"

Taylor took a long, deep breath. She filled her lungs until they should have popped like balloons. It should have sent her into a coughing fit with her asthma, but somehow she was fine.

"I...I want to meet my mother. If you can help me, that is."

Danny sucked in a breath.

"I don't like to stray far from home," Mr. Fountain said. "But I'm sure Danny would prove a capable guide."

"M-Mr. Fountain, I don't know about this...."

"Come, now, Mr. Underhill. You knew this was a possibility."

"B-but I can't just drop her at Mrs. Redmane's feet!"

"No," Moe said, "I don't suppose you can. Although I imagine you could take the long way around, if you wanted to. I hear Pilot Knob is pretty this time of year."

Danny's expression seemed suddenly awake. Wheels were turning inside his head. Possibilities were unfolding.

"What's Pilot Knob?" Taylor asked.

Moe Fountain smiled. He got up, slipped back inside the house, and returned almost immediately with a golden delicious apple. He set it on the table between his chair and Danny's. He gave Danny a subtle smile.

"Well, I'm glad that's settled," he said. "I'm going fishing! Pack yourselves a lunch before you leave. Danny, I assume you know the way?"

Before Danny could answer, Moe started down the stone path into the spring. In an instant he had vanished beneath the water.

Taylor's eyes darted between Danny and the apple. Danny looked like he had seen a ghost.

"So...what's the deal with the apple?" Taylor asked. She left her seat on the swing to sit in Moe Fountain's rocking chair.

Danny sighed. "Remember what I said yesterday about faery food?"

"You said something about it being a commitment, whatever that means. Is that what you're talking about?"

"Right." Danny squirmed in his seat. "You see, fae society is all about reciprocity."

"Reciprocity?"

"Like for like, give and take. You scratch my back, I'll scratch yours."

"I ask you five questions, I owe you five answers in return?"

"Exactly." Danny paused, considering how to proceed. "The thing is...Faery food works sort of the same way. It unlocks a fae's powers. The reason you've been sickly all your life is you're malnourished, magically speaking."

"But...?"

"But it also sort of...binds you to the Wonder. They say if you eat enough of it, Topside food won't even taste good any more. Even if you only eat a little, though, it changes you."

Danny looked her in the eye. "It's usually only changelings that happens to, but you've lived Topside so long, Taylor...I don't know what might happen to you. You don't want to eat it unless you're sure."

Now both of them were staring at the apple Moe Fountain had set in their midst.

"Persephone," Taylor said.

"What?"

"Not what, who. Persephone. In Greek mythology, she ate six pomegranate seeds on a visit to the Underworld and ever after she had to spend six months of every year down there as the wife of Hades."

Danny sat silently. Taylor's heart beat like a drum. Finally, Danny said, "It's your call, Taylor. If you really want to go to the Summer Court and meet your mom, you're gonna need all the magic you can get. But please please please don't do it unless you're sure. I mean absolutely sure."

"This is what Moe meant by 'buying in,' isn't it?"

"Yeah. Once you eat your first faery food, you've bought in. You're truly one of us." He sighed. "Look, maybe in a few days this will all work out and you'll be able to go back to your Topside life...but like I said, faery food changes you. It's hard to predict how, but it does."

"You can take me to the Summer Court."

"It's hard to say.... I mean, they move around a lot, and there are lots of places they might be..."

82

"Danny, that wasn't a question. You were supposed to take me to my grandmother *yesterday*. You know perfectly well where the Summer Court is right now. You *can* take me to them."

"Yeah," Danny said, defeated. "I can take you to their rath."

"Do you have to say it that way? I'd rather not think about their wrath."

"Not wrath as in anger," Danny said. "Rath as in fort or castle. Mrs. Redmane is waiting for us at her rath at Dunhoughkey...if that makes you feel any better."

Taylor frowned. "Not especially." She picked up the apple. "Dad always says, if you can't go over your problem, or under it, or around it, then the only thing to do is go through it." She didn't give herself time to chicken out. She took a bite of the apple. It was the most wonderful apple she had ever tasted. The meat felt cool and tingly going down. Even the crunch sounded like music to her ears.

"That's delicious," she mumbled.

She took another bite. Danny watched in silence.

"Take your time," he cautioned.

Taylor slowly and deliberately finished off the entire apple. She couldn't decide if she felt any different. Her ears didn't suddenly turn pointy or anything, but with every bite she wondered if her senses were somehow being adjusted— heightened, or maybe tuned to different frequencies. The colors on the walls seemed a bit more vibrant. The rich aroma from Moe Fountain's empty coffee cup filled the air. Even her breathing registered in her consciousness in ways it never had before, like she was breathing properly for the first time in her life, drawing into her body not only oxygen but power, vitality, magic.

Then again, maybe it was just her imagination.

She set the apple core on the table and licked her fingers.

"Okay," she said. "Let's go meet my mom."

Chapter 10

Glamour School

Like all pookas, Danny thrived on chaos. He was never more energized than when things were moving in a hundred different directions at once. But even he wasn't sure he liked the way things were shaping up.

On the porch that morning, Moe Fountain confirmed a lot of what he had feared. All over his valley, the songbirds had tweeted the news that things were heating up between the Summer and Winter Courts. A recent spate of tornadoes in Tennessee weren't just a fluke of nature but a skirmish between competing factions of spriggans. A family of angry and paranoid merpeople capsized a boat somewhere in Alabama when they mistook its crew of vacationers for Gentry spies.

Danny cursed himself for not paying more attention when his mother tried to teach him the language of the birds. Maybe he'd have heard some of this back in Macon. Maybe he'd have been better prepared.

At the center of the storm stood Danny. Or, more properly, stood Taylor Smart—the biggest trophy either Court could hope to possess.

But if Taylor was the center of the storm, then Danny had a ringside seat. One thing was certain, however. There was no way he could protect this frail girl on his own. She had to learn how to take care of herself in the Wonder—and fast.

As soon as Moe mentioned Pilot Knob, Danny began to hatch a plan. He'd take her there and see what the fae who lived there could do for them. But first he had get Taylor started learning magic.

She seemed truly relieved that leaving Moe Fountain's place didn't require diving underwater. Danny could feel her dread, however, when she found out the spring in front of Moe's house was a portal into the Wonder, the same as the mushroom ring back home. She grabbed Danny's arm and gritted her teeth as the two of them stepped through the sparkling wall of light and, rather than falling into the water, vanished into thin air.

In the pre-dawn gray, scenes passed through Danny's consciousness in quick succession: woods, rivers, and small towns. Taylor began to whimper. Danny tried to travel as gently and directly as possible toward his goal. At last, he slipped out of the tornado and back onto solid ground.

He braced himself in case Taylor had another asthma attack. She didn't. Even so, she didn't look too good.

"How do you do that?" she moaned. She stumbled off of the large boulder they landed on.

"It takes practice," Danny said. "Stepping straight in is a lot easier than sliding around the edges."

"I mean, how do you do that without puking all over yourself?"

"Huh? I never thought about it before."

Danny looked around. There was no ring of mushrooms or natural spring, only a flat hunk of rock sixteen feet across, jutting out of the ground and covered with strange markings. It was circled by wooden posts, and there was some kind of platform wrapping around it in a semicircle. He spied the surrounding woods. Nothing seemed out of the ordinary.

Taylor pulled her windbreaker close around her body. The air was cooler here than in Grubb, South Carolina, and the hills were steeper. They were somewhere in the mountains. The sky was purplish gray, with the first hints of sunrise peeking out behind the trees to the east.

They followed a gravel road through meadows and low hills. There was farmland all around them. Before long, a cluster of tiny cottages interrupted the landscape, like shadowy building blocks a giant preschooler might have dropped.

"Okay," Taylor said. "How much farther to the Summer Court?"

"You're not ready for the Summer Court yet," Danny said. "If you want a fighting chance, I need to teach you some magic first."

The look on Taylor's face said she hadn't thought about that.

"Magic," she said. "You mean glamour?"

"You remembered the word. That's good. Yeah, glamour—among other things. And then there are some people we need to see, but we can talk about that later. For what it's worth, it looks to me like you've already figured out a little about glamour on your own. That thing you do where you get all intimidating? That's called presence. It's a pishogue: a glamour trick. You project an aura of power and confidence. People find it hard to stand up to you."

"Really? I've already been using glamour?"

"Pretty impressively, too," Danny said. "But we need to start at the beginning. You need to learn something more basic."

"Go on, Professor."

Danny gestured forward through the trees. The two of them circled around the perimeter of the valley, keeping close to the trees. They gradually made their way closer to the cottages.

"The whole point of glamour is to bend the minds and perceptions of people around you—Our Kind or Topsider," Danny explained. "Bryn is able to take your place at school today because she's using glamour to plant the suggestion that she's really you."

"Don't remind me," Taylor said.

"It's tricky to try something that specific, but it comes pretty easy for a huldra like her. That's why I requested her for this assignment. It's easier just to pass as a human generally, like I did at school."

"But I already look human!"

"I know, but if you do it right, there are other pishogues you can do with glamour. The most basic is to use it to keep people from noticing you at all."

"You mean invisibility?"

"True invisibility is really hard to pull off," Danny said. "What I'm talking about is simpler. If you make a loud noise or call attention to yourself, the spell is broken and anybody can see you. And if somebody's looking straight at you, it won't ever work on them. You'd have to distract them first, make them look away for a second. It ain't perfect, but sometimes it's all you need.

"What I'm talking about is more like...well, you know how Shelby Crowthers pretends she doesn't even see the unpopular kids? Then if she bumps into you in the hallway, she acts like it's your fault you weren't watching where you were going? It's like that, only the person *literally* can't see you. You use glamour to make yourself as uninteresting as possible, so you just kind of get lost in your surroundings. Maybe you look like a bush or a slab of rock or an old tire. Maybe you don't look like anything at all."

"You think I could learn to do that?" Taylor asked, wide-eyed.

"I know you can," Danny said. "This is kindergarten stuff for Our Kind. You'll pick it up right away. The trick is to get used to feeling glamour. It's around us all the time. It sort of oozes out of the Wonder, like all faery magic. Now that you've bought in, you'll become more aware of it. Think of it as a mist or an aura that surrounds you everywhere you go. You just need to learn to draw on it, take it into yourself. Once you can feel it, you can make it do what you want. It helps if you can imagine letting yourself to be wrapped up in a veil or a blanket."

Taylor stopped to give it a try. She closed her eyes and breathed deeply. "Nothing is happening," she said.

"You're doing fine," Danny encouraged her. Then something caught his attention. He sniffed the air and smiled. "Tell you what, you deserve a treat, this being your first official day as one of Our Kind and all. You see that house in the valley? The one closest to us?"

They were no more than half a mile away from the nearest cottage. It was small but tidy, wrapped in the waning night and with not a light on inside. A vegetable patch grew in neat little rows in the back yard. The house had an old-fashioned porch with a porch swing, a wooden rocking chair, and a hand-made wind chime dangling from the ceiling. An older model car was parked in the driveway.

"I see it," Taylor said. "What about it?"

"Friendlies live there," Danny said. "Can't you smell it?"

"Smell what? What are Friendlies?"

"Topsiders who still believe in the Fair Folk. There aren't that many these days, and a lot of them are just plain crazy, to be honest. But they're good people. They know what it means to respect nature, to be open to things that most Topsiders can't explain. And they still have their uses. Point your nose toward the house and give it a good sniff."

Taylor did as Danny told her. She struck him as a city girl, not used to the earthy smells of the countryside: grass wet with dew, natural fertilizer, healthy soil, growing things. She looked at Danny, confused. He encouraged her to try again. She took another sniff, and then it hit her.

"I smell cookies!" she gasped.

Danny simply grinned. "They leave us offerings like that. Why don't you go up to the porch and have some."

"You're kidding."

"I'm as serious as a troll attack. They want you to take them. That's why they leave them out. Just make sure nobody sees you."

"Seriously?"

"Seriously. I'll wait at the edge of the garden. Help yourself. Just remember, 'wrapped up in a veil.'" Danny pantomimed pulling a veil over his head.

They crept up on the cottage without another word. Danny glamoured himself, although Taylor could still see him as plain as day. Or at least as plain as dawn.

He stopped at the edge of the garden and motioned for Taylor to go on. She took a deep breath. Danny watched as magical mist began to swirl around her, spreading from her shoulder blades out over her entire body. He strained his eyes to see her as she appeared to any Topside observer. She slowly faded from sight.

Switching back to his normal vision, Danny watched as Taylor tiptoed toward the house. At the bottom of the porch steps was a plate of cookies and a glass of milk. She flashed Danny a look that said, "This is ridiculous!"

She took another step, then stopped in her tracks as a light flipped on inside the house. A moment later, the latch of the back door rattled. Taylor froze where she stood.

Just stay calm, Danny thought. Taylor's glamour seemed to hold up.

The door slowly opened. A tiny hairball of a dog bolted out, then stopped in its tracks a few feet short of where Taylor was standing. It circled around her, whining and sniffing.

"Make it quick, Chester," the old lady said. Taylor looked the woman squarely in the eyes. She tried to be as still and quiet as possible—which was not easy with a dog sniffing around her feet. But as much as the dog complained about her presence, the old lady didn't seem to have a clue there was a stranger standing in the middle of her yard.

Taylor glared down at Chester. He gave a subdued yelp and trotted away, did his business, and returned to the house.

The glamour collapsed just as Chester threaded between his mistress's legs.

When the door closed behind them, Taylor looked back toward Danny. He urged her on. She inched forward.

The picked up a cookie as if she were a cat burglar stealing a diamond necklace. She took a nibble. She smiled.

She drank about half the milk and scooped up the remaining cookies. Stealthily, but somewhat more quickly, she tiptoed back to the edge of the garden.

Taylor couldn't help but giggle.

"Not bad," Danny said.

"I think the dog saw me."

"Animals usually at least sense that something's not right. Babies are the worst, though. I swear, if they could talk.... Oh, and for the record, you slipped a little bit at the end. Don't worry—she didn't see you. But when you got to the porch steps, you were plain as day."

"I guess I need more practice." She wolfed down a second cookie and offered Danny the third one. It was chocolate chip, and homemade by the taste of it. Most Friendlies could be counted on for leaving a decent treat.

"And sugar. Using magic can take a lot out of you. Sweet snacks can help keep up your magical energy. Carbohydrates, you know? But you didn't do bad at all for your first try. Just remember: it's a lot easier to glamour yourself when there's nothing more at stake than a handful of cookies. If you're serious about finding your mom, Taylor, you may have to hide from people—and things—that are trying to kill you."

"Yeah," she said.

"Oh," Danny said. "Look at this. The poor lady's got worms in her watermelons." He held up a leaf for Taylor to inspect. It was yellowed and half-eaten by some sort of creepy-crawly.

"We're going to have to do something. We can't let a nice lady like that lose her garden."

Danny rubbed his hands together and blew on them a couple of times. He assumed a spread-leg stance, elbows slightly raised and hands facing outward as if he were getting ready to catch a ball.

He quietly hummed a sing-songy tune, soon adding words that Taylor couldn't quite make out. After no more than about a minute, he pushed his hands toward the watermelon patch with a flourish, at the same time expelling a forceful puff of air. Smoke curled around his fingertips.

"That's better," he said.

Taylor looked back at the leaves. They were perfectly green and healthy!

"Whoa," she breathed.

"All part of a day's work for a pooka," he said. "Help the nice ones, make life miserable for the naughty ones."

"And eat lots of cookies?" Taylor quipped.

"When we can."

"Wait a minute," Taylor said. Something was definitely familiar about this scenario. "You do good things for nice Topsiders. You play tricks on the naughty ones."

"Yeah, so?"

"And they give you cookies and milk?"

"What's your point?"

"Well, isn't that an awful lot like San—?"

"You're right, Taylor. You need a little more practice," Danny said brusquely. "I only wish you knew your true name."

"My what?"

"Your true name. All of Our Kind have one. Concentrating on your true name helps focus your magic. It lets you get the most from it."

"So what's your true name?"

"Taylor, don't even joke about that!" Danny said. "You never want to reveal your true name to anybody you don't trust with your life. Heck, plenty of Our Kind get nervous about sharing their everyday names with fae they don't know! Knowing your own true name strengthens your magic, but if somebody else learns it, they can use it against you."

"I see," Taylor said. "And you don't trust me."

"Look, don't feel bad. It's just not an appropriate thing to ever ask."

The more Taylor thought about it, the more she saw Danny's point. She had secrets she would only share with Jill. There were others she wouldn't even share with her best friend. "I understand," she said. "I'm sorry."

"We've got to travel another two hundred miles or so. Then we'll see if we can meet...people." He still wasn't terribly enthusiastic about the people they would be meeting. He knew Moe Fountain was right, though. They needed these people—more than Taylor could guess.

"How about a game of hide-and-seek?" Danny said. "I'll count to twenty. You head into the forest and see if you can glamour yourself to hide from me."

Taylor hesitated. "Are you sure?"

"One...two...three..."

Taylor grinned. She whipped around and charged into the woods. Danny turned away, but kept his ears open, following the sound of her footsteps as they went deeper into the forest.

On twenty, Danny opened his eyes and sniffed the air. His sense of smell wasn't as acute in his normal form as it was as a dog, but it wasn't hard to pick up the scent of Taylor's clothes—not to mention the chocolate chip cookies.

He hiked up the side of the hill, moving as silently as possible. He came to a stop and spied around in every direction. He looked up into the trees. Someone was there, he was sure of it.

He stalked on, but turned back when he heard a rustling of branches. There was Taylor, standing in the Y of a maple tree about five feet off the ground.

"Gotcha!" he said.

"I think I'm getting better," Taylor said.

"You're not bad at all. Keep practicing and you'll be all right."

"Good," Taylor said. "So, when are you going to tell me about Pilot Knob?"

"Ah, that."

"Somebody lives there that Moe Fountain thinks can help me. Right?"

"Something like that." Danny wasn't sure how much to say, or when would be the best time to say it. He balanced Taylor's need to know with the way she was likely to react if she knew too much.

"I'm listening," she said.

Danny sighed. "Another two hundred miles. Are you ready?"

"Not particularly," Taylor admitted, "but come on. Let's get it over with."

They walked back to the boulder with the markings. But something was wrong. Danny held out his hand, and Taylor stopped abruptly. *Wonderful!* he thought. He made his veil gesture again, and Taylor concentrated on glamouring herself. She peered through the trees and discovered what had captured Danny's attention.

Someone else was already waiting for them. In fact, two someones stood watch on the wooden viewing platform. Taylor was visibly frightened but managed not to make a sound.

They were shorter than Danny, five feet tall at the most, and dressed in what looked like Boy Scout uniforms. But if they were Boy Scouts, they were working on their merit badges in ugly. They had crooked, skinny bodies. Like Danny, there was something animalistic about their appearance. They had arched bushy eyebrows, big bat-like ears pointing straight up, and unkempt hair: one black, the other reddish-blond. They had long knives strapped to their belts—or maybe they were short swords. Either way, it was pretty obvious they were bad news.

Danny made a shushing gesture, but Taylor had already figured out making noise would be a gigantically stupid thing to do.

"This is nuts," one of the creatures said. He may have been the size of a child but his voice was a deep baritone. "We've been here half an hour. The sun's already rising."

"We're just supposed to guard the place, Jory, not ask questions. And what do you care, anyway? Guard the threshold and let Mr. Cornstack know about anything suspicious. Pretty easy duty if you ask me."

Mr. Cornstack! Danny thought. They were with the Winter Court. This couldn't be good.

Jory answered with a burst of profanity. "Boring duty! Come on, Kev, you mean you wouldn't rather be doing something fun? Blighting crops? Snatching Topsider whelps?"

Danny made another shushing gesture. That rock was the portal to Pilot Knob. He had to draw the guards away so he and Taylor could get to it. He blinked away in a swirl of shimmering dust, leaving Taylor to crouch down behind a tree and hope her glamour held up.

"What I'd rather be doing," Jory answered, "is anything but this! How come we pull the lousy duty while other spriggans get all the excitement? Would it have killed Mr. Cornstack to send us to Georgia instead of Bill and Pasco and that bag-man— what's his name? Enrique?"

"Don't forget Lyle," Kev added.

"See? Even some stupid troll gets to see more action than we do!"

Danny reappeared high in the trees and tried to collect his thoughts. The bag-man had to be the one that tried to grab Taylor, and the troll was the one camped outside her back yard back in Georgia. From the sound of things, Crom Cornstack had also put a couple of spriggans on the case.

"The way I hear it, Enrique botched things up," Kev said. "That's the only reason Bill and Pasco got sent in."

"Even better!" Jory said. "We coulda gone in and fixed Enrique's mess, maybe gotten a little bit of respect from the boss. Instead, here we are guarding some stupid rock."

"You gotta look at the big picture, Jory. Say the feud between the Summer and Winter Courts really is heating up again. If that's so, then both sides will want to control this 'stupid rock,'" Kev explained. "Judaculla is the oldest and most powerful portal into and out of the Wonder for five hundred miles."

"Fine," Jory grumbled.

"Just keep alert. If there's—" Kev stood suddenly alert. Danny had snapped a twig to get their attention.

The two guards glanced at each other. Magical mist swirled around Jory and Kev, masking their appearance until they looked like ordinary human Boy Scouts. Even the sheaths of their weapons shrunk to the size of utility knives like campers might carry.

None of that mattered to Danny, of course. He knew exactly what he was dealing with. He dropped from his tree branch.

Combat magic is hard. You have to work your rage and aggression up to a fever pitch and then push it even further till you could shape all that negative emotion into something to throw at your enemies. Danny didn't figure the spriggans would have much trouble with that technique. For his part, he preferred to be a little more creative.

As soon as he hit the ground, he assumed the form of a black, shaggy goat and bounded into the clearing, bowling both spriggans over with a single pass.

Not bad, he thought to himself. *Now if you morons would just follow me...*

His eyes glowed with yellow fire. He wheeled around and launched into a second attack. One of the spriggans had already summoned energy for a blast. He gestured toward Danny, pushing a shimmering swirl of magic in his direction. There was a flash of white light, but Danny had changed direction five feet short of his targets and narrowly missed being struck.

He rolled on the ground and reverted to his everyday form.

Getting blasted was one of Danny's least favorite things in the whole world. With Taylor to protect, he couldn't afford to get hit. He sprung to his feet as the spriggans hurried toward him.

"What's the big idea?" one of them said. But Danny just grinned and gave the spriggans a rude gesture.

"I'm gonna kill you!" the creature said.

"First you'll have to catch me," Danny said. He broke into a run, but then suddenly blinked out of sight.

"Get him!"

Danny reappeared deeper into the woods. The magical Boy Scouts took off at a run. The one in the lead stomped toward him. He grabbed a tree by its trunk and pushed it down until it snapped in two.

"You think you can hide from us?" he bellowed.

Danny took a deep breath. Of course, he already knew that spriggans were incredibly strong. That wasn't quite the same thing has having a couple of them chasing him through the woods howling for blood. He blinked again—and wished he had eaten a couple more cookies. The spriggans stopped only long enough to catch a glimpse of the flash of light where he reappeared.

Danny dropped from the trees into a small clearing.

Perfect! he thought. He quickly got his bearings. The rock was no more than about fifty yards in front of him. Now if he could just egg them on a little bit more...

"I'm not hiding!" he taunted. "Why should I hide from a couple of pipsqueaks like you?"

The first spriggan drew his blade and lunged at Danny, who darted away in the form of a horse. As the second spriggan approached him, Danny turned and kicked him square on the chest. The spriggan fell back spread-eagle on the grass. His partner attacked again, but Danny dodged his blast by blinking away once more. That was it, though. He was really starting to feel drained. One more blink was about all he could count on. He just couldn't let them know how tired he was. From a safe distance, he chuckled. "Oo! I'm really scared now! The teeny weeny little spriggans are about to get me!"

"I'll give you teeny weeny!" the first spriggan growled.

Danny smiled. Now it was all just a matter of timing.

The spriggans scrunched their faces and balled their fists. All at once, they began to grow taller. They passed normal human height and kept going until they might have been over ten feet tall.

Danny called them a rude name. They stormed after him once again. This time, their ponderous footsteps sounded like a miniature earthquake.

Spriggans could grow to gigantic size at will, just as pookas could assume different animal forms. This ability, combined with the gigantic strength they possessed at any size, made them fearsome warriors.

What most fae didn't realize—and what Danny had only learned the hard way, after numerous bruises and broken bones over many years—was that a spriggan's height could also be a liability.

Moe Fountain had once tried to explain it to him mathematically, but it just gave him a headache. The long and the short of it was that as a spriggan's height increased, so did his weight. In fact, his weight increased faster than his height. So even though a spriggan got even stronger as he grew, he also got slower for having to lug all those extra pounds around.

Double the height worked about to about half the speed and agility. And speed and agility were a pooka's bread and butter.

He would never try it in a confined space, but in the open woods, Danny knew that as soon as the spriggans grew to giant size, he had the advantage. He sprung into his horse form, bounding between the legs of the nearest spriggan. Then, just as the spriggan was bending down to grab him, he resumed his two-legged form and jumped up onto the shoulders of his other attacker, only to dive off, spin in midair, and land safely on the ground. The second spriggan twisted as if swatting at a mosquito. In fact, he twisted right into the path of the first spriggan. They slammed into each other, and both fell flat on the ground with a thunderous thud.

But Danny didn't stay around to hear it. He only had a matter of seconds to get back to the rock, collect Taylor, and escape. He blinked away, appearing directly in front of Taylor, his eyes still glowing with yellow fire.

"Hurry!" he shouted.

They ran to the rock, stopping only long enough for Taylor to get a strong hold on Danny's arm.

"Come back here you stinking pooka!" a spriggan hollered. The two guards had blinked into the clearing, once again normal sized. They bolted toward Danny and Taylor with murder in their eyes.

"Gotta go!" Danny yelled, and turned to face the rock.

Then, just as Danny stepped through the portal, one of the spriggans grabbed Taylor's ankle.

Chapter 11

The Rules

Taylor had reached a conclusion. As bad as ring-travel was for her stomach, ring-travel with an unwanted hitchhiker grabbing her by the ankle and screaming bloody murder was even worse.

She might have imagined it, but it seemed Danny was moving through the Fair Folk's ring system even more erratically than he had before, no doubt trying to throw off their passenger. Taylor watched as they passed over fields and villages, deep valleys and stony mountaintops. When she couldn't bear to watch any more for fear she'd throw up all over Danny, she shut her eyes as tightly as possible.

The trip must have lasted at least twenty minutes, but at last their attacker lost his grip. Actually, he didn't loose his grip at all. But Taylor's shoe lost its grip on her foot, and away he spun, shoe and all, bellowing curses into the Wonder.

"Hold tight!" Danny cried. The two of them bounced around for a few more minutes until finally coming to an abrupt stop. The initial impact knocked Taylor's exposed sock clean off her foot. She wished her stomach could evacuate the scene as well. They rolled head over heels along a grassy slope, finally coming to rest in a field of clover.

Taylor rolled over onto her stomach. "You've really got to work on your landings," she sighed. She struggled mightily not to throw up.

"Sorry. Couldn't be helped. I had to shake that spriggan."

Taylor pulled herself up until she was kneeling on the grass. She stumbled up the hill toward her errant sock. It felt weird to walk in only one shoe. On the way back she hopped along while she unstrapped the other one. By they time she got back to Danny she was barefooted—and mostly over her motion sickness. The grass was cool between her toes. She hoped a trip to a shoe store was somewhere on Danny's agenda.

"Can you hold onto this for me?" she asked, offering him her shoe.

"Sure." He shoved it into his backpack.

Then she realized that something was wrong. The sun was already going down. When they left, it was still morning. How could it already be afternoon?

"Where are we?" she asked.

"North Carolina."

"H-have we been at this all day? Did I pass out or something?"

"You didn't pass out," Danny said, exhausted. With some difficulty, he regained his feet. He pointed into the distance and started walking. Taylor followed.

"It's just that crossing a threshold can be tricky. If you're not careful, you can time-skip."

Taylor stared at him.

"Okay, you know those stories about Topsiders who stumble upon a ring, and go in and party with the Fair Folk for a couple of hours, but then when they leave, a hundred years have gone by?"

Taylor gulped.

"Now, don't worry. We haven't skipped more than a few hours—a day and a half, tops. Most of the time, Our Kind don't have any problems at all. It's when Topsiders try to cross a threshold that things get really messed up. But that spriggan... I had to ride a little reckless to shake him off. I guess I should have paid a more attention."

"It's not your fault," Taylor said. "Do you know where we are?"

Taylor looked around. They were even higher in the mountains than they were before. It must have been pretty close to suppertime, although it should have only been late morning. Danny suggested they eat the lunch he had packed for them at Moe Fountain's place.

Taylor wasn't especially hungry, but she also didn't feel like moving. Plus, Danny must have used up a lot of magical energy leading those—did he call them spriggans?—away from her. Since his magic was the only thing keeping her alive at the moment, she figured it was best for him to refuel. She nodded her agreement.

He opened up his backpack and doled out an assortment of fresh fruit, bread, and cheese. He opened a thermos and poured Taylor a cup of cool, fresh water from Moe's spring. Danny drank from the thermos.

Taylor started peeling an orange. As with the apple, everything about it seemed perfect—the aroma was sweet and refreshing, the juice glistened in the sunlight like liquid gold.

"What were those things?" she said at last.

"Spriggans," Danny said. The word seemed to leave a bad taste in his mouth. "All the Courts like to use them for guards and soldiers and what have you. From the way they were talking, they're with the Winter Court. They answer to Crom Cornstack. Bunch of no-account snatchers if you ask me!"

"Snatchers?"

Danny took a bite of his apple. "Common kidnappers. They steal children for their bosses."

"Really? How dreadful!" Taylor rolled her eyes.

"Hey, there's a difference between switching and snatching! A spriggan's just a thug who'll grab a kid and blink away. They almost always get the Topside police involved, and lots of times they have to take the kid back because too many people got suspicious. What I do takes planning, intelligence. There's a reason Mrs. Redmane's kept me under contract. I'll have you know I've completed ninety-eight switch-outs in the last forty years, with nary a hitch."

"Until yesterday," Taylor observed.

"Yeah, well...," Danny muttered under his breath. "The point is, I take pride in my work. Switching is an art. What spriggans do is more like a carjacking. No style at all."

"You've really given this some thought," Taylor said. She didn't know if she should be revolted or simply mystified.

"I don't mean to brag," Danny said, "but I'm pretty much the best at what I do. Even Mrs. Redmane knows that. Sure, following my rules takes a little longer, but the results speak for themselves."

"Rules?"

"There's rules for switching just like there's rules for anything else. Respect my four rules and you'll succeed every time."

"So what are these rules?"

"Come on, and I'll tell you," Danny said. He took one last swig of water and put the thermos back in his backpack. The two of them continued up the slope.

"The first rule is the one most of Our Kind forget: Knowledge Is Power. If you want a quick, clean switch-out, you gotta know everything about your target. Get on the inside, let the target show you the best way to proceed."

"That's what you were doing at my school," Taylor said. "Getting to know me, my habits, my friends." She trembled at the thought of being studied like that. The Fair Folk really were monsters, she decided. Even the nice ones.

"Okay, so what's the second rule?"

"Timing Is Everything. The best time to switch somebody out is before anybody even realizes it's happened."

"Wouldn't somebody know it if their own child is missing?"

Danny grinned. "You figure your parents have noticed that *you're* missing?"

Taylor gasped. "Bryn?"

"Exactly! Of course, your situation was a little bit...ah... different. For your switch-out, we needed somebody like Bryn to impersonate you short-term until you've had your talk with Mrs. Redmane. Whenever I switch out an older kid with magical talent, I like to use a placeholder until he or she decides whether or not to buy in. And, of course, there are times we leave one of our own babies in place of the target. I think I already explained about that. But usually it's easiest just to use a fetch."

"A what?"

"A fetch," Danny explained. "You take a piece of wood, you see, or a little clay figure, or something like that. Magic it up until it looks and acts human. It's very complicated—potions, spells, and you need a sample of the hair or fingernails of the target. Then, when you take the target, you leave the fetch. A really top-of-the-line fetch will last for months—maybe years—and the parents will never catch on. Looks just like the real thing.

"Danny, that is about the sickest thing I've ever heard! How can you do that to some poor family?"

Danny shrugged. "I prefer to think about the kid who's getting a better life out of the deal. You should see some of the kids I've switched out over the years, Taylor. Their parents might have beat them, starved them, or basically treated them like dirt. You ever heard of crack babies? Fetal alcohol syndrome?" Danny gritted his teeth. For a second, his eyes glowed with their eerie, yellow light. "I ain't gonna feel bad about giving kids like that over to a fae family who'll take care of them."

"Ouch!" Taylor stepped on a sharp rock and nearly bowled Danny over. She definitely needed to go shoe shopping!

"Anyway, the third rule is Create a Diversion. You've got to keep everybody looking in the wrong direction until it's too late to do anything about it. Of course, we didn't really get the chance to set off our diversion in your case because of the bag-man. But we had it all worked out. We had a trampoline, some pumpkins...it would have been awesome!"

"I'll take your word for it." Taylor was feeling sick to her stomach. Was she really one of these people? They seemed to take such a flippant attitude toward things, like the lives or concerns of puny Topsiders didn't even matter.

"You said there were four rules."

"Did I?"

Danny looked straight ahead and continued to walk. Apparently the discussion was over. The two walked in silence for several yards. "I think we're close," he said. "Come on."

They hiked further up the mountain. Danny may have been through talking about his rules, but there was something else on Taylor's mind.

"So...Pilot Knob?"

He regarded Taylor silently. "It's one of the largest eldritch settlements in North America," he said. "Apparently Moe Fountain thinks there are fae there who'll be willing to help you."

"But you're not so sure."

"Okay, here's the story," Danny said. "The good news: the Pilot Knobbers are like Moe in that they don't give a rip about the sídhe Courts. Add to that the fact that they have a reputation for siding with the underdogs."

"Sounds like our kind of people," Taylor said. She gave Danny her hand as he helped up over an outcropping of rock. She gingerly stepped over it. "And the bad news?"

"Let's just say they have kind of a history with the daoine sídhe. Taylor, once they find out who your grandparents are, they're not likely to trust us. They might think either the Redmanes or the Hellebores sent you, that we're trying to pull something over on them."

Danny continued. "You remember what those spriggans said? The Summer and Winter Courts are on the move. There's trouble brewing—and I'd bet anything we're at the center of it. I don't know if the Pilot Knob fae will be very friendly if it means getting in the middle of a war."

"I see," Taylor said. Still, they had come too far to turn back. "So, where do we find them?"

"I'm not exactly sure," Danny said, "and that spriggan threw us off course. I've never been here myself, but we're in the right place: Pilot Knob, North Carolina. We need to look around for some kind of threshold."

"Like that rock in the park, or Moe's spring?"

"Yeah, some kind of portal between Topside and the Wonder. I don't think it would be a spring, though. More likely a cave, even a deep crevice in the rock somewhere."

"Then let's get going!" Taylor said.

The sun had sunk even further toward the horizon by the time they found the portal. They wandered all around the mountain ridge—it was actually pretty hard to decide where one specific mountain stopped and the next one began—for over an hour. Danny poked his head into half a dozen small crevices, but to no avail. Taylor tried to squint and shift her vision to see any entrances disguised by glamour. Either she wasn't as good at it as she thought she was, or there was nothing to be seen.

Finally, Danny found the entrance to a cave, partially covered by vines and bushes growing out of cracks in the rock. "This has got to be it," he said to himself.

Taylor looked for signs of glamour, but didn't see any.

"Are you sure?"

"No, but it's the closest thing to an entrance we've seen today. Besides, it will be dark soon. We'll need a safe place to sleep."

"Okay," Taylor breathed. Danny stooped and entered the cave with Taylor right behind him.

They had only gone a few feet when the cave floor sloped down and around to the right. Sunlight began to fade as they plunged deeper into the earth. It wasn't long until it was pitch black.

As well as Taylor seemed to manage seeing in the dark that morning, she was surprised at how black things got in the cave, and how quickly. She waited for her eyes to adjust, but they didn't. Before she could complain, a dim light appeared in front of her. Danny held open his hand, palm up. A tiny, glowing glob of light floated silently above it.

"You've got to teach me that trick," Taylor said.

Danny grinned. They kept creeping into the depths of the earth. The tunnel soon opened up wide enough that the two of them could nearly walk side by side. The ceiling was still so low, however, that they both had to stoop to keep from hitting their heads.

As far as Taylor could tell, the tunnel was a natural feature, a passageway (if that's what it was) carved by erosion over thousands of years rather than the work of any miner. The floor was uneven and slick with slime.

After about a hundred feet, the passage forked. Danny and Taylor looked at each other with uncertainty.

"Left or right?" Taylor said.

"No way to know," Danny confessed. "Split up?"

"Not on your life!"

"Okay," he said. "Then let's try this." He cupped his hand around the ball of light he had been carrying. He tossed it underhand as far as he could down the left passage. It ran out of momentum about thirty or forty feet ahead of them and floated, suspended in mid-air.

"See anything?" he asked. Taylor studied the area Danny's light illuminated. It looked as gray and boring as the part of the tunnel they had already passed through.

"Nothing."

Danny gestured, and the ball of light floated silently back into his hand. He tossed it down the other passage. This time it traveled a bit farther and then stuck to the ceiling.

"I can't tell any difference," Danny admitted.

For a second, Taylor was tempted to try eeny-meeny-miny-moe, but that seemed like an awfully stupid way to make a decision.

"Do you think you could go as far as your light-thingy and throw another one?"

"Sure. And I call it a spunkie, though I s'pose 'faery fire' is the proper term"

"Well, whatever it's called, maybe if we could see a little farther, we could decide which way to go."

"Right."

"Just don't get out of my sight," Taylor said. "Understand?"

"Perfectly," Danny said. He inched down the right passage toward his fiery orb. Every third step, he looked over his shoulder to nod toward Taylor.

Forty feet ahead, his fire was slowly dimming and sinking toward the ground. He paused to lift it to the ceiling. At the same time, he recharged its brightness. He walked no more than three paces past the orb and formed another one in his hand. As Taylor had seen twice before, he gave it an underhand toss deeper down the tunnel. This time, the orb curved around a bend to the right. She could still see the glow, but the orb itself had passed from her view.

Danny crept forward toward the second light.

"Not too far!" she whispered.

"Don't worry," Danny whispered back. "Believe me, Taylor, the last thing I want to do is let you out of my—"

Suddenly, everything went dark. Someone had thrown something over Taylor's head. Rough hands grabbed her around the waist and lifted her off her bare feet. She kicked and screamed, but couldn't pull free no matter how hard she tried. Her shoulders and legs banged against the cave walls.

The last thing she heard was Danny calling out her name.

Chapter 12

Trapped in an Iron Cage

Taylor screamed, kicked, and twisted her body every way she could trying to break free, but her abductor was far too strong. She bounced along on his broad shoulders, banging knees, feet, shoulders, and head into the cave wall at least a hundred times.

Still, she didn't know what to do but fight. She cried out for Danny until her throat was raw. Then she couldn't scream any more because she couldn't catch her breath. *Rats!* she thought. There was never a good time for an asthma attack. This had to rank near the top of the list of worst times. Whatever kind of bag she was in, it was full of dust—and dust was always the worst.

The harder Taylor tried to breathe, the harder it got. She gulped and wheezed, but it was like she was sucking air through a straw. She started to panic. She lurched and kicked, trying to break free not so she could escape but simply so she could breathe.

"Dwally! Move aside!" the gravelly voice of Taylor's captor demanded.

There was a murmur of voices, all equally harsh.

"What's the matter, Nabby?" someone called.

"I've found a trespasser," Taylor's captor—Nabby—said. "Clear out the supply locker, and be quick about it!"

There was a general commotion. Furniture was being moved around. Footsteps headed in different directions. Then there was a rattling and clicking sound of metal striking metal. Taylor was dumped on the ground, and the sack that had covered her head and shoulders was pulled off. All the while, Taylor coughed and wheezed.

Get a grip! she told herself.

She fell to the ground, drowning in a sea of air. She tried to scoot away, but it was all she could do to keep from passing out.

"She looks sick," someone said. She peered upward into the face of a nightmare. He was nearly as tall as a normal man, with a nose that seemed way too big for his face. He was bare-chested and dressed in grease-stained work pants and clunky boots. He sported a tangle of jet-black hair and a full beard that looked like he hadn't washed or even combed it in months. His skin was as pale as chalk, like a vampire but without the good grooming. Taylor didn't think he was one of those lame, sparkly vampires, either.

"Asthma...," she wheezed. "Please...." Why did she ever let Bryn take off with her inhaler?

"Well, that's no good," the pale man said. "We can't interrogate her if she's dead. Blain, can you do anything?"

"Let me see her," another voice said. Another creature muscled in where the first had stood. He was the same sort of thing—pale as death, black-haired with a tangled beard, solidly built, big-nosed, and wearing grubby workman's clothes—but his most distinguishing feature was the patch over his right eye.

"What's your name?" he asked.

Taylor tried to speak, but she couldn't catch her breath.

"I don't know what I can do without her name, Dwally," Eye Patch said.

"Just try."

The creature with the eye patch placed his huge hands on either side of Taylor's head. She flinched, but couldn't pull away. His rippling muscles were as hard as stone.

The creature started to hum in a low, rumbling drone that set the entire room to vibrating. The rest of them joined in. Eye Patch looked straight at her with a single eye that was as deep and black as onyx. Then he opened his mouth and began to sing. Only it wasn't quite singing. It might have been closer to chanting—a strange singsong like nothing Taylor had ever heard before:

By the earth below,
By the stars above,
I adjure you, Panting Sickness!
I hunt you from wights, from beasts,
From birds, from every living thing,
To the deep pools I hunt you,
To the murky swamps I hunt you,
To the heart of the earth I hunt you,
Where no wight walks,
Where no beast wades,
Where no bird flies.
If you do not obey me,
I will burn you in my forge,
I will pierce you with my tongs,
I will pound you with my hammer,
I will bend you on my anvil,
I will drown you in my pail.
I order you to leave this girl—whatever her name is—
And torment her no more!

The longer the creature chanted, the more he raised his voice in an eerie, animalistic howl. A couple of the others swayed from side to side as they stared up at the ceiling. The last line came out like nothing remotely resembling a human voice. Then again, it was pretty obvious the singer was not human.

Taylor slumped back to the floor. She felt oddly warm. A tingle in her chest reached all the way up to her nose and into her sinuses. It took her a second to realize she was no longer gasping for air. Nearby, people were chuckling. She willed herself to calm down. With any luck, the worst was over.

At last she sat up and took stock of her surroundings. She was in a workshop, a blacksmith's shop, to be precise. There was huge brick furnace in the center of the chamber as well as three wooden workbenches and a massive anvil on a stand. The benches were littered with the tools Eye Patch mentioned in his song—tongs and hammers and such. Even more tools dangled from spikes driven into the walls.

She was in an enclosure of some kind, separated from the rest of the chamber by metal bars. One of the creatures was padlocking the door. The one with the eye patch stood to one side, either dazed or exhausted. Maybe both.

"That'll hold her," the first creature said. Taylor shared her cell with numerous crates and a bank of shelves against the far wall. Despite the fire in the furnace, she felt unnaturally cold.

Four others gathered around the door. Each was as ugly as the first, pale and twisted and not entirely human. They were dressed similarly, but three of them wore leather aprons that covered them from their torsos to their knees. The fourth had on a threadbare tee shirt.

"Let's have a look at you, little girl," one of the creatures said. He spoke with a distinct nasal twang. Given the size of his nose, Taylor wasn't that surprised. She realized all of her captors had the same kind of voice, the kind that would have given her choir teachers fits.

Taylor eyed them from behind her bars. She inched up the wall, using the shelf for support. Her whole body ached from being slammed against solid rock so many times. Plus, she was exhausted from her asthma attack.

"Let me go!" she gasped. The creatures murmured to themselves.

"Not likely," the one in the tee shirt said. To his comrade he said, "You say you found her trespassing?"

"That's right," Nabby answered. "She was poking around out by the south entrance. And that's not all."

"Yeah?"

"She wasn't alone. There was a fae tossing fire orbs in the tunnels."

"A fae!" a different creature spat. "I thought we had a deal! Nobody from Pilot Knob is supposed to come near our caves without permission!"

"You can't trust a stinking faery!" a fourth creature chimed in, the tallest of the group.

"Then she's one, too!" the leader said. Was his name Dwally?

Taylor's head was pounding, but she had to get a grip. She tried to call forth enough glamour to try a death-glare. "Presence," Danny had called it. An aura of confidence. Power. If she could intimidate them, maybe she could convince them to let her go.

"I said, *Let me go!*" she growled.

All five creatures became suddenly silent—then burst out laughing.

"Listen, little girl," one of the creatures—the tallest one again—chided, "your little glamour tricks aren't going to work around here. Or are you so dense you haven't even realized where you are?"

Taylor didn't know what to say to that, but her face must have told her captors everything they needed to know. To more sneering and joking, the creature who had spoken to her pulled some kind of metal scraper from a pocket on his apron and ran it across the bars of her makeshift cage.

"What Otter is trying to say," Dwally explained, stifling laughter, "is that you're trapped in an iron cage. Iron!" He said it as if it was the punch line to a joke Taylor should have understood, but didn't.

She tried once again to imagine a veil of magical mist resting on her shoulders, draping over her. Nothing happened. It was as if she had used up her daily allotment of glamour. She had run out of magical steam.

"What kindred d'you figure she is?" another creature asked. He was nearly as tall as the one who rattled her cage and built like a brick wall.

"Too ugly to be a huldra," a stout creature in an apron said.

"Too stupid to be a sídhe," Nabby added. Taylor fumed. "I think the other one was a pooka, though."

"She could be a puke," Dwally mused. "If I was going to send a spy, I'd definitely send a puke."

"They're tricky, that's for sure," Otter, the cage-rattler, said.

"I'm not a spy!" Taylor protested. She limped forward. "Now please, *let me go!*"

It was no use. She simply couldn't intimidate them. She grabbed the icy bars and shook them in frustration.

"Dwally," Nabby said, "do you want me to get hold of Tewa? Find out how much ransom he's willing to pay to get his spy back?"

Dwally scratched his chin. "Not yet," he said. We need to find out what she knows—and especially where her buddy is. Blain, any ideas?"

The creature in the eye patch snapped out of his daze at the mention of his name. "Not sure," he said. "Give me a minute." His gaze turned in Taylor's direction. Taylor shuddered. For an instant it felt as if he were looking straight through her.

"We don't have a minute," Dwally said. "Blain, Finn: get back in the tunnels and round up the other one. I don't want him making it back to Pilot Knob. Understand?"

"Sure thing, boss," Eye-patch said, shaking himself awake. He gestured to his stoutly built colleague. He picked up a big leather satchel that jangled as he heaved it to his shoulder, and the two of them darted out a sturdy wooden door on the far side of the chamber.

That left Taylor alone with Dwally, the leader; as well as Nabby, apparently the one who caught her in the first place; and Otter, the tall one with the metal scraper.

Dwally swaggered over to her. "They're starting them young these days. What are you? Twenty? Twenty-five?"

Taylor started to protest that she was only thirteen, but thought better of it. She had already seen that the Fair Folk aged more slowly than ordinary humans, but she had no idea how that worked out in terms of how foolish and immature her actual age would make her seem to these creatures—whatever they were.

"I'm not a spy," she said.

"You keep saying that," Dwally said. "I just don't believe you." Nabby and Otter murmured in agreement. "You Pilot Knobbers make a big show of letting us dwarves live in your neighborhood. You trade for our goods. But we both know you'd give anything to learn our secrets."

"I'm trying to tell you, I'm not from Pilot Knob. I've never even been—wait, did you just say you all are *dwarves*?" She gazed up at Otter, the tallest of the group, who could have been nearly six feet tall.

"Well, what did you *think* we are? Wood nymphs?" Otter laughed in derision.

"No!" she protested, blushing. "It's just...I always thought... never mind."

"The state of education these days," Dwally sighed, shaking his head. "I bet she doesn't know a thing about dwarf-kind except what she's seen in those Topsider movies where we're all short, proud, warrior guys with Scottish accents."

"Ignorant stereotypes!" Nabby added. "I blame Dungeons and Dragons." The others murmured agreement.

"Like it would kill them to portray our culture with any sense of integrity!" Otter said. "Hoot mon!" He broke into a ridiculous Scottish brogue. "Gie me an axe so Ah can lop aff the head o' the wee fae lassie!" Dwally and Nabby laughed out loud in spite of themselves.

"Yeah...," Taylor said nervously. "Lame, right? Totally unrealistic."

"You can say that again," Nabby said. He turned to Dwally. "So, what do you figure we should do with her?"

Dwally considered her for a moment, then said, "I doubt she knows anything. Why don't we just kill her and be done with it?"

"What?"

"Otter, you got your axe handy?"

"I just sharpened it yesterday, boss."

"Wait a minute! What about all those negative cultural stereotypes?"

"What about them?" Dwally said. "We're not short. We're not proud warrior guys. None of us has a Scottish accent."

"We're just going to kill you to protect our secrets," Nabby added.

"It's what we do," Otter said, now hefting a fierce-looking hand axe. "No need to take it personally, little girl. It's just business."

"Business!"

"Teach you faeries a thing or two about boundaries," Nabby added.

"But I don't even want to know your secrets!"

"Too bad," Dwally said, "'cause we've got some really great ones." He pulled a key ring off the wall and started for the supply locker.

There was a sudden commotion somewhere outside the chamber that grabbed the attention of the three dwarves. Someone yelped in pain, followed by the barking of an angry dog.

Danny! Taylor thought.

Nabby and Otter looked to Dwally. There was a rumble like an earthquake or a small explosion, then more shouts of anger and confusion.

"We better go see what's wrong," Dwally said. "The girl can wait. She's not going anywhere."

"You got that right," Otter said with an angry glare. The three filed through the wooden door behind them.

Taylor still felt weak, bruised, and sore, but being alone in the dwarves' workshop gave her new energy. She spun to face the shelves. There had to be something here she could use to escape.

She rummaged through the shelves. There were leather aprons, work boots, and grease cloths. There were tools Taylor had only seen in period movies, awls and hand drills as well as other things she didn't recognize. There were boxes upon boxes of metal scraps and fittings: iron nails and screws, copper rivets and wire, brass doorknockers and bathroom fixtures, and even some gold and silver trim of some sort. It was like a tiny, underground home improvement store.

She turned to the crates on the floor. The first one she saw was addressed to "Wormfield & Co. Fine Metalworking, c/o D. Wormfield, Proprietor." The lid had already been pried off. Inside, she found a collection of tools and dies.

I could really use a lock-pick set, she thought.

Then she saw it. Behind the crate, kicked up under the shelving, was some kind of tool, a fancy set of pliers with the handle grips hollowed out to make room for extra fittings. Taylor's dad had something like this in his toolbox back home. He called his a multi-tool. It reminded Taylor of an overgrown Swiss army knife. It had all kinds of gadgets and doodads: a screwdriver, pliers, scissors, wire cutters—just about everything. This one made her dad's look like a kiddie toy. It must have had at least thirty different tools. Plus, it must have been expensive. The handle was black as the tunnels, and the metal parts looked like they could be silver.

She flipped the contraption this way and that, looking for any tool that might prove useful. The wire cutters were too small. The screwdriver was too big. The toothpick dispenser was no use at all. The compass might come in handy later, but first she had to get out of her cell.

"Aha!" she breathed. She flipped open an attachment on one of the handle grips. It was an old-fashioned key, three times as long as any ordinary key, with a long shaft with a metal casting near the base that looked like a tiny human skull.

A skeleton key? Taylor thought it was worth a try. She reached around the outside the bars and fiddled to get the key inside the padlock. The bars were still cold, but that was the least of her complaints. She slid the key into the lock and twisted it around until she heard a click. She took a breath and pulled the lock open.

Okay, she thought. *Now, which way out?*

She decided her best bet was to go out the same door the dwarves had. On her way out, she fiddled with the multi-tool, looking for something that might serve as a weapon. Cork-screw? Metal file? Eyebrow tweezers? She pushed a stud on one of the handles, and the end opened up like the iris lens on an old-fashioned camera. A beam of soft, white light struck the wall in front of her.

"Now we're talking!" she whispered. She didn't know if her flashlight was powered by double-A batteries or by dwarvish magic, and she didn't really care. At least now she'd be able see where she was going.

She pushed open the door and glanced at the compass on the other handle of the multi-tool. She started down the passage. It wasn't long before she heard sounds of a commotion. Angry dwarves were heading her way.

"He must have doubled back!" one of them called.

"Split up!" another said. It must have been Dwally. "Nabby, Otter and I will check the workshop. Finn and Blain, guard this fork in the tunnel.

Taylor hadn't seen any of the dwarves yet, but they were on their way. She scrambled in the opposite direction as quickly as she could. On the other side of the workshop door, the tunnels forked again. She ducked around the corner.

Another door was just ahead on the right. She tried the handle and sighed with relief when it creaked open. She slipped inside as quickly as she could and pushed the door shut.

The room's ceiling was made of glowing orange rock. Taylor thought for a second it was made of lava, but it didn't give off any heat. She was just as cold as she was before. Outside, booted feet trudged past and angry dwarven voices echoed along the rocky corridors. She slipped the multi-tool into the waistband of her skirt so it rested securely against the small of her back.

Taylor found herself leaning against a bookcase. Every wall was covered with them, and a large wooden table took up most of the center of the room along with a couple of globes and some other instruments she didn't recognize. She was in a library.

Despite the danger, curiosity compelled her to scan the spines of the nearest ones. The titles were written in several languages and even in different alphabets: Greek, Arabic, and even in runes, the strange angular letters the Vikings used to use.

The titles she could actually read were at least as bewildering as the ones she couldn't. These dwarves apparently held a wide array of interests. Naturally, it seemed, there were books on mining and metalworking, geological science, and machine tooling, but also books on natural history, cooking, philosophy, and more. As she wandered around the room she found titles like *A Brief History of Sage* and *The Compleat Pyromaniac.*

She nearly picked up that last one until the door suddenly burst open. She started to shout before remembering she was hiding. Instead of a shout, she gave a startled squeak.

"Shh!" Danny ran forward and clamped a hand over her mouth.

"Glamour," he whispered. "They're coming back. We gotta to use glamour. Fast!"

Taylor tried to settle herself. After her glamour failed so miserably in the dwarves' workshop, she wasn't sure what good it would do, but she closed her eyes and imagined the magical mist wrapping itself around her. Danny pulled her out of the library and into a side passage across the hall Taylor hadn't noticed before. A second later, heavy footsteps clunked past them.

"Nothing in here," one of the dwarves called as he ducked his head into the room Taylor and Danny had just left. Taylor thought it might have been Otter, the big one with the axe. He and his two friends passed on down the corridor.

"Get ready to move fast," Danny whispered. "And whatever you do, don't let your glamour slip."

He summoned a handful of faery fire and sent it floating down the side passageway. At the same time, he pulled Taylor back out into the main passage. In the bright light of Danny's orb, she could see Dwally, Nabby, and Otter thirty feet ahead. They whipped around as soon as they saw the light.

"That way!" Nabby shouted. They stomped back the way they came. Taylor held her breath, but thankfully they didn't notice her or Danny. All they were interested in was the light Danny had conjured, which he now sent further down the other tunnel.

Danny pushed her forward. The two of them now crept away through the tunnel the dwarves had originally chosen. At the first bend, Danny conjured more faery fire to light their way. This time, he kept it very dim, barely enough to see by.

"How'd you get away?" he whispered. "Never mind. You can tell me later. We've got to find a way out of here. But help is on the way."

"It is?"

"Seeing stone," Danny explained. "Pilot Knob is sending somebody, but we've got to find a safe place to wait for them."

These tunnels, Taylor noticed, were different from the ones where they first went underground. They had been widened, no doubt by dwarven tools, and every now and then a wooden door broke the monotony of the cold, gray stone. Unlit torches were mounted in iron braces along the corridor.

"There they are!" a dwarf yelled. Taylor could see the shadowy figure approaching off a side passage. He was big and stocky and armed with a dagger. Behind him was the short dwarf with the eye patch. Finn and Blain.

"Keep going!" Danny yelled. He turned back to face their pursuers. Taylor ducked into the nearest doorway. She fumbled with her multi-tool. There had to be a knife or something in there she could use to defend herself!

The dwarves lunged at Danny, but he vanished in a flash of light, reappearing behind them and kicking Blain in the pants. By the time the two had turned around, Danny had assumed the same goat form he used against the spriggans. He rammed into Finn, catching the strap of his leather apron on his horn and yanking him this way and that like a rag doll.

Blain reached into his satchel and brought out a coil of metal chain. He flung it in Danny's direction and it seemed to come to life, snaking around the pooka's body and flinging him against the far wall. Danny slumped back to the ground, dazed and in his usual shape.

Taylor gave up looking for a knife. She needed the skeleton key to get inside the door she was crouching against. She found it just as Danny let out a pitiful whimper. She flung the door open and closed it quickly behind her. She slipped the multi-tool back into her waistband. She was once again trapped in utter darkness, but hopefully the dwarves wouldn't find her.

"Blain! Finn!"

It was Dwally's voice. That meant the other three dwarves were there, too.

Oh, great! Taylor thought.

"The girl escaped!" another said. Finn, maybe? "I saw her go this way!"

The dwarves' footsteps came closer and closer. Taylor found the wall with her hand and edged away from the door. She concentrated on being as uninteresting as possible.

There was a jangle of keys.

"Get your axe ready, Otter," Dwally said. In the distance, Danny shouted Taylor's name. He sounded hurt, dazed.

There was a metallic click.

The door flew open.

Chapter 13

Tsuwatelda

Danny couldn't do a thing.

Why didn't I warn her about iron? he thought. Iron messes with fae magic. Tied up in iron chains, he couldn't shapeshift, couldn't blink, couldn't do anything but roll around on the ground shivering. He was shaking so badly he could hardly breathe. Even through his clothes, his bonds were so cold they burned his skin.

"Let me go, you ugly maggots!"

The nearest dwarf kicked him in the gut.

"Who're you calling maggots, faery?"

"Taylor!" he yelled, but his voice had no hope of carrying over the echoing shouts of the dwarves and Taylor's frightened screams. They had burst into the room where she was hiding and yanked her out into the corridor.

"Not a spy, huh?" the leader said.

"No!" Taylor cried. "Just let me—"

"Listen here, little girl! We know you're with the puke! Tell us what you're up to and we *might* let you live!"

They slammed Taylor onto the floor in front of Danny.

"So what's it going to be?"

"I'm trying to tell you..."

"Wait!" a short dwarf wearing an eye patch held up a hand. All eyes darted toward him. "I heard something... Somebody's—"

The tunnel was suddenly ablaze with scarlet light. The dwarves spun in every direction, lowering their weapons toward the newcomers.

There were about a dozen of them, approaching out of the shadows along all three corridors. Danny craned his neck to see the one nearest him.

Taylor squealed with fright, and with good reason. The warriors of Pilot Knob were a sight to see. They carried war clubs and tomahawks with flaming heads that crackled in the suddenly silent corridors, although the fire didn't seem to harm them at all. Their enemies wouldn't be so lucky.

They were dressed in loincloths, leggings, and colorful cotton shirts adorned with ribbons and cinched with wide beaded belts. The one in front, with steel-gray hair but full of vigor, wore a red headscarf—in fact, he was dressed in black and red from head to toe. Others wore either multicolored headscarves or a feather or two tied at the crown of their heads. All of them had multiple earrings circling the rims of their ears. With their stern expressions, it was obvious they weren't paying a social call.

The tallest dwarf rushed forward. He lifted his axe above his head and moved to bring it crashing down on the head of the nearest warrior. Instead, a flaming tomahawk parried his blow. The warrior twisted his weapon, yanking the axe from the dwarf's hands and flinging it away into the darkness.

"Enough!" the fae in the red headscarf shouted.

The dwarf leader cursed. "How dare you!" he growled.

"You have no quarrel with these two, Wormfield," the fae said. "They lost their way in the tunnels trying to find our domain. It was an innocent mistake."

"Lies!"

"I never lie. It was a mistake." The fae was calm and poised. Danny wasn't sure he was using presence. He may not have needed to. He was clearly in charge of the situation, outnumbering the dwarves better than two to one. He had no need to twist anyone's perceptions on that matter.

The dwarf leader hesitated.

"Let them go," the fae said.

The dwarf leader grumbled as he nodded to one of the others, the dwarf with the eye patch. He gave Danny's chain a tug, and at once it loosened and retreated from Danny's body, coiling around itself into a roll that quickly disappeared into the dwarf's satchel.

The dwarf yanked on Danny's collar and hauled him to his feet. He thrust him forward into the main circle of fae warriors. He glanced around. They had also turned Taylor over to the nearest group of rescuers.

"This isn't over," the dwarf muttered.

"Indeed, it is not," the fae answered. "This isn't the first time you have mistreated our guests. The bonds of hospitality may mean nothing to you, Wormfield, but rest assured Tewa will not be pleased."

With that, the fae nodded to his companions. Someone grabbed Danny by the arm, and everyone blinked away.

They slipped through tiny cracks in the rock, across a deep chasm, and through a labyrinth of natural tunnels. Danny could have never navigated such a maze! At last they reappeared in the open air.

They were in a vast expanse of rolling hills surrounding a well-watered bottomland dotted with fertile fields. In front of them was a town surrounded by a wooden palisade. Above them, the sky was bright and turquoise and dotted with puffy clouds that glowed purple and pink in the last light of the setting sun. Birds flew overhead, huge crows that trailed rainbows behind them as they flew off toward the north.

They had made it safely into the Wonder. Danny sighed with relief. Taylor leaned into him, woozy from blinking. He offered her his arm, but she waved him off and pressed on.

Strong girl, Danny thought. *I hope she's strong enough.*

Danny, Taylor, and the Pilot Knob warriors approached the palisade. It opened with a gesture from the fae in the red head-scarf. Inside was a town, a jumble of wooden and stone houses circling a cluster of high artificial mounds. The returning party escorted Taylor and Danny down a wide avenue running east to west straight to the middle of town.

As soon as they entered the settlement, Danny, Taylor, and the returning warriors were surrounded by hundreds of curious Fair Folk. Most were nunnehi, Native American fae who had lived at Pilot Knob for thousands of years. But there were a good number of others as well: fae and other beings seemingly from every corner of the world.

"The White Chief will want to speak with you. Soon," the fae leader said. "I trust you will enjoy your stay at Tsuwatelda."

Danny nodded. He tried to remember the little he knew about how the nunnehi did things. He had completely forgotten the native name of Pilot Knob—if he had ever known it. Nothing came to him except something about them having three different chiefs ruling at the same time. But he didn't have time to think about such things. He was too worried about Taylor.

"Are you all right?" he asked her.

She nodded, speechless. Here eyes were like saucers. Danny realized this was the first time she had ever really seen the Wonder in all its glory.

"It's...beautiful...," she sighed. "But...where are we? Those mountains in the distance—is that where we started?"

"Yes and no," Danny said. "The Wonder isn't exactly a place. I like to think of it more as a frequency. Most Topsiders don't have the equipment to tune into it."

"But we're here!" Taylor protested. "And there are doorways between here and the outside world."

"It's complicated," Danny said. "See, there's the world you know." He held up his left hand at chest level, like he was demonstrating the depth of water in a swimming pool. "But that's just the skin of the onion. There's a bunch of other levels underneath." He waved his right hand vaguely to demonstrate. "That's what we call the Wonder. The two worlds are never entirely in sync, but there are places where the connection is pretty close. Usually high in the mountains or deep in the woods. Some are even underwater, like the entrance to Moe Fountain's place. Before, when we were ring-riding, we only slid around the edges of the Wonder." He winked and smiled. "This is the real thing."

They reached the main thoroughfare and strode down it like a parade. At the door of every house, fae of all ages peered at the visitors in their Topsider clothes. At the center of town was a vast, open plaza. At the far end, Danny spied a dozen or more fae warriors practicing archery. Closer by, children played a game of chase, laughing and egging each other on.

"Are you all right?" Danny said again. "Dwarves can be pretty rough on strangers, especially Our Kind. They didn't use iron on you, did they?"

Taylor shuddered. "They put me in a supply locker. They said something about iron, but I didn't understand."

"I'm sorry," Danny said. "I should have warned you. Iron does a number on fae magic. You've got to be careful around it."

"What?" Taylor stumbled forward. "What kind of lame weakness is that?"

"I said I'm sorry."

"You darned well better be sorry! I'd kind of appreciate knowing that going into a hardware store could be harmful to my health, you know? Would have been nice to know before I got kidnapped by a bunch of homicidal blacksmiths!"

"I-I just didn't think of it," Danny said. "All this comes second nature to me. I forget it's all new to you."

They stumbled on. Taylor still looked awfully shell-shocked from the whole experience.

"So, is there anything else you've been meaning to tell me? Do I have to watch out for crosses or wooden stakes or anything like that?"

"What? No, don't be silly: that's vampires. But I would be careful around church bells if I were you. The ringing sound makes some of us really sick."

"Okay. Iron. Church bells. Anything else I should try to avoid?"

"There are some plants that are poisonous to Our Kind. Rowan berries—of course, they taste awful anyways. Saint John's wort. You're not taking any antidepressant medications, are you? 'Cause the active ingredient might be—"

"I don't even know what you're talking about."

"Okay then." Danny counted off the items on his fingers. "Iron. Church bells. Rowan berries. Saint John's wort. That's about it. Well, salt, obviously."

"Salt? What will that do, melt me like a slug?"

"Don't be ridiculous," Danny said. "It's just bad for your blood pressure. You'll take a hundred years off your life if you're not careful."

Taylor sighed. "Well, thanks for the warning."

They came to the foot of the mound at one end of the central plaza. Above them was the town's Council House, circled by a cluster of individual houses, the living quarters of Pilot Knob's leaders.

A nunnehi girl approached them. She looked about Taylor's age. She was at the head of a gaggle of children.

"Ayoka!" the fae with the red headband called. The girl trotted up to him as if he were an old friend and not someone who could slice and dice a roomful of dwarves in about half a second.

"This is Ayoka," the fae told Taylor. "And Ayoka, this is...?"

"Taylor."

"...This is Taylor. She is a guest of your grandfather. Can you make her feel at home while the Chiefs speak to her friend?" He gestured toward Danny.

Ayoka smiled. "Sure. Come on! This way!"

Chapter 14

The People Who Live Anywhere

Normally, Taylor would protest being thrown into a group of strangers, even if they were all kids about her age—especially if they were all kids about her age! But her head was still spinning from the events of the past several hours to the point she didn't have it in her to raise a stink about anything. She had been kidnapped by dwarves, rescued by scary Native American Fair Folk, and taken to their mountain stronghold. Now she was mesmerized by the onslaught of amazing sights and sounds.

The first thing she noticed was the people. There must have been thousands of them! Most of them looked Native American, but others where white, black, Hispanic, and even Asian. More than a few were of mixed heritage. Some were human-sized. Others, clearly adults, were as small as children. Some had pointed ears like Danny, but most would have looked like anybody walking down the streets of any city in America.

At least, they would if nobody paid attention to their clothes. Many wore traditional Native American clothing. Others—only a few, but enough for Taylor to notice—were dressed like they had just finished posing for the pictures in her history book, in styles from colonial times to the Civil War to the roaring twenties to the present day.

Ayoka, the girl who had greeted her, was dressed in denim shorts, a bright white cotton shirt, and something Taylor could only describe as a shawl made out of shiny green feathers. She was barefooted, as were most of the children who gathered around her. The whole gang—about six or seven of them—ran across the plaza, laughing and chasing each other.

The archers at the far end of the plaza caught her attention. They were practicing on wooden targets that levitated around the practice area ringed by burning torches. The fae shot off arrows faster than anything Taylor had ever seen. Whenever they had one arrow nocked, they held four or five more ready in their hands. Then, as soon as they fired the first arrow, they were able to get the next one ready in about a second. They spun around the practice area, firing off arrow after arrow into the moving targets.

They practiced shooting while running backward or even while jumping off a raised platform in the center of the practice yard. Some vanished in a flash of light—the same trick Taylor had seen Danny do—and reappeared to strike a target with three or four arrows at point-blank range.

"That's amazing!" Taylor said.

Ayoka grinned. "My cousin is the one jumping off the platform," she said. "Good shot, Tsisgwa!"

A young man who looked about twenty years old smiled and waved, then quickly pulled five more arrows from his quiver and ran to the next station.

"Wait a minute." Taylor just noticed something. "There aren't any arrows sticking out of the targets. Where did they go?"

"They're using elf-shot," Ayoka explained. Her expression said Taylor should already know this.

"Elf-shot? Sounds like something you'd load in your twelve-gauge."

""I suppose," Ayoka said, "though a bow gives you better range. But it isn't meant to cause physical wounds, just deliver some kind of curse: maybe a muscle cramp or paralysis. Confusion. Even death if the spell is powerful enough."

"Whoa. And the arrow just vanishes?"

Ayoka nodded. "Exactly."

A boy approached Taylor. He looked to be about eleven years old, and his long, black hair was tied in a braid that reached to below his knees. He had pointed ears, a weak chin, and a quirky smile, but the most distinctive thing about him was that he only came up to Taylor's waist.

"Hi!" he said, gazing up at her.

"Hello."

"Are you a friend of Chief Tewa? My name's Ikegwa."

"Taylor. Nice to meet you." Try as she might, she couldn't help but stare at the tiny boy in front of her. He must have caught on she had never seen anything like him.

"Don't they have little folk where you're from?"

"Oh, we have little people," Taylor said. "We just don't have... little people."

Ikegwa puzzled over that. After a few seconds, he gave her a shrug.

"If that's a riddle, I don't know what it means," he said. "But anyway, come join us!" He bolted away into the swirl of other children. They were playing some sort of tag, and Ayoka was apparently "it." She darted this way and that across the plaza. Anytime someone got close enough to tag her, however, she vanished into thin air, and the rest of the children loudly counted to three. On three, Ayoka was apparently required to remate-rialize, but she always appeared a few yards away from where she had started and heading in a different direction. Many of her chasers also disappeared and reappeared as they tried to anticipate her next move and head her off.

Taylor realized they were turning invisible—not merely evading notice like Danny had taught her to do, but actually turning invisible. She could hear their footfalls, and sometimes Ayoka even called out taunts to the kids who were trying to catch her.

Taylor joined in half-heartedly. When Ikegwa finally tagged Ayoka, he became "it." Even without the ability to disappear, he was faster on his little legs than Taylor would have thought possible. It wasn't long before she was completely frustrated with her inability to compete.

Another child eventually tagged Ikegwa. This one was an older fair-haired boy with pointy ears. He wore jeans and a green camouflage tee shirt.

Ayoka signaled for time out. She must have noticed that Taylor was having a hard time keeping up.

"Let's do something else," she suggested. The children batted a few ideas around. Some wanted to play something called chunky, which Taylor had never heard of. Ikegwa voted for stickball, and offered to lend Taylor a set of sticks. Ayoka must have seen the apprehension on Taylor's expression, though, because she quickly grabbed the hands of her two nearest playmates and began to sing. Taylor couldn't understand the words, but apparently it was a favorite of all the children, because most of them joined in right away.

Soon, everyone had joined hands in a circle. Taylor found herself between Ikegwa on her left and a black fae girl on her right. They danced a simple rhythmic circle dance and repeated the song over and over.

One or two other children soon joined them, including another boy as small as Ikegwa, who beat out the rhythm on a tiny drum as the others continued to sing and dance.

The song transformed over time. Some sang a melody line while others added a descant. Taylor paid attention to the syllables the girl beside her was singing and on the fourth time through dove in and began to sing along.

The song somehow touched Taylor's heart. She didn't understand a word of it, but it refreshed her. She couldn't help but smile. A warm breeze brushed her face. For the first time in twenty-four hours, Taylor dared to enjoy her surroundings.

Taylor found herself trying to imitate the simple dance steps of the other children rather than simply being carried this way and that. It was a beautiful song, whatever it meant. She kept up as best she could. The others smiled encouragement.

"You're really good," Ayoka said.

"Thanks." Singing was one of the few things to which Taylor gave a total commitment.

"Could you teach us a song from your kindred?"

Taylor paused. "I don't think so."

"Please?"

"It's just that...I'm pretty new to all this 'kindred' stuff...."

"But you're a fae, aren't you? All fae love to sing. You're bound to know a song you can share." Ayoka's deep brown eyes sparkled. The other children urged Taylor on.

She thought for a second. She couldn't help smile at the warm welcome the Pilot Knob children had given her.

"Well, here goes." She took a breath, then launched into the first song that came to her mind:

'Tis the gift to be simple, 'tis the gift to be free
'Tis the gift to come down where we ought to be,
And when we find ourselves in the place just right,
'Twill be in the valley of love and delight.

When true simplicity is gained,
To bow and to bend we shan't be ashamed
To turn, turn will be our delight
Till by turning, turning we come 'round right.

She chuckled to herself. Mrs. Peterson, her Chorus teacher, would be proud she remembered all the words. She sang the song a second time. This time, the boy with the drum picked up the beat, and by the time the chorus came around again, two or three of the other kids were singing along.

Ikegwa improvised a simple dance step to go along with the music, but nobody could make sense of what foot they were supposed to put where. Before long, most of the kids had tumbled to the ground, laughing at themselves.

When she finished, they asked for another. And then another. These kids were really into music, and it didn't matter what kind: they warmed up to an old Beatles song just as much as the latest release from Katy Perry or even another traditional hymn Taylor remembered from church. She found herself lost in the joy of singing. After three songs, they taught her another one of theirs.

Something happened as she enjoyed herself on the plaza. She began to see the Fair Folk as real people and not just sinister forces who were out to get her. If this was what the fae were really like, it might not be so bad to be one of them.

At the same time, she wondered about her parents and her friends back home. What would she do if she got stuck in the Wonder and couldn't go back?

The younger children soon drifted away as their mothers called them to supper. Soon, only Ayoka and Ikegwa sat on the grass with Taylor.

"They'll call for us soon," Ayoka said, looking across the plaza toward the large round building. "My grandfather wants to hear your story."

"Your grandfather's the Chief?"

Ayoka nodded. "I overheard him talking about it to Chief Inali. He's the one who led the rescue party."

Taylor arched her eyebrows. "Wait, you all have *two* chiefs?"

"Three," Ikegwa said. "Ayoka's grandfather is the ranking Chief, what we call the White Chief. But Chief Inali is Red Chief. It's their job to argue with each other about whether to fight or make friends."

"It's not their job to argue, Ikegwa," Ayoka said. "Grandfather and Chief Inali have been best friends for centuries. It's their job to explore every possibility before reaching a decision."

"But if they can't agree," Ikegwa spoke up, "it's up to Chief Kalahu to decide."

"Right," Ayoka said. She went on to explain, "Chief Kalahu is Medicine Chief."

"That sounds kind of complicated," Taylor admitted.

Ayoka shrugged. "It's just how we do things. Besides, my mother says the sídhe have *four* chiefs, one for each season of the year—and nobody even gets to vote on them."

"That's crazy," Ikegwa said. "No wonder the booger fae are so messed up."

"Ikegwa!" Ayoka scolded. "That's not a nice word. Especially not with..." she trailed off, glancing at Taylor.

"I'm sorry, Taylor!" Ikegwa said. "I forgot...I mean, I hope you're not mad at me. Everybody is welcome in Tsuwatelda. I don't think of you as a...a..."

"Booger fae?" Taylor said. "What does that even mean?"

"Well," Ayoka said, composing herself. "Like I said, it's not a very nice word. It's what some people call the Fair Folk who came here from Europe."

"Not all of them, though," Ikegwa said. "Only the mean ones, the ones who try to push everybody else around."

"I see," Taylor said, bristling. "Well, I'll try not to be mean to anybody."

"Ikegwa, you're not helping," Ayoka said. "Taylor is our guest. You should learn to be more—"

"Ayoka!" A gray-haired fae suddenly called. He stood near the big, round building in the middle of town. His voice boomed across the plaza. "Bring our guest and come to supper!"

Ayoka bid her goodbyes to Ikegwa and escorted Taylor across the plaza. They skirted around the house, which Ayoka identified as the Council House, and caught up with the gray-haired fae as he was entering one of the adjacent buildings.

Even in the near-dark, Taylor could see he wasn't your ordinary fae. He was dressed in dazzling white from head to foot: cap, feathered cloak, belted tunic, buckskin trousers, moccasins. This must have been Ayoka's grandfather. He looked down upon Taylor with a grim expression.

What now? Taylor thought.

"Taylor Smart," he said. "I'm pleased to meet you. My name is Tewa. I am the White Chief of Tsuwatelda. I trust my granddaughter has made you feel at home? Come sit with us, please. We have much to discuss."

He led Taylor into a large room, apparently a combination living room and dining room where Ayoka's grandfather welcomed company. Danny was already seated on a wooden stool at one end of a long, low table weighed down with food of every kind. Ayoka's grandfather seated Taylor across from Danny and then took his seat at the head of the table between them. Ayoka sat further down the table between a couple that must have been her parents. A woman in a beaded buckskin dress took the seat next to Taylor. At the far end of the table, Chief Inali, the fae in the red headscarf, sat between two of his warriors. Across from Ayoka and her family sat a third older fae in an ornate cloak with a mass of beads and amulets around his neck.

The banquet spread before her was more food than Taylor had seen since Christmas dinner—assuming, of course, that her family would ever serve Christmas dinner for about two dozen houseguests! There was cornbread, some kind of corn chowder, roast meat, sausages seasoned with exotic spices, not to mention vegetables and fresh fruits of every kind. An attendant—who stood no taller than two and a half feet and whose braided black pigtails fell nearly to the floor—set before her a small gourd filled with water.

Taylor debated eating any more faery food. After Danny explained about "buying in" that morning, she didn't want to overdo it. But she had hardly eaten since the night before. She was famished, and all that food smelled fantastic.

Chief Tewa stood and sung some sort of grace in a foreign language. When he finished, he nodded, and everyone began to dig in. Taylor reached for a roast chicken leg and set it on the plate in front of her. That corn chowder looked awfully good, too. And so did the mushrooms. And she had to try one of those sausages that smelled so delicious...

She only looked up from her plate when Chief Tewa spoke to her. "Your friend has informed me of your quest," he said.

"And our Red Chief, Inali, has also shared what he knows of your recent encounter with the dwarves." He indicated the warrior in the red headscarf.

"Thank you for saving us," Taylor said. Chief Inali nodded.

"Is it indeed your plan to go looking for your birth mother?" Chief Tewa said. "Experience tells us your people are not to be trusted."

"With all due respect, sir," Taylor said, "I already figured that out on my own."

Chief Tewa chuckled.

"It sounds like you've met some of my relatives," Taylor continued.

"Every now and then," Chief Tewa sighed. "They first arrived in the Nunnehi Lands when I was a small boy."

"Nunnehi Lands?"

"Our people are called nunnehi," Chief Tewa explained. "It means, 'People Who Live Anywhere.' When I was young, we were practically the only fae in this region. We kept good relations with all the other inhabitants of the Wonder. We never had any trouble with the yunwi tsunsdi or any of the other tribes of little folk, and of course the other fae kindreds regarded us as their equals. We often visited with Topsiders and enjoyed their company on many occasions."

"We were too trusting," Chief Inali said with a grimace.

"Perhaps," the fae with the amulets said.

"This is Kalahu, the Medicine Chief of Tsuwatelda," Chief Tewa explained. "And he is quite right. In the past, we nunnehi were too trusting of the European fae."

"The sídhe and the other white fae arrived on this continent long ago—long before their Topsider cousins," Chief Kalahu explained. "At first, it was just a trickle of settlers in search of a better life. An odd pooka here and there made little difference to us," he glanced at Danny, "indeed, there are native kindreds very similar to the pookas, nixes, and others who began to settle in the Nunnehi Lands. They learned our ways and adapted quite well to life here."

139

Chief Tewa continued the story. "We were happy to share with them, to welcome them into our midst. But as their numbers grew, it seemed the sídhe weren't content to sit with us as equals. They intended to rule us, as they had ruled the fae of Europe for thousands of years."

The more Taylor learned about her relatives, the less she liked them.

"Mr. Tewa...Your Majesty...Sir, Danny's probably told you I grew up Topside. Heck, I've only known about the fae and magic and stuff for about twenty-four hours."

"Don't misunderstand, Taylor," Chief Tewa protested, "I don't hold you responsible for the sins of your ancestors."

"I'm glad, but that's not what I was going to say." Taylor tried to compose her thoughts. She tried to project an aura of confidence, but she wasn't even sure presence would work on Chief Tewa.

"My parents—my Topsider parents—never hid the fact that I was adopted. But they also couldn't tell me anything about my biological parents. They didn't know anything to tell. I always figured when I turned eighteen I'd try to find out what I could about where I came from. Not that I wanted to turn my back on my parents or anything, but just, I don't know, just to satisfy my own curiosity.

"Well, yesterday I learned about my birth mother five years earlier than I expected to. Her name is Shanna Hellebore. I also learned that my biological father was Aulberic Redmane, and that he died before I was even born.

"Maybe my birth parents were just as bad as everybody else in my family apparently is," Taylor frowned, "but Shanna is still my mom. And she's in trouble. Her mother-in-law—my grandma—is probably going to kill her. So it looks like if I'm ever going to meet her at all, it has to be now."

There was a long silence. Chiefs Tewa, Inali, and Kalahu traded knowing glances. Ayoka considered Taylor with and expression of both wariness and concern.

"Please don't make me pass up my once chance to...to find some answers."

"As I have explained to Danny," Chief Tewa finally said, "I do not intend the white fae to win. Not this time." He turned directly toward Taylor. "It isn't fair for you to be used the way you have been. We nunnehi never take people from the Topside world without their full permission. We certainly never split up families or deprive children of their mothers."

"Agreed," Chief Inali said. His balled fists were braced on the table as if he were holding it down. "Say the word, and fifty of my best warriors—"

"Would not stand a chance assaulting Rvne Rofke," Chief Kalahu said. "*Thluh-nee-thlof-kee*," he repeated slowly at Taylor's confused expression.

"Or at least, that's where Mr. Underhill says the Summer Court is currently residing," Chief Tewa added.

"Well, we say it 'Dunhoughkey,'" Danny said, "but yeah. That's where they are. And Chief Kalahu is right. No offense to you, sir," he turned to Chief Inali, "but Dunhoughkey's pretty well defended. The Summers ain't really lived there in big numbers for over a century, but they've always kept a garrison there so it would be ready in case of emergencies."

"Like invading nunnehi?" Taylor quipped.

"Well," Danny blushed, "like Mr. Chief Tewa said, the two kindreds ain't really been on speaking terms for the past few hundred years."

"But...you *are* going to help me, right?" Taylor asked.

"What you need is not force but knowledge," Chief Tewa said. "You need a way to enter Rvne Rofke unobserved and locate your mother."

"A little force would be nice, too," Taylor muttered.

"Find me a hole," Danny said. "A crack in the rocks, anything. Even if it's as tiny as an ant hole, I can blink through it."

"I'm pleased our talk hasn't discouraged you," Chief Tewa said.

"Oh, I'm plenty discouraged," Danny confessed. "But I don't have much choice in the matter. I promised Mrs. Redmane I'd bring Taylor to Dunhoughkey."

All eyes suddenly fixed on Danny. Taylor gasped.

Danny grinned. "I don't think I said anything about bringing her through the front door."

"Excellent!" Chief Inali smiled. "Then all we need is to find Mr. Underhill his hole."

"I have an idea about that," Chief Tewa mused. He sat up straight and kept his peace for several heartbeats.

"Well?" Taylor said at last.

"There is one sure source for knowledge about all things under the earth," Chief Tewa said.

"No," Chief Inali gasped.

"What?" Taylor said.

"We must, Inali. Taylor must be absolutely sure. Her life depends on it."

"What?" Taylor said, a bit more forcefully.

"They'll need some convincing," Chief Kalahu said. "The information we seek will not come cheaply."

"Of that I'm quite sure," Chief Tewa said.

"*Will someone* please *tell me what you two are talking about?*" Taylor growled. A wave of presence radiated outward from her. Most of the fae at the table scooted backward. Danny whimpered. Only the three chiefs seemed unaffected.

"Dwarves," Chief Tewa said.

"D-dwarves?"

"If anyone knows a secret entrance to Rvne Rofke, it is the dwarves," Chief Kalahu explained.

"Then it's settled," Chief Tewa said. "I'll set up a meeting at once."

Chapter 15

Second Thoughts

Chief Tewa offered his guesthouse to Danny. At Ayoka's insistence, he permitted Taylor to spend the night with her family. Before Taylor went to bed, however, she paid a visit to Danny. He had mentioned as he left the table that he needed to check in with Bryn. Taylor was not going to miss that conversation!

As he had before, Danny whispered Bryn's name and breathed across the face of his seeing stone. Taylor rested her hand on his shoulder. The ghostly form of Taylor's stand-in appeared to both of them.

"Hey, Danny. 'Sup?"

Danny quickly filled her in on what they had learned about Taylor's parents and the plan to sneak into Dunhoughkey so she could meet her mom.

"Wow," she said. "That's a lot to get hit with all at once. Is she holding up okay?"

"I'm doing fine," Taylor interrupted. "What's going on there?"

"No problems," Bryn said. "The troll came by again right after dark. I'm pretty sure some spriggans followed Jill and me home from school."

"Yeah, we ran into some of their cousins," Danny said. "It looks like the Winter Court means business."

"It does," Bryn said. "But they haven't tried to capture me. I think that means they know I'm not really you."

"What about my parents?"

"I'd never let anything happen to Mom and Dad, sweetie."

"I wish you'd quit calling them that," Taylor said.

"Anywho, I'm pretty sure I passed that math test today."

"*Pretty sure?*"

"I'll admit I was a little rusty. By the end, it was all coming back to me. At least, I'm pretty sure it was..."

Taylor gritted her teeth.

"Oh, and that Jared boy seemed really interested in whether I was going to his party tomorrow. When we were sitting together at lunch, he—"

"You sat with Jared McCaughey at lunch?" Taylor was dumbstruck.

"Well, to be honest, I only did it because of the way that Shelby girl was acting. She's really kind of rude, isn't she?"

"What does Shelby Crowthers have to do with you and Jared—?"

"Oh, she was rattling on about her party at some stupid country club and how losers like me—er, you—weren't invited. Anyway, she was saying all this to some boy named Tom. He's on the football team. So, what else could I do?"

"Uh, Bryn?" Taylor said. "I think you skipped a couple of steps in there. What *did* you do?"

"I just told Shelby that Jared's party was going to be way cooler than hers."

"And...?"

"And nothing. I just asked Tom what he thought. Can I help it if he took my side? Anyway, I introduced Tom to Jared so he could get the scoop on the party, and that's how Jared, William, and I ended up sitting together at lunch."

"Wait a minute! You sat with Jared McCaughey *and* William Matthews?"

"Yeah, and there were some other boys there, too. I don't remember all their names. Some of them were pretty cute, though."

"I can't believe this is happening," Taylor sighed.

"Oh, and Jill and I had a great time at the mall tonight. Dad drove us. That was kind of tricky, being inside a car and all, but I wore a hat and tried to keep my head down. I don't think my glamour slipped."

"Inside a car? Oh, you mean because of all the steel?"

"Exactly," Danny interrupted. "Steel is mostly made of iron, after all. Cooped up in a rolling iron box is no fun for a fae, I'll tell you that!"

"To tell you the truth, Taylor, I think Jill already suspects something's different about you."

"Do you mean 'me' me or 'you' me?"

"'You' you," Bryn said. "I only put it together after you called last night, but Jill and William are twins, aren't they?"

"Y-yes?"

"Twins!" Danny said. "How did we miss that?"

"What's wrong with twins?"

"Nothing," Bryn said. "It's just that some Topsiders are more likely than others to have Second Sight."

"That means they can detect glamour," Danny said, "maybe even see through it."

"And twins tend to be better at it than most," Bryn said. "Oh, she may not be able to see much. She definitely didn't notice those spriggans on the way home from school today. But if she's known you very long, Taylor, I'd bet she at least has a hunch that there's something different about you. William, too."

"W-William?"

"Oh, and one more thing, Danny. Mrs. Redmane contacted me not too long before you did. She wanted to know what's happening."

"What did you tell her?" Danny sounded frantic.

"There wasn't much I could say. I told her about the bag-man, the troll, and the spriggans. I made it sound like the Winters are everywhere."

"Must have been a challenge," Taylor quipped.

"So what did she say?" Danny asked.

"She understands you can't take the direct route to Dunhoughkey. But she's getting impatient. I mean seriously impatient. It won't be long till she expects to see you."

"The nunnehi are trying to get us some information," Danny said. "If everything works out, we can be there tomorrow morning."

"Well, good," Bryn said. "And good luck."

"Thanks," Danny said.

When Taylor returned to Ayoka's house, the nunnehi girl's mother had a message from Chief Tewa.

"You and Danny are to meet Chief Tewa in the Council House early tomorrow morning," she said. "The dwarves will want to conclude their business before sunrise."

Ayoka's room was about the same size as Taylor's own back in Georgia. Two mats had been rolled out on the floor and covered with colorful woven blankets. Ayoka loaned Taylor some pajamas, and both girls eventually settled down for the night.

Of course, the last thing on Taylor's mind was sleep. It wasn't just that her nerves were frazzled after everything that had happened with the spriggans and then the dwarves, the time-skip in between had given her a serious case of jetlag. She felt like she could stay up for another three or four hours, easy.

She lay on her mat, staring up at the ceiling in the dark, trying to make sense of everything. She didn't even hear when Ayoka started talking to her.

"Huh? Did you say something?"

"I just said I hope you're not mad at Ikegwa...that thing he said."

"Don't worry about it," Taylor said, but she couldn't help being sarcastic. "Now that you've heard my story, you can decide for yourself whether I'm a booger fae."

"Of course, you're not!" Ayoka protested. "You didn't do all those terrible things. And you've acted perfectly sweet ever since you got here."

"Yeah, well.... I'm a little off my game. It's been a rough couple of days. Usually I'm a lot more prickly."

"You hide it well."

"And I like to get my way about things."

"Who doesn't?"

"And if you ever did something really, really stupid, I guarantee you I'd be telling you about it. And I'm warning you: I don't do subtle."

"Neither do I. Look, Taylor. I'm trying to offer to be your friend. So just shut up and let me, will you?"

"Okay, okay!" Taylor smiled. "Man, are the Fair Folk bossy or what?"

"Go to sleep, Taylor."

"In a minute," she said. After a pause, she said, "There's something I need to ask you first."

"Yeah?"

"Do you know much about dwarves?"

"Not really," Ayoka said. "Just that they don't really like Our Kind. They're very suspicious, always thinking we're trying to steal from them or take advantage of them. Grandfather says it's partly because of how they've been treated by the European fae."

"What did they do?"

Ayoka shrugged. "He never said. But he told me you should always try to be as polite and honest with a dwarf as possible to show them we're not all that bad."

"I see," Taylor said. "Well, then I guess I'd better not try to steal anything from them."

Ayoka laughed. "Not unless you want them to curse it against you! We'd better get to sleep. Good night." She gestured toward the lantern on her dresser and extinguished its light.

Taylor rolled over and pulled the blanket snugly around her shoulders. She sighed deeply, wondering if the dwarves had discovered their multi-tool was missing. It was all she could think of the rest of the night.

Chapter 16

Crom Cornstack

Bledrus Dingle tried to project more confidence than he had. The Primus insisted on frequent updates whether there was anything to report or not.

Unfortunately, this meeting was going to fall into the "not" category.

The spriggan was in no hurry to tell the Primus that there was still no sign of the girl or the pooka since the fiasco that morning at Judaculla Rock. He took his time shuffling down the wide, stone corridors of Cair Cullen, the seat of the Winter Court, despite efforts by his changeling escort to speed him up.

You didn't just walk blithely into Crom Cornstack's council chamber and tell him you didn't know any more than you did that morning. The Winter Primus was usually slow to anger. The problem was that he had been angry since January. This was April. There was no reason to expect he would get over it before Bledrus reached the throne room.

Not for the first time, Bledrus wondered if the Autumn Court was hiring.

I could be an Autumn, he told himself. *Not as much drama. Christmas off. I ought to look into it.*

The Autumns were so much easier to get along with. Sneakier, maybe, but not quite as vindictive. Bledrus thought he really ought to look into it. He might even take up a new field: maybe arcane secrets or Friendly relations. Pasco Tanwhistle could keep on trying—and failing—to earn his merit badge in dentistry, and for once it would be somebody else's problem.

But first he had to face Crom Cornstack—and every warbler, thrush, and chickadee had been busy all day tweeting the news: they almost had them at Judaculla, but the girl and the pooka had managed to escape. It wouldn't be long until everyone in Arradherry knew what had happened. The Primus would not be happy. Bledrus started to tremble, thinking about what he should say. He took slow, deep breaths. He practiced in his mind how to explain himself so as to escape blame.

Far too soon, they arrived at the great double doors to the council chamber. His changeling escort stood at attention on either side. There was nothing for it but to step in.

Mr. Cornstack sat upon his throne like a dark and foreboding mountain. The throne itself, or at least the part that wasn't cushioned in red velvet, was made of yellowed antlers linked together to form a frame that strained beneath the weight of the occupant's imposing figure. The fae who sat on it remained motionless except for the tap-tapping of his fingers against the armrest, hopefully more out of boredom than impatience.

Before he even said a word, Bledrus sensed the power of the Primus's formidable presence. The two fae looked each other in the eye—which Bledrus immediately realized was a mistake. Those piercing blue eyes demanded his undivided attention. The Primus gestured for Bledrus to approach—an easy, graceful motion. Crom Cornstack was utterly in control of this audience.

As usual, the room was dim. Only a few weakly flickering orbs of faery fire kept the council chamber from being plunged into total darkness. Around the edges of the room skirted some of the Primus's other minions: trolls and goblins mostly. They murmured comments Bledrus could barely hear and certainly couldn't understand.

He bowed his head in the presence of his superior, but could not bring himself to avert his eyes.

The Primus was, after all, arrestingly good looking in the eerie way that all daoine sídhe were. His bright eyes and fair skin practically glowed in the dim light of the council chamber.

His regal attire only added to the effect, for he insisted on wearing his full regalia of office: a red cloak lined with harp seal fur, a wreath of holly adorning his white-blond mane, an obsidian-topped mace in his massive hands. You'd have never guessed the Winter Assize ended two months ago.

By his side sat his wife, the Chief Matron, dark-eyed and brooding, beautiful as a flower yet cold as ice. She, at least, had put away the flowing white robes of her office. Instead, she wore a luxurious dress of shimmering black. Her silver jewelry sparkled in the orb-light. Her mouth twisted into a dismissive grin as Bledrus slowly approached them.

Bledrus felt a trickle of sweat tickling the back of his neck.

"Primus," he began.

"Captain."

The Primus gazed down at him. In the dim light, the blue and black geometric shapes tattooed across his face gave the impression that Bledrus stood before a living mosaic. Those bold, angular lines seemed to amplify every subtle change of expression—and Crom Cornstack's changes of expression were always subtle.

"I take it there is still no sign of the girl and the pooka?"

Bledrus braced himself against the Primus's imposing presence. "Th-that's correct, Primus. They vanished from Judaculla Rock this morning. One of my spriggans chased them as far as New Avalon before they threw him off."

"I see," the Primus said, still glaring into the core of Bledrus's being.

"K-kevern Gwenbrith—he's the one who chased them—only just fell out of the rings about an hour ago. Time-skip, you know. With any luck, sir, he'll be able to remember something and—"

"Are you telling me that my Captain of the Guard is reduced to relying on luck to fulfill his duties?"

"N-no, sir," Bledrus backtracked. "It's just...now that we know she's no longer at her home Topside...we've got to rethink our strategy...sir." It sounded so reasonable when he practiced telling it to himself. Now, as he gave his report, Bledrus felt like an idiot. What did that even mean? Obviously, he would have to rethink his strategy—his strategy flew out the window the moment Enrique the bag-man failed to capture the girl yesterday afternoon. The last thing that went right on this mission was when the oaf blasted the girl's friend with a stomach bug to get her out of the way.

He tried to explain, to justify his lack of anything further to report, but it wasn't long until he stopped being convincing even to himself. The Primus had a knack for dissecting everything he said. With a single dismissive sigh, he made him feel about as dense as a common troll.

Although come to think of it, even the trolls lurking in the shadows tittered at Bledrus's pathetic rambling.

"We all know where the girl is headed, Crom," the Chief Matron said. Her only visible ink was a spidery frame of Celtic knotwork around her left eye that writhed like a snake when she arched her eyebrow.

"I've already got men patrolling around Dunhoughkey," Bledrus said. "I can send more if you like, take 'em off Judaculla and Macon, for instance."

"The girl is key, Captain. I shouldn't have to explain that to you. Find her, and she will lead you to...the other one."

He can't even say her name, Bledrus thought. Then it occurred to him that the Primus hadn't just been angry since January. He had been angry for the past fourteen years.

He shuddered when he thought what it must be like to carry around such hatred. Was a Gentryman's honor really worth all that?

"We will reclaim what the Summers have stolen from us, by Danu," the Primus continued. "And *she* will pay dearly for her little escapade."

"Yes, Primus."

"Leave your spriggans at Judaculla. I wouldn't be surprised if the pooka decides to show his face there again."

"Y-you really think so, sir?"

"It's a major ring-portal just a few stops from Dunhoughkey. And in case you haven't noticed, Captain, pookas are always up to something," the Primus mused. "If we could find out what this particular pooka has up his sleeve...I have a feeling it might help us resolve this whole unfortunate matter." His expression was impassive, but Bledrus knew that meant very little as far as the Primus's actual state of mind.

"As for Macon, however, I'm not entirely sure.... What do you think, Mara?"

The Chief Matron leaned toward he husband. "The huldra they've left there obviously knows something. Perhaps we should observe her for a little while longer."

The Primus stroked his beard.

"Perhaps, Mara. But I fear we may need all our forces at either Dunhoughkey or Judaculla. If there's no change in Macon by morning, Captain, you may recall your team from there and send them to Dunhoughkey. One way or another, the girl will show up there sooner or later."

"As you command, Primus."

"And Captain?"

"Yes, Primus?"

"Don't disappoint me again."

"Of course not, Primus. I'll get right on it...I mean...first thing in the morning...at least, I'll tell Bill and Pasco to head to Dunhoughkey first thing in the morning...but I'll get right on telling them those are your orders...as you said...sir."

Bledrus bowed his way past the changeling guard and out of the council chamber. As soon as he stepped outside, his head began to clear.

What are the chances of snatching the girl before Mrs. Redmane gets hold of her? he thought. He was confident that was the only chance his spriggans would get. Once she made it to Dunhoughkey, Bledrus held little hope that anyone would ever see the girl again.

And if the girl was key to reclaiming Shanna Hellebore, his own job prospects—and maybe his life if the Primus wasn't in a forgiving mood—rose or fell with her.

He ambled toward the mess hall, even though he had lost his appetite long ago.

I'll get my seeing stone and scry Bill and Pasco, he thought. *Then I guess it's off to Dunhoughkey.* No sense leaving the situation there to his subordinates since his head was on the block if there were any screw-ups, anyway.

But as soon as this mission was over, he was definitely sending his résumé to the Autumn Court.

Chapter 17

How Iron Came to Be

Long ago when the world was young, there lived a wise, old fae who sought to find the true names of everything under the sun.

For one hundred years, she studied the ways of every animal until each divulged its true name. "You are called *ager*," she said to the goat, "and you are called *harrz*," she told the bear; and so on until she had mastered every name. And by mastering their names, she mastered their forms, their powers, and their natures.

For the next hundred years, she studied the ways of every plant until each divulged its true name. She announced to the sunflower, "Your true name is *eúgi*." She commanded the maple tree, saying, "Your true name is *asdiar*." And so she proceeded until she had mastered every name. And by mastering their names, she mastered their forms, their powers, and their natures.

For the next hundred years, she studied the ways of every rock and metal until each divulged its true name. To gold, she said, "You are *aehori*." To flint, she said, "You are *suhaez*." She thus studied every rock and metal until she had mastered every name. And by mastering their names, she mastered their forms, their powers, and their natures.

The more the wise, old fae learned, the more powerful she became, and as she shared her knowledge with others of her kind, her entire kindred prospered.

But the blood of the earth was the most willful and obstinate of rocks. "I will never be mastered by any fae!" it declared. And, true to its word, it refused to divulge its true name to the fae no matter how long she studied it.

One day, a Topsider was digging deep in the ground in search of copper, and the blood of the earth whispered in his ear. "Dig me out of the earth," it said, "and I will show you how to best the Fair Folk." Now, Topsiders had come to fear the fae, for they had become the masters of every kind of animal, plant, rock, and metal. So the man was eager to learn whatever secret the earth's blood might tell him.

As soon as the Topsider brought home a pile of the reddish rock, it whispered to him again. "Smelt me in your furnace," it told him. And so he did. He heated the furnace hotter than it had ever been, and the earth's blood flowed like water. And as it flowed, its nature changed.

"Cast me in your mold," it whispered. And the man complied. He poured the molten metal into a mold he had used to fashion swords of bronze. As it rested in the mold, it became cold, hard, and gray as twilight in winter.

"Now I am iron," the sword whispered, "the bane of the Fair Folk. I will never bend to the will of the fae, but to your kind I will freely submit from now until the end of time."

Enthralled with his new weapon, the man went out in search of Our Kind, to drive them far from his Topside village. He dared to stand at the threshold of the Wonder and challenge the old fae who had learned all the secrets of nature.

"Who dares approach me?" the old fae demanded.

"I do," said the man, "for I have something to show you that you have never seen!"

"I doubt that, deathling," the old fae said, "for I have become the mistress of all things." And with that, she turned into a she-bear and snarled at the man.

But the Topsider held his ground and held up his sword so the fae could see it. Immediately she reverted to her two-legged form, for the sword had already begun to work: the fae felt a shiver down her spine in the presence of the iron. She knew in her heart she must never touch it.

"What is this?" she said, and her blood turned as thin and weak as water.

"Something you can never master," the Topsider said.

"I am the mistress of everything under the sun," the fae said. "And I will be the mistress of your strange, cold metal."

"You may be the mistress of all that exists in nature," the man said, "but you can never master iron, for I have made it! The blood of the earth has shared its secret with me alone, and iron is now mine to command!"

The old fae knew the man was telling the truth. With a curse, she vanished from his sight.

And so it was that the fae have become the master of all that exists under the sun—except for iron, which has cast its lot with the Topsiders.

Chapter 18

Dickering with Dwarves

Danny awoke long before daybreak. He washed his face, brushed his teeth, and did his morning exercises. First, he became a goat. Then he became a horse. Then a dog. He reverted to his true shape and repeated the same pattern in reverse. He yawned and stretched. He went through the same routine again from the start.

It was going to be a long day, and everything told him it wouldn't be a very good one. He needed to be ready for anything. You didn't just stroll into a fortified stronghold of the Summer Court. You certainly didn't try to pull anything over on Anya Redmane. Somehow, that was exactly what he was planning to do.

"And with the help of a bunch of dwarves!" he muttered.

Most of all, he hated involving Taylor in all this. She had grown on him over the past couple of days. If anything happened to her...

And yet, the end was so close! *One more switch-out,* he thought. *Just one more and my contract is up. I can go where I want, do what I want.*

The fact was he needed Taylor more than she knew—more than he could afford to tell her. He wasn't looking forward to how this day might end.

Danny was glad that his hosts had provided him fresh clothing. The Topsider school clothes were necessary to make contact with Taylor, but he never liked them. He left them folded on his sleeping mat happy never to wear them again. He slipped on the buckskin trousers and loose cotton shirt he found on his dressing table. He found a pair of moccasins as well and pulled them on. *That's what a shoe is supposed to feel like*, he thought.

Next, he went through his school backpack, rummaging for anything that might prove useful. He took his seeing stone, a piece of chalk, a bronze-bladed penknife, a small hammer and chisel, a collection of jars and tins of potion ingredients, a flask of whiskey he had been saving for a special occasion, and the last of his rations from Moe Fountain. He scooped them up and into a leather shoulder bag decorated with beautiful nunnehi beadwork. He considered the fireplace opposite his bed and the rack of firewood beside it. He poked around until he found a round, thick piece of wood about two or two and a half feet long—pine, he thought. He used magic to split the wood into two sections. They also went into his bag wrapped in his bed sheet.

He joined Taylor about halfway to the Council House, the large circular building on the plaza. She had also changed into fresh clothes: jeans, a belted blue woolen tunic, and a leather purse much like Danny's but smaller. Danny grinned to see she had managed to acquire some Topsider tennis shoes, no doubt a gift from Ayoka.

"Good morning." Taylor yawned.

Danny grunted.

A couple of stray spunkies floated lazily above the rooftops. They got loose like that sometimes.

"These dwarves... Do you think they'll help us?"

"If the price is right."

"And Chief Tewa can afford to pay them? Because I sure can't!"

"First of all, 'pay' is kind of a dirty word for fae and dwarves alike. We don't do things for pay, leastways not the way Topsiders understand it."

"It's like at Moe Fountain's, then?" Taylor asked. "Give and take? Exchanging favors?"

"Exactly. The things is, what dwarves treasure most is knowledge. That makes them very useful for our purposes. They know things, but they don't like sharing what they know."

"I see."

The inside of the Council House was a prefect circle with a fire pit in the center flanked by four massive wooden posts. The only furnishing, if one could call it that, was a raised two-level ring of compacted earth along the wall. This platform was decked out with ornate cushions on which the leaders of Tsuwatelda sat—although at present the only people present were Chiefs Tewa, Kalahu, and Inali. They held seats of honor on a somewhat higher platform, directly opposite the door, sculpted in the shape of a great bird of prey. The only other person in the room was a middle-aged fae who tended the fire. Spunkies flitted to and fro, enhancing the dim light.

At Tewa's welcoming gesture, Danny and Taylor took their seats to one side. No one said anything for several minutes.

Then two dwarves trudged down the corridor that led into the central chamber. They were wrapped in thick, black cloaks that covered their entire bodies from head to toe. Danny wondered how they could even see in them. An attendant ushered them into the presence of the three Chiefs of Tsuwatelda. They doffed their cloaks, but refused to let the attendant take them away. They simply let them fall to the floor behind them.

They no longer wore their crude work clothes. Instead, both dwarves had on tunics striped in purple and gray with black trousers and polished black boots. They had even taken the time to comb out their beards. The leader had braided his with silver thread.

The leader of the dwarves, Dwally Wormfield, had come with the short dwarf with the eye patch. Wormfield didn't look any happier than he did the day before.

"We appreciate you coming," Chief Tewa said.

Wormfield merely grunted.

Chief Inali sat silently with his arms folded.

Chief Kalahu kept his hands on his knees.

Taylor leaned forward, sitting on her hands. She seemed nervous, and who could blame her?

"I do not appreciate the liberties you take against our kind nature," Wormfield said.

Danny scoffed. All eyes darted in his direction. Taylor held back a smile but everyone else—fae and dwarf alike—shot glares of anger. He shrunk back into his seat and studied the floor for several uncomfortable seconds.

"I don't know what you're up to," Wormfield continued, "but I will not be a part of it. Find a pawn somewhere else for this game of yours."

"I assure you, Mr. Wormfield, this is no game," Chief Tewa said. "We have called you here, as I explained, in order to acquire information about the faery rath at Rvne Rofke."

"Is that so?" Wormfield said. "And you're telling me this girl has nothing to do with it?" He jabbed a chalky white finger toward Taylor.

"On the contrary," Chief Tewa said. "She has everything to do with it."

"So you admit she's a part of your plan! Don't try to pull one over on a dwarf, Tewa. I promise you, it won't end well. While she was in our care, my colleague Mr. Stamp performed a healing spell upon her. Do you understand? Their souls touched—if Your Kind even have souls—although only for an instant. But that was enough, Tewa. He *knows*."

Danny glanced at Taylor, whose eyes were about to jump out of their sockets. He wanted to ask, "Knows *what*?" He was clueless about how dwarf magic worked, but among the fae, healing magic tended to create a bond between the healer and the patient. Was that what he was talking about?

"If your colleague truly knows about the girl, then he knows she is no threat to him or to you," Chief Tewa said, his tone even and controlled, even casual.

"No threat? She's a threat to all of us!" Wormfield shouted. "You think I don't know what's been going on? The sídhe Courts are at each other's throats, Tewa. War is coming—and she's the reason!" Once again he gestured toward Taylor.

"You're trying to game this for your own benefit, aren't you, Tewa? You're trying to get one over on the Redmanes. Why else would a sídhe girl ever set foot in Pilot Knob? Yes, we know her kindred. As I said, Blain knows. He has seen her past, her present, and her future."

Taylor grabbed the bench as if she would fly into the air if she didn't hold on.

"You're going to send her to Dunhoughkey as part of some plan, aren't you? Admit it!"

"Mr. Wormfield," Chief Tewa said, "I assure you my only concern is to see the girl safely to Rvne Rofke. No harm will come to you or your kind."

"And you promise your protection if you're wrong?" The dwarf turned to Inali the Red Chief.

Before Chief Inali could respond, Chief Tewa said, "I believe that is a fine place at which to begin our negotiations. Tell us what we want to know and, should the Summer Court move against you or your comrades, the nunnehi shall come to your defense."

"And what precisely do you want to know?" The dwarf with the eye patch spoke for the first time.

"A way to enter Rvne Rofke without being detected," Chief Tewa said.

Eye Patch sucked in a breath. Stamp, they said his name was. Wormfield eyed Chief Tewa. There was a glint of something lively in his black, beady eyes. Maybe he was imagining what Chief Tewa might give him in exchange for such knowledge.

Wormfield pulled Stamp aside and whispered something in his ear. The other dwarf whispered back, a look of concern on his face. Wormfield said something else. Stamp nodded. The dwarves once again stepped forward.

"We are prepared to bargain for such information," Wormfield said.

"Yes?" Chief Tewa said.

"You realize, of course, that you are asking for significant and potentially dangerous knowledge. Misused, it could lead to open hostilities between your people and the Summer Court. Not to mention the chance Blain and I are taking even discussing the matter with you. I have no love for the sídhe, but I would prefer they simply leave us alone rather than storming our mountain home, howling for our blood, should they discover where you received your information."

"I'm waiting, Mr. Wormfield."

"An even trade would seem in order. Knowledge for knowledge."

The hairs on Danny's neck stood on end at the smug tone of the dwarf's voice. He might as well have been licking his lips.

"You have a young granddaughter, don't you?"

Chief Tewa leaned forward, his hands on his knees.

"I can get you inside Dunhoughkey. In return, suppose you tell me your granddaughter's true name?"

Chief Inali breathed a curse and slipped his hand to the knife on his belt.

Chief Kalahu held out a hand to keep Chief Tewa from springing to his feet.

Danny could almost literally feel the White Chief's anger boiling over. The Council House shook, and everyone could feel it. Taylor squeaked.

"We're done here!"

"Forgive me," Wormfield said. "I thought you were serious when you asked us to risk our lives by implicating ourselves in whatever ill-advised scheme you're hatching against the sídhe. Now I see you were only joking."

"Mr. Wormfield," Chief Kalahu said, "I doubt you seriously expected Chief Tewa to agree to divulge such information."

There was a tense silence. Danny studied the body language of the three chiefs and the two dwarves as they sized each other up. Chief Inali's hand hovered over the handle of this sheathed knife.

Chief Tewa and Wormfield stared into each other's eyes as if daring each other to blink.

Wormfield didn't really want to bargain—why else would he make such an outrageous demand? But then, why even come to the meeting?

Stamp's good eye stayed trained on Chief Kalahu. Those two seemed to be the most even-tempered people present.

Danny bit his lip and hoped somebody would do something. He had to know what the dwarves could tell him.

"Let us make a good-faith offer," Chief Kalahu said at last. "We will show you how serious we are...if you are willing to bargain in good faith."

Stamp whispered something to his boss. They talked among themselves for a moment before Wormfield finally turned back to the three nunnehi chiefs and nodded.

Danny sighed with relief, and the real negotiations began.

The dwarves didn't get anybody's true name, obviously, but the nunnehi made a very generous offer to disclose knowledge the dwarves did not have. The dwarves made counter-offers, and eventually the price was set.

In exchange for information about the defenses of Dunhoughkey, the nunnehi promised to defend them against any future sídhe attacks. They also agreed to grant access to certain ancient tomes of astronomy and herb-lore, teach them the Cherokee syllabary, divulge the foundational principles behind fae healing magic, and explain the lyrics to a Topsider song called "Louie, Louie."

After ninety minutes of haggling, Wormfield smiled. "You are too kind," he said. "And there is, in fact, a passage directly into the lowest level of the rath of Dunhoughkey."

Danny leaned forward. "Well?"

"It's behind the reflecting pool, of course. I'm sure it's glamoured as strongly as anyone could manage."

"Which is quite strong," Stamp added.

"But beyond the illusion of a solid rock wall, you'll find a tunnel. Follow the tunnel to the end, and the door you'll find there will open with the correct password."

"Forgive me for saying so, Mr. Wormfield," Chief Inali said, "but I find it hard to believe you could possibly know such a thing."

"The sídhe turned to dwarves to upgrade the locks and other security measures when they largely withdrew from the rath a hundred years ago," Wormfield said. "It wouldn't do for Topsiders to stumble upon anything they had no right to see, would it? Best to button things up tight before pulling out the bulk of your forces, you know. And I happen to know someone who knows someone who worked on the project."

In other words, Danny thought, every dwarf east of the Mississippi could probably sneak into Dunhoughkey if they felt like it.

"And the sídhe," Danny said. "Do *they* know about this secret entrance?"

Wormfield smiled. "You'll find that security specialists often leave themselves a back door...just in case. They rarely divulge this information to others."

"I see."

It was starting to look like this plan might actually work.

"We'll need the password," Danny said.

"Cracker Jacks."

Seriously?

"Uh, one more thing."

Two pairs of beady black eyes turned on Danny.

"I'm thinking we're probably gonna need a way out, too. So where does this passage go—and how do you open it from the inside?"

"The other end of the passage is inside a supply closet," Wormfield said. "At the end of the corridor nearest the statue of Uasal Redmane—assuming they haven't moved the old crone. The same password should work at both ends."

166

Danny sat up straight. Beside him, Taylor took a deep breath. She turned in his direction. He gave her a wink and a smile, but she seemed just as nervous as before. Maybe more.

"Mr. Wormfield," Chief Tewa said. "We are grateful for your kindness."

Wormfield nodded. He and Stamp began to collect their cloaks from the floor.

"Wait!" Taylor said. All eyes turned in her direction.

"The sun will soon be rising," Wormfield said. "It's time we go."

"Not yet," Taylor said. "I also know something. Something you'd be very interested to find out."

"I doubt that," Wormfield said. He pulled his cloak over his shoulders.

"I know the answer to a question you don't even know to ask," Taylor said.

Danny gazed at her. What was she talking about? Did she know what she was getting into, trying to bargain with a dwarf?

"Before, you said Blain—Mr. Stamp, was it?—learned things about me with his healing spell. I'd consider sharing what I know with him."

"I don't see what you could possibly know that would be of interest to us," Wormfield said.

"Perhaps not," Taylor said. "Go on home then, if that's what you want to do." She sat up straight and folded her hands in her lap. "It would sure be a shame if I'm right, though."

There was a pause. Danny couldn't decide if Taylor had been using presence or not, but he could tell Wormfield was suddenly interested in what she had to say.

"Mr. Stamp said he knows about me," Taylor continued. She leaned slightly forward. "It sure would be nice to hear what he knows..."

The dwarf with the eye patch stepped toward her.

"You say there is a question that we don't know to ask?" he said.

Taylor nodded. "If you knew, you'd have asked it already. Since you haven't yet, I can only assume—"

"You're bluffing!" Wormfield said. "It's nearly sunrise. We must go."

"Have it your way," Taylor said. "I'll find a way to put what I know to use. But, to be honest, I'd rather hear what Mr. Stamp has to say about my past, present, and future."

"I believe I'll tell her," Stamp said.

"She's using a glamour trick!"

"Perhaps... Do you swear you have the knowledge you claim?"

"On my honor," Taylor said.

Danny's eyes darted between Taylor and the dwarf in the eye patch. There was a tense silence while the pale creature gazed into her eyes.

"As you your past," he said. "You are a sídhe princess of two noble bloodlines, although you are not truly part of either."

Taylor nodded.

"In the present, you are not a spy. You barely know what you are—or what your existence even means. You are, however, a pawn in schemes far larger than yourself. You hate this, but you know it is true."

"And my future?"

Stamp sighed. "The quest you are on will change your life forever. And the lives of others as well. You, my dear, are quite possibly the most dangerous fae alive today. You have the power of life or death on your tongue."

"I *what*?"

"Don't ask me to explain, but that is what I sensed. You have to but say the word, and bring either life or death to others."

Taylor gulped. Danny could see that she was trembling.

"We must be going, young lady," Stamp said. "As soon as you have honored your vow."

"What? Oh." Taylor said. She fumbled with her purse. She pulled it off her shoulder and sat it in her lap. "The answer to the question you didn't know to ask."

Stamp and Wormfield leaned forward.

"The question you might have asked is, 'What ever happened to that multi-tool'"?

"Multi-tool?" Wormfield said.

"You mean the one Nabby lost a few weeks ago?" Stamp said.

"Could be," Taylor said. "The answer is, 'That sídhe girl used it to escape.'" She pulled from her bag a bulky dwarven tool. Danny cursed under his breath.

"Thief!" Wormfield bellowed.

"If I were a thief, I wouldn't be willingly returning this, now would I?" Taylor said. She held the tool in both hands and extended it toward Stamp.

Stamp allowed a sly smirk to cross his face.

"Well played, girl," he said. "Well played."

"This is ridiculous!" Wormfield said. "Chief Tewa, I would thank you to exert a bit of control over your guests! It's bad enough you bring a sídhe girl into your midst. Now she is revealed to be a thief!"

"It sounds to me like she found a tool you didn't even realize was missing," Chief Tewa said. "Although of course if you would like to put a curse on it now, you're certainly welcome to do so."

"Now listen," Wormfield sputtered.

"But seeing as it is now back safely in the hands of its rightful owners, I'm not sure what good that would do." Chief Tewa crossed his arms. Danny thought he noticed the slightest trace of a grin.

Wormfield's eyes bulged. His face came very near to flushing pink.

"Taylor has returned your property, and for a finder's fee that seems quite reasonable," Chief Kalahu said.

"But—"

"And, as you have already reminded us, Mr. Wormfield," Tewa said, "the sun is about to rise. I suggest you go home while you can. I'm grateful for the help you have given us." The White chief bowed cordially but never took his eyes off the dwarven leader.

Wormfield finished pulling on his cloak. Stamp did the same, and it wasn't long before they were both trudging out of the Council House and presumably across the plaza back to the front gate of Tsuwatelda.

"That was...different," Taylor said.

"Gratifying," Chief Tewa added.

"Freaking awesome," Danny said with a grin.

"Taylor, I suggest you be on your way as quickly as possible," Chief Tewa said. "I expect your greatest challenge is still ahead of you. It won't be easy to find your mother, even with the dwarves' help."

Danny gulped. The reality of what he was about to do sunk in again. He was about to march into Dunhoughkey on an impossible mission. He was about to defy Anya Redmane.

It would probably be the last thing he ever did.

Chapter 19

Reunions

Taylor ate her breakfast in silence at Chief Tewa's table.

This was it. She was about to sneak into a magical fortress, evade the guards, and look for the mother she had never met. She wasn't overwhelmed; she was terrified. But she didn't see any way to go but forward.

After breakfast, she drifted away to spend some time by herself. She sat under a tree on the plaza, not quite crying but definitely not far from breaking down completely. She took several deep breaths.

"Ready to go?" It was Ayoka. She smiled at Taylor.

"Ready as I'll ever be."

"Probably," Ayoka said. "You'll feel better when you're moving again."

Taylor looked at her. "What makes you say that?"

"Grandfather says you're only thirteen years old. That means you're bound to be very restless. Never satisfied. Always looking for more out of life."

"What are you talking about? And what are you, anyway? Thirteen? Fourteen, tops?"

"I'll be twenty-six in two months."

Taylor's jaw dropped open.

"You must be in a fearsome hurry to grow up, to be this big and only thirteen."

"I-I don't understand."

"You're a fae, aren't you? Our Kind only grow up as quickly— or as slowly—as we want. I put off being a teenager until I was twenty, personally. I guess it took me a while to get used to the idea of handling more responsibility, the expectations grown-ups put on you. And, of course, boys." Ayoka blushed and grinned.

Taylor was having a hard time taking all of this in. "You mean, you can stop getting older whenever you want?"

"Mostly," Ayoka explained. "Eventually, childhood gets old. That sounded strange, didn't it? But you know what I mean, right? It's nice to live with your parents and have them take care of you, play with your friends all day, and so forth. But nobody can go on like that forever, not even one of Our Kind. Eventually, we decide it's time to grow up."

"I was brought up Topside," Taylor said. "I never really knew what you're talking about was an option."

"Oh, well that explains it. I just figured, as young as you are, you must have been awfully restless."

"Maybe I was... But it might have been nice spending a couple more years as a little kid."

"Childhood definitely has its advantages," Ayoka admitted. "But I think I'm going to like being a teenager just as well. I might give it a try for a couple of decades."

"You'll have to let me know what you decide."

"My grandfather told me what you're about to do," Ayoka said. "It sounds very grown-up for a thirteen-year-old."

"I guess so." Taylor didn't feel very grown up at that moment. She would have given almost anything to fly into her mother's arms back in Macon. She wished she could turn the clock back and be eight or nine years old again with not a care in the world.

But then she realized she had plenty of cares when she was eight. She worried about monsters in her closet or not getting the toys she wanted for Christmas or whether her parents would give her back to the adoption people if she broke the rules one more time. She had outgrown all those things. (Although given the circumstances, maybe she needed to re-examine the whole monsters-in-the-closet thing.) But other worries still haunted her. She also worried about not fitting in at school, about how out of place she always seemed to feel.

She wondered when she would be old enough not to have worries like that.

It must have been nearly ten o'clock before Danny and the three nunnehi chiefs approached. Time to go.

They walked in silence toward the palisade. They passed through the gate to the circle of standing stones just outside the village.

"Where is this place anyway?" Taylor asked.

"Dunhoughkey?" Danny said. "Actually, it's not too far from where you live. Bald Mountain, I think the Topsiders call it."

That didn't ring any bells.

"Bald Mountain is the Muskogee name," Chief Tewa said. "That's the English translation of 'Rvne Rofke.' White folks call it 'Rock Mountain.'"

"Stone Mountain," Chief Kalahu corrected. "They call it 'Stone Mountain.'"

"You've got to be kidding me," Taylor said. "Stone Mountain? *The* Stone Mountain? With the putt-putt and the train and the ginormous carving of old Civil War guys?"

"You've heard of it?" Chief Inali said.

"Heard of it? I've been there like a dozen times! You're telling me a bunch of evil fae live in a state park outside of Atlanta?"

"It's more like a vacation home," Danny said. "They keep a garrison there. Some commoners live thereabouts: miners and stonemasons, mostly. Most of the year it's fairly empty, though."

Taylor shook her head. "You might as well shoot me now, because things can't get any weirder."

"Nobody's going to shoot you," Danny said. "Look, we'll just ring-travel over...and play it by ear, okay?"

"Yeah." They had arrived at the stone circle.

"I guess this is it," Danny said.

Taylor tried to express her gratitude to the chiefs, although she couldn't find the right words. She ended up just mumbling "Thank you" and giving them each a timid bow.

"Just...hang on tight," Danny said.

Taylor clung once more onto Danny's arm. "Just give me a soft landing this time?"

The ring erupted in a dazzling swirl of light.

Danny stepped into it. A blur of sharp colors flashed by as Danny rode the rings to Dunhoughkey. Thankfully, this ride was fairly smooth. Maybe Danny was being extra careful. Maybe she was getting used to it.

They reappeared in the center of a circle of standing stones. That surprised Taylor; she didn't know there was anything like that at Stone Mountain. They were deep in the woods, apparently on the slope of the mountain itself. Its great bald granite top was clearly visible above them, golden in the morning light. They must have been in the Wonder, approaching the mountain at a different "frequency" than she was used to.

Danny led her up a path of pink marble flagstones that ended in a broad cleared area where a wall of solid rock rose almost straight up. Into this wall was carved a great, ornate door—a foreboding entryway three stories tall, carved into the living rock itself.

Danny nudged her forward. They strode up the marble steps. The closer they got, the larger Taylor realized it actually was.

They soon got close enough for Taylor to see details. Beneath the monstrous archway was a set of double doors at least twenty feet tall set with fittings of polished bronze. In front of it was a gate of silvery metal. It reminded Taylor of the entrance to a medieval castle.

The only sound she heard was their breathing and their soft footsteps on the hard stone pavement.

She looked around. If this really was Stone Mountain, they weren't anywhere near the reflecting pool. Were they even in the right place? Did Danny know what he was doing? The thought arose in her mind that they should be leaving—and fast. They needed to find the reflecting pool. More important, they needed to get clear of that door before anyone saw them.

She glanced at the pooka, who kept his eyes focused straight ahead.

"Shouldn't we—?"

Danny shushed her without looking at her.

He slipped his hand around her arm near the elbow.

"Where—?"

Danny shushed her again. They were almost to the gate. With his free hand, Danny reached forward. The gate slowly rose into a groove at the top of the archway. As soon as it cleared the doorway, the double doors swung open toward from them. On the other side of the door was a great open chamber, as big as an auditorium, flanked with doors and passageways and lit with dozens of bright glowing torches and wandering orbs of faery fire.

Taylor tried to pull away.

Danny expelled a labored breath. As they stood in the doorway, he finally turned to look her in the eye, then down at the ground.

"Mrs. Redmane," he said, "I brought you something."

Taylor couldn't believe her ears. Half a dozen figures materialized all around her, and she couldn't believe her eyes.

The guards were dressed in muted shades of green and brown, with steely eyes and pointed ears. They swarmed around her at once. They were armed with shotguns—antique-looking pieces with bronze barrels and ornate wooden stocks that were polished till they shone in the dim light of the entrance chamber. They aimed their weapons straight at Taylor as if daring her to flinch. Danny slipped out of their way to stand before the only other figure in the courtyard.

She was fair-skinned, tall and slender, with a wild expression: a lioness ready to pounce. The folds of her green silk dress shifted and rippled in the slightest breeze. Her red hair fell in luxurious waves around her shoulders.

"I suggest you stay where you are, child," she said, "unless you want my guards to fill you full of elf-shot." She turned to Danny as if only then realizing he was there. "Well done, Mr. Underhill. Although you took your good time getting here."

"Couldn't be helped, Ma'am," Danny said. "The Winters were on our back practically the whole time. They nearly got us at Judaculla Rock."

"So I've heard."

She strode toward Taylor, who kept her hands firmly against her sides to keep them from shaking.

"Good morning, dear. I've been waiting to meet you."

"D-danny?" Taylor whimpered.

"Sorry, kid." Danny sighed. "Business is business. Try not to take it personally."

"Y-you're giving me to her?" Sweat ran down Taylor's neck. "You're just handing me over to Mrs. Redmane? After all you—"

"You mustn't blame Mr. Underhill," Anya Redmane said. "He had little choice in the matter. Nor do you, I'm afraid."

Taylor turned toward Danny. "What are you doing? Danny? Answer me!"

Anya Redmane grabbed Taylor by the shoulders.

"Look at me when I'm talking to you!"

"Danny, what's going on?"

"I said look at me!" She raised a hand. There was a flash of white light, and Taylor felt the sting as if someone took a baseball bat to her face. She spun in mid-air and fell to the floor, dazed. She spit blood onto the flagstones. She heard Danny groan as if he were the one who had been struck.

She almost choked on a broken tooth. She spit that onto the floor as well.

Mrs. Redmane's dainty, slippered feet were right in front of her.

"You will learn to treat me with respect, you horrible child, if it is the last thing you do!"

Taylor wanted to say something snarky. As soon as she opened her mouth, however, she had second thoughts. She did

176

not want to cross this woman. She didn't want to speak badly of her either, for some reason. Something about her was so compelling it couldn't be ignored.

"Watch your mouth," Mrs. Redmane said. "Or I'll watch it for you."

She eyed Taylor's broken tooth. With a sly grin, she stooped and snatched it up.

"That will be all, Mr. Underhill," Anya Redmane said.

"Begging your pardon, ma'am..." Danny bowed his head. "Seeing as she's my ninety-ninth switch-out and all, I was hoping we could go ahead and finish our business?"

"That eager to be rid of me, eh, Mr. Underhill?"

"No, ma'am, it's not that. It's just...well, I've been making plans, and—"

"No need to make excuses, Mr. Underhill. You are quite right." She extended her right hand toward Danny like she was swearing an oath.

"Dandan Underhill, you have completed your obligation and repaid your debt to the noble house of Redmane. The oath between us is hereby dissolved. You are free to go."

Danny looked like a hundred-pound weight had been lifted off his shoulders.

"Thanks, Mrs. Redmane. Now, if you don't mind, seeing as how I've paid my debt and all—"

"Yes, by all means, go. I will, of course, provide you a good reference, should you need one. Do come back and see me sometime." She smiled as if this were just a normal day at Dunhoughkey.

Danny didn't even look at Taylor as he slid past the wall of guards surrounding her.

"You know where to take her," Anya Redmane said. She turned to Taylor. "I'll send for you shortly, child."

Two guards grabbed her from behind. She struggled, but they were too strong. Her screams echoed throughout the cavernous courtyard. She called Danny every vile and filthy name she could think of and then made up some new ones. She twisted and kicked and stomped on the guards' booted feet. If they felt it, they didn't let on.

She was half-dragged, half-pushed through another large door, along several corridors, and down several flights of stairs. She screamed till her lungs were raw, but it didn't seem to phase her guards in the slightest.

At last, they arrived at the bottom of the last flight of stairs. They pushed her down another corridor to a door overlaid with dull, gray metal.

They pinned her against it as one of the guards fiddled with the key. She felt a sudden chill down her spine. Iron.

The door swung open, and Taylor toppled in. Just as quickly, the door slammed shut. She rolled onto her back and roared a primal scream.

There was nothing left to do but cry.

Chapter 20

A Dinner Invitation

Taylor sniffled and rolled onto her belly, tears already flowing freely. She heaved and sobbed and barked out harsh, raspy, mournful moans. She started to shake, in part because the room was so chilly, but mostly out of fear.

"Selena?" a feminine voice whispered.

Taylor wasn't alone. She tried to pull herself together, but she just couldn't stop shaking. She sat up. A pair of pale blue eyes looked down on her.

"It is you! Are you all right?"

The young woman knelt beside her, grasped her hands, helped her to her feet. She took in Taylor's frail body from head to toe. "No broken bones," she said. "Let's get you cleaned up."

She vanished into a side room—the bathroom—and returned with some towels and a damp washcloth. She patted down Taylor's bloody lips and chin.

She was dressed in a black miniskirt, with a blue sleeveless V-neck blouse. Her hair was black, cut short on the sides until it was almost a Mohawk, but full and wild on top, and sporting pale blue highlights the same color as her eyes. A diamond stud adorned her left nostril. A circle of tattooed thorns wrapped around her right arm like an armband, and a stylized image of a tiny wren flitted across her right calf.

"I'm so, so sorry," the young woman said. She guided Taylor to a chair and eased her into it. She knelt at Taylor's feet. She couldn't take her eyes off of her.

"Would you like some water?"

179

Taylor nodded, still shaking. Her mouth throbbed.

Her cellmate padded off again toward the bathroom.

For the first time, Taylor looked around the room. Apart from the ironclad door and iron bars set at intervals along the outer walls, the room looked more like an old-fashioned parlor than a dungeon cell. The furniture could have come out of a historical museum. The walls were festooned with paintings of nature scenes and with black-and-white photos of men and women in all manner of poses: sitting in a portrait studio, standing over a dead...*something*—a creature part dinosaur and part mountain lion—surrounded by a retinue of waist-high servants.

Three doors led off the main room. From one of these, Taylor's cellmate returned with a glass of water.

"This will make you feel better. When Claudia comes, I'll have her bring you a healing potion. I'm sorry, Selena. This is all my fault."

Taylor looked into those pale blue eyes, so much like her own.

"You're my mom, aren't you? You're Shanna Hellebore."

She nodded.

"My name is Taylor."

"Taylor." Shanna Hellebore said. She seemed every bit as frightened as Taylor felt. "It's a pretty name, Taylor." She brushed the side of Taylor's face. "When you were born, I named you Selena."

"Oh."

Shanna sat on the floor in front of Taylor. She didn't look that much older than Taylor herself—twenty or twenty-five, tops. She remembered what Ayoka had said about how fae could control their own aging and wondered how old her mother really was.

Her eye shadow and dark blue lipstick highlighted her fair skin. In addition to her nose stud, she wore silver earrings and a silver necklace with a pendant shaped like a fancy Celtic knot. Taylor could imagine her working at some trendy music store in the mall—and getting hit on by every boy who came in.

"I'm so, so sorry."

"You said that."

"Since you're here, I take it you know...?"

"About you and my dad? Yeah."

"And how my parents kept me locked up?"

Taylor nodded.

"I escaped after Midwinter. The first thing I did was try to find you."

"But the Summer Court found you first."

Shanna bowed her head. "Danu! I should have been paying more attention. But I was almost there! South of Dunhough-key, I could feel that you were close. You were all I could think about—you're all I've thought about for the past thirteen years."

"Shanna," Taylor whispered. "M-mom."

She slipped out of her chair and joined Shanna on the floor. They held each other tight. They wept both with the joy of reunion and with fear for the future.

There was a sound of metal scraping metal. Someone unlocking the door. Shanna pulled away. Both she and Taylor stood up.

The door opened, and in walked a tall black woman in a blue business suit. She stepped inside and bid two little people attendants to enter, each carrying a tray of food.

"Lunch time. And good afternoon to you, Miss." She bowed slightly toward Taylor.

"Sel- Taylor, this is Claudia," Shanna said. "Claudia looks after me here."

Taylor said nothing. The little folk carried their trays through the sitting room into another part of her mother's quarters."

"Claudia, I'm afraid my daughter had a bit of a...," she stroked her lip. "That is, when she arrived here..."

"My grandmother beat me up," Taylor said. "Do you think you could bring me a healing potion?"

"Of course, Miss Hellebore," Claudia said. She and the two little folk departed.

"'Miss Hellebore,'" Taylor said. "That sounds so weird."

"What are your Topsider parents' names?"

"Smart. Fred and Julie Smart. Most Topsider couples just share the one name. I know that works different for you guys... for Our Kind."

"I knew that," Shanna said. She led Taylor into the dining room. It was nothing fancy, just a small wooden table, a sideboard, and more paintings and odd photographs.

Taylor ate slowly. Her mouth was still sore, especially when she forgot and chewed on the side where she lost her tooth. She tried to make the most of her Jell-O salad and her sweet tea, but didn't dare bite into anything as tough as the pork cutlets or the dinner rolls.

Claudia arrived in due time with a steaming cup of liquid, which she offered Taylor with another respectful bow.

Taylor took a sip. It actually wasn't bad, though it tingled in her mouth. It tasted more like vegetable broth than any kind of medicine. She nodded in appreciation and downed the rest.

"That'll take the swelling down and do something for the pain. I'll find something for that tooth, too," Claudia said. "It shouldn't take longer than a day or two, and I'll bring it right to you."

"Claudia is a genius when it comes to potions," Shanna said. "She says it's something she learned from her mother."

"If you don't need me any more, Mrs. Hellebore, I'll be going now."

"Of course, Claudia. And thanks for everything."

As soon as she was gone, Taylor said, "She seems so nice for a..."

"A fae?" Shanna finished. "Don't judge all of us by your grandmother. But Claudia's situation is a little...complicated. Her mom wasn't even Our Kind."

"Her mom was a Topsider?"

"A Friendly," Shanna nodded. "And pretty magical, apparently. Good with roots and herbs and such. But yeah, Claudia's great. If you have to be stuck in prison, she's the jailer you want.

"You were telling me about your Topsider parents."

Taylor explained about her parents, her school, her friends, her entire Topside life. Shanna asked questions about everything. Living in her own parents' dungeon for the past thirteen years hadn't robbed her of her curiosity. She wanted to know everything she could about her daughter's life—even though most of it must have seemed very strange.

Around the time the little people returned to take up the lunch trays, Shanna had begun talking about her own parents. She shared about the time she first met Aulberic Redmane, about how they fell in love.

"Of course, Dad hit the roof," she said. "There was no way he was going to let any son of Anya Redmane near his daughter."

"They really hated each other, huh?"

"Not just that. With Our Kind, inheritance passes from mother to daughter. That's why we don't take our husbands' names when we get married: it's the mother's line that counts. Dad rules the Winter Court because he married into the right family."

"Your mom?"

Shanna nodded. "The Hellebores are the ruling house. Whenever the throne is vacant, succession goes to the husband of the next Hellebore woman in line."

Taylor's mind was racing. "So, when your dad dies..."

"If I'm married, my husband becomes Primus of the Winter Court. Dad couldn't stand the idea that his power would pass to a Redmane. He just wouldn't allow it."

"But you married Aulberic anyway."

"Mom and Dad wanted me to marry one of my second cousins. Mold Cornstack." Shanna's face scrunched up as she pronounced the name.

"Mold? Seriously?"

"He's probably an okay guy, even with the unfortunate name. But he's not very bright, to be honest. And as soon as I met your father..."

"Bye bye, Mold."

"You got it. Aulberic was everything my family wasn't: cheerful, upbeat, spontaneous. I wish you could have known him."

"He must have been great."

"He was. But then..." She hung her head. "Let's talk more about your dad later, okay?"

"Sure."

Shanna's eyes suddenly brightened. "I've got something for you!" She got up from the table. Taylor followed close behind. They whisked through the sitting room and through the door to the bedroom. Like the rest of Shanna's cell, it was furnished in an odd, antique style. By the bed was a low bookcase that served as an end table.

Shanna pulled a small, leather-bound book from the shelf.

"This was mine when I was your age," she said.

Taylor held the book in her hands. The paper had yellowed over the years, but it was still in good shape. The title was *Timely Tales for Young Fae*, written in raised gold letters in an odd, angular type. Beneath the words was an engraving of a group of people gathered around an enormous tree.

"It's a story book," Shanna said.

Taylor opened the book and found the first chapter. "The Song of the World Tree?"

"That was one of my favorites," Shanna said. "When I was little, my own mom used to read to me from this book every night before I went to bed. I've practically got the whole thing memorized. When I escaped, I brought it with me. For you. I can't tell you how many times I wished I could have read you these stories when you were little."

Taylor flipped the pages. Other chapters bore titles like "The Pooka and the Water Horse," "The Changeling Prince," and "How Iron Came to Be."

"It's like a book of faery tales—oh, sorry! I hope that's okay. I know 'faery' isn't always a good word."

"It's okay. Our Kind are a little too touchy about things like that, if you ask me. We're very prideful, and the daoine sídhe are probably the worst. Sometimes they even call us the Children of Pride." Shanna placed a hand on Taylor's shoulder. "Whatever happens, Taylor, I hope you'll keep this...and have time to read it."

"Yeah."

Those last words brought Taylor back to reality. She was still in her grandmother's power. She was stuck in a prison cell inside an enemy fortress. The one friend she thought she had in the whole Wonder had sold her out.

"Why did he do it?" she said, tears welling up once again in her eyes. "I thought Danny was my friend! Or at least, I thought he would never just hand me over to that woman. He knew she hates me!"

"Danny? Is that the pooka?"

Taylor sniffled. "You know him?"

"I've heard of him."

Taylor slumped onto the bed. Her mother sat beside her. "Anya Redmane is very persuasive," Shanna said. "It's hard for anybody to tell her no. If he was somehow in her debt..."

"No!" she yelled. "He sold me out, do you understand? He doesn't care anything about me. He doesn't care about any Topsider! None of you do. We're just 'deathlings.' Pets or...or curiosities to Your Kind. You don't even think of us as people!"

Shanna sighed and pulled Taylor into her arms.

"I'm not defending him," Shanna said. "And I'm certainly not defending my mother-in-law. But we're not all like her."

Taylor sobbed into her mother's shoulder. She thought about Chief Tewa, his granddaughter Ayoka, and the other Fair Folk of Tsuwatelda. Then she thought about Jill and William and Mom and Dad.

"I just want to go home."

"I wouldn't blame you if you did."

For the longest time, they said nothing to each other. They just lay there on the bed in silence. Once, Taylor opened her eyes to see that Shanna was staring at her, as if she were trying to memorize her face. She was softly humming a tune that

185

seemed oddly familiar, like something barely remembered from a dream.

Taylor's messed-up sleep schedule finally got the best of her, and she drifted off into a fitful sleep.

The next thing she knew, Shanna was gently patting her on the shoulder.

"Wake up, Taylor."

"Huh? What?"

Taylor sat up on the bed. Shanna sat next to her. Claudia stood over her, a frilly pink dress on a hanger in her hand.

"It's time for supper, Miss Hellebore," Claudia said.

"Alright," Taylor said. "Just give me a minute. I'll meet you in the dining room."

"You're to come with me, Miss Hellebore. Mrs. Redmane has requested your presence."

Taylor was suddenly wide-awake.

"And she asks that you dress appropriately." She held forward the dress.

"You've got to be kidding."

Chapter 21

A Cruel Choice

The dress was not quite as awful as Taylor feared. It was awful, all right. Just not quite as bad as it might have been. It wasn't a huge, hooped monstrosity like the Civil War dress she tried to wear at Moe Fountain's place. It didn't have a low neckline—which Taylor would have hated—and it wasn't too tight. It was sleeveless, however, which made Taylor self-conscious about her pale, scrawny arms, and it swept the floor like a formal ball gown. She tried to persuade Claudia to let her wear her tennis shoes, but her jailer insisted she put on the matching pink flats she provided.

"Great," she complained, "I'm going to my fate dressed like a flamingo."

"Maybe this will help," Shanna said. She slipped a silver chain around Taylor's neck. The pendant was in the shape of a flower crafted in silver with purplish-pink gemstones for petals.

"Your father gave it to me," she said. "Do you know what it is?"

Taylor shook her head.

"It's a hellebore. They bloom in winter, you know. No matter how cold or harsh the weather, all it takes is a little bit of sunlight and up they come."

Taylor smiled in spite of herself.

Claudia and a couple of Mrs. Redmane's armed guards escorted her through the labyrinth of stairs and passageways. This time, she was able to pay attention to her surroundings. The whole rath was decorated like a medieval castle. Tapestries adorned the stone walls. Lanterns in metal sconces sprung to life as they drew near and extinguished behind them when they passed.

"It will be best if you show the utmost respect," Claudia said as they climbed what must have been the fourth or fifth staircase. "You are not their equal; they will be deeply offended if you suggest otherwise."

"They?"

"Mrs. Redmane has invited the other members of the Triad to dinner. The Triad's role is to uphold the Eldritch Law of the daoine sídhe. Think of them as something like your Topside Supreme Court, only with more power."

"Am I being put on trial?"

Claudia pondered her answer for several steps. "Not exactly," she said at last. She swung open a massive wooden door at the top of the stairs. The four of them entered a long, brightly lit rotunda. "But Mrs. Redmane is a stickler for the formalities. She takes her position very seriously."

They passed through an archway and began to walk down a long corridor.

"Do these guys ever talk?" Taylor hadn't heard her guards say a single word. They just marched along behind her and Claudia, shotguns resting on their shoulders, with bored expressions on their faces.

"Changelings aren't always the most talkative bunch," Claudia said. "Isn't that right, Bob?"

Neither guard's expression changed. Whichever one was Bob remained a mystery.

"Changelings? You mean humans?"

Claudia nodded. "The Redmanes prefer to employ changelings in their personal guard. They say they find them more loyal than Our Kind."

"Yeah, Our Kind don't really like taking orders."

"So you understand."

"Yeah, I understand. The Redmanes prefer to use guards who won't quit on them just because their bosses are a bunch of psychos."

"Perhaps," Claudia admitted.

They finally arrived at the dining room, and Taylor could only stand in awe. It was vast and full of color. A dozen high windows were cut into the stone walls on one side, letting in the light of the setting sun upon a garden of vines and flowering plants: azaleas and hyacinths and tulips. Between the windows were colorful tapestries of matchless workmanship.

The ceiling was high above them. A warm breeze blew through the open windows and tickled the hair behind Taylor's ear. Butterflies fluttered above, a swirling rainbow of life. Hovering globes of faery fire drifted about, bathing the room in a warm, yellow glow. In one corner, a fae played a haunting melody on a golden harp.

In the center of the room were two C-shaped tables facing each other so that they formed a donut shape with enough space for servants to walk between them. Claudia led Taylor to the nearest of the tables. A single chair had been provided. As soon as Taylor sat down, Claudia drifted into the background. Taylor craned her neck to watch her standing by the door. She gave Taylor a subtle nod of affirmation.

At the other table, three women sat, each dressed in fine, tailored business suits. Anya Redmane was in the middle, cradling a black cat with a little tuft of white on its chest. It licked at a tattooed length of ivy that snaked up her grandmother's neck and curled around her ear, but she didn't seem to notice. To her left was a dark-haired woman about the same age as Mrs. Redmane, with full, red lips that curled into something halfway between a smile and a condescending sneer. To her right was a younger blonde woman, maybe as old as Shanna—although with the fae, who could tell?

Mrs. Redmane shooed the cat to the floor and clapped her hands. A troop of little folk entered the dining room with trays of food and pitchers of drink. One of them set a silver plate full of roast beef, potatoes, and peas in front of Taylor while another filled her silver goblet with milk.

Taylor couldn't even think of eating. She just looked across the divide at the three women facing her at the other table, and especially at Anya Redmane glaring back at her.

The three women nibbled at their food. Taylor barely picked at hers. Apart from the clinking of goblets and the scraping of silverware, supper passed in silence. Taylor looked around at the tapestries—anything to keep from making eye contact with her grandmother. They were exquisitely made; the figures were so lifelike they almost seemed to come to life. Mrs. Redmane herself featured prominently in one of them, seated next to a handsome older man, sharply dressed, with blazing green eyes. Her grandfather, she imagined.

"State your name," Mrs. Redmane said.

"What?"

"Your name, girl." Mrs. Redmane continued to glare at her, like she didn't think Taylor was bright enough to answer the question. On either side of the Chief Matron, her cohorts eyed her with obvious discomfort.

"Taylor Smart."

"Not that name."

"The Chief Matron is asking for your...your fae name," the young blonde fae said. "The name you were born with."

"And she is apparently unfazed at how forward a request that is!" the darker woman added. She and Mrs. Redmane exchanged hateful glares.

"Far be it from me to upset the Chief Matron's little game," she added with a dismissive wave of her hand. "Answer or don't. It doesn't matter to me."

Taylor looked from one to the other of her inquisitors. She swallowed.

"Selena," she whispered. Then louder: "Selena Hellebore." How odd that name sounded on her lips.

Mrs. Redmane smiled for the first time. At the same time, her cat had wandered over to Taylor's table. It nudged Taylor's leg and looked up at her as if to say, "What are you doing here?"

"I have been asked to explain," Mrs. Redmane said, glancing at the black-haired woman to her left, "that this is not an official meeting of the Summer Triad. My colleagues are merely present to serve as witnesses."

"Okay."

"Furthermore, you are to understand that you are not being accused of any crime. The purpose of this meeting is...personal. My purpose is simply to ascertain your intentions with respect to eldritch society."

"I-I don't think I understand," Taylor said.

Mrs. Redmane sighed. "You were raised Topside, were you not?"

"That's right."

"Although you are, in fact, a full-blooded fae? A duine sídhe and, in fact, a descendant of the house of Hellebore?"

"We all know who she is, Anya," the black-haired woman said. "Why must you be so punctilious about this?"

"I will handle this interview as I see fit, Dubessa," Mrs. Redmane snapped.

"That's right," Taylor said, strong and clear. She surprised herself by saying it, but it was the truth. Why bother denying what they all already knew?

"Good," Mrs. Redmane said. "Good. And then perhaps you know about the feud between our two families?"

"You mean *my* two families, don't you? I'm just as much a Redmane as I am a Hellebore." Taylor put as much confidence as she could into her voice. She was tired of this stupid posturing. She was tired of being talked down to her like she was an idiot.

Her boldness got Mrs. Redmane's attention, though. The Chief Matron gazed at her with murder in her eyes.

"*You. Will never. Be a Redmane,*" she said. The words vibrated with primal energy that washed over Taylor from head to toe. She sat back in her seat, eyes glued to her grandmother. Her own 'death-glares' seemed about as intimidating as a newborn puppy next to her grandmother's. Anya Redmane was beautiful, to be sure, but there was something foul and monstrous about her. She was not someone to play games with.

"And therefore, I must know what to do with you."

"Yes, ma'am." She silently cursed herself. She hadn't meant to be so polite. Where did that come from?

The cat leaped up onto Taylor's table. Taylor scooted her chair back with a start.

"You mustn't mind Loppy, girl," Mrs. Redmane said, her voice once again even and reserved. "He's merely curious whether you have a soul he can steal. How cute!"

Yeah, the little fuzzball's adorable, all right.

"As I said, I've brought you to discuss your plans."

"My plans, Ma'am?" *Ma'am?* Crap! She did it again!

"It is actually quite straightforward, child. Do you choose to remain in the Wonder as a duine sídhe, or do you choose to foreswear your heritage and rejoin the Topside world?"

Taylor didn't know what to say. There was a trick here, she was sure of it.

"What happens if I decide to go, M-Mrs. Redmane? You'll let me, right?"

"Of course I'll let you. As I would have expected Mr. Underhill explained to you, the final decision will be yours to make and yours alone. That I have sworn by my own true name," Mrs. Redmane grinned. "But understand that once you leave, you are never to set foot in Dunhoughkey or any other rath in the Chiefdom of Arradherry ever again."

The blonde woman fidgeted on Mrs. Redmane's left.

"Does this bore you, Nuala?"

"Not at all, cousin. But you are being a bit overly dramatic, don't you think?"

"It's in her blood," the black-haired woman said. "And hardly befitting the Chief Matron of the Summer Court, if you ask me."

"I didn't ask you, Dubessa," the blonde said. "When you are Chief Matron, you can show us how the house of Fairchild would handle such matters. For now—"

"For now, we are wasting time," Mrs. Redmane said. "I will hear the child's answer."

All eyes turned once again to Taylor.

"Begging your pardon, Ma'am," she began. She bit her lip. What had gotten into her? "What happens to Shanna?"

"Shanna?" Mrs. Redmane said.

"Shanna. M-my birth mother. If I go back to my Topside parents, what happens to her?"

"If you choose to walk away from Dunhoughkey, I hardly see how that is any of your concern." Mrs. Redmane's eyes flashed, and she licked her lips like someone had set a chocolate sundae in front of her—or maybe a sacrificial lamb in a black miniskirt.

"I see. So...what if I decide to stay?"

"Now, that would be interesting," Mrs. Redmane said. "As a member of fae society, you would, I'm afraid, be subject to our laws. All of our laws. Including those laws concerning reciprocity and blood vengeance.

"Reciprocity." Taylor remembered her exchange with Moe Fountain. "Like for like."

"Indeed," Mrs. Redmane said. "When family honor is at stake, the offended party has the right to demand fitting retribution from the family that is at fault. 'Like for like,' as you say. And I should inform you that Our Kind hold honor very highly, child. Very highly."

"Go on, please." This wave of politeness was getting ridiculous!

"The house of Hellebore delivered an unforgiveable blow to the Redmane honor," she said. "They didn't merely kill my child, they destroyed him—and in my presence. Can you grasp what that is like, to watch your own child, your own flesh and blood, ripped away from you before your very eyes?"

"What the Chief Matron is trying to say, child," the black-haired woman said, examining her nail polish, "is that she would very much like to kill you in the most unimaginably horrible way. Although, one way or another, someone is going to pay for the crimes committed against the house of Redmane."

"You say that as if you wouldn't do the same should anyone dishonor the house of Fairchild, Dubessa."

"Perhaps I would," she said. "Then again, the house of Fairchild is on the rise, while your noble house.... Well, let's just say it has seen better days."

"Be that as it may, Dubessa," Nuala said, "it is hardly relevant. Anya is right that the Hellebores must pay for their crime. The Eldritch Law must be upheld. Therefore, the girl must decide what she intends to do."

Taylor remembered what Blain Stamp had told her: she had the power of life or death on her tongue. She had to but say the word, and bring either life or death to others. She speaks, and Shanna either lives or dies.

"What if I refuse to decide?"

"Ah, but you must." Mrs. Redmane extended her hands. An ornate wooden box, like a tiny casket, appeared from nowhere in front of her. "You have no choice, you see."

She brushed a butterfly away and opened the box. With her thumb and forefinger she produced from it a tiny speck of white. Taylor's hand instinctively found her mouth. Her missing tooth was there in Mrs. Redmane's spidery fingers.

She drew two other objects from the box: a block of clay and a long, thin silver dagger.

"I doubt you've learned much of anything about Our Kind, so let me give you a brief lesson about the principle of contagion. You see, things that were once part of each other can never truly be separated. This tooth, for example. It's still part of you, magically speaking. And the person who has it, has you."

As she spoke, she worked the clay, pinching here, flattening there. Taylor realized it was vaguely taking on the shape of a human body.

"Oh, it would be easier to control you if I possessed your true name," she said. She began to work the tooth into the thickest part of the clay with her thumbs. All the while, she continued to speak to Taylor.

"But that can only be given willingly, and I doubt you would be so obliging. I do appreciate, however, the way you surrendered your common name so readily, Selena. 'Selena Hellebore,'" she said, exactly matching Taylor's own cadence and pronunciation. "A fine name to conjure with. Paired with this little memento from our first meeting, I don't think I'll have any trouble compelling you to choose."

With the knife, she traced a line across the back of the tiny clay figure from top to bottom. At the same time, sang some kind of charm or chant under her breath in a language Taylor couldn't understand. She cut additional lines touching or crossing the first line at various angles. Her eyes never left Taylor.

Finally, she held the clay figure at eye level, still repeating her eerie melody. She snapped her fingers, and a tongue of fire sprung from them. This wasn't cold faery fire, though. She could tell in an instant it was real fire, hot enough to burn.

Mrs. Redmane held the clay figure above her flaming fingertips. All at once, Taylor felt the room grow warmer. She started to sweat. In a matter of seconds, it felt like she was in an oven. Her vision blurred. She groaned in pain.

Mrs. Redmane blew out the flame, and the pain left Taylor as quickly as it had come upon her. She returned the figure to its box. Taylor took huge gulping breaths. She was sure an asthma attack was coming on. The sensation soon went away—but not the dread that caused it.

"You will decide at dawn tomorrow, in this chamber," she said. "Or else."

"Yes, ma'am."

She cast a glance over Taylor's shoulder. Claudia approached. Apparently, the interview was over. She had until dawn to decide whether to let her mother die, or to die herself in her mother's place.

She started to tremble as Claudia helped her to her feet and escorted her from the dining room. The two changeling guards fell into step behind them.

"She's enjoying this," Taylor said. Without Mrs. Redmane gazing over at her, she no longer felt the need to use her best manners.

"What was your first clue?" Claudia said.

"It's not fair!"

"You said it yourself, Miss Hellebore: like for like. That's the way it is with Our Kind. In the end, everything has got to balance out. Debts *will* be paid."

"One way or another."

They wound through the corridors and descended the stairs once more. At the bottom of the last staircase, Taylor noticed the marble statue of a severe looking woman in flowing robes with a garland of flowers in her hair that seemed totally out of place. Taylor stopped to study it more closely. The golden plaque at the base identified her as Uasal Redmane.

"That's Mrs. Redmane's grandmother," Claudia said. "All the American Redmanes are her descendants."

"And they remember her by putting up her statue in the dungeons?"

"Folks that remember her say it suits her."

Taylor studied the statue's frowning face. It wasn't hard to imagine Mrs. Redmane's grandmother feeling at home in the moldy darkness beneath Dunhoughkey.

They arrived before the iron door to Shanna Hellebore's cell. Claudia unlocked it with a gigantic silver key. She dismissed the guards and followed Taylor inside.

Shanna leaped up to greet Taylor. She guided her to the sofa and sat beside Taylor as she told her story.

She listened with growing alarm as Taylor and Claudia explained what happened before the Summer Triad, the cruel choice that Anya Redmane had forced upon Taylor.

"You've got to save yourself," Shanna insisted. "Tell her you'll leave. I'm the one she really wants."

"I can't," Taylor said. "I want to... Believe me, I wish I could just walk away and forget any of this ever happened."

"Then do it," Shanna said.

"No. That's not an option. Not anymore. Now that I've met you... Before, you were just a name to me. You might have been just as cruel and heartless as my grandmother. But you're not. You're...normal. If I leave, your death will be my fault. I couldn't stand to live if that were true."

"You've got to listen to reason, Taylor," Shanna said. "There's no reason for you to die so young. You're only thirteen years old!"

"You're not much older."

"I'm older than I look," Shanna quipped. "I'm also your mother. I know you've barely met me, but I remember when you were born. I've loved you all your life. If I live to be a thousand, I'll still love you. You're my daughter." Her voice began to break. "I'm not about to let you throw away your life for my sake."

She turned to Claudia, and Taylor only then remembered that the two of them were not alone.

"Claudia," Shanna said, "we need a way out of this. Do you have any ideas? Is there anything I'm missing? Any way you see to get Taylor out of this mess?"

There was a quiet knock at the door. Taylor didn't hear it the first time, but Claudia did, and sprung up to answer it.

"Could be, Mrs. Hellebore," she said.

She cracked open the door. "Leastwise, if anybody can get the two of you out of here, he's the one to do it."

Danny Underhill stepped inside and shut the door behind him.

197

Chapter 22

The Pooka

Danny felt like a monster, turning his back on Taylor back in the courtyard. He deserved every name she called him, and he knew it. But it couldn't be helped. He had a job to do, the biggest he ever had.

He passed through the stone circle at the entrance to Dunhoughkey and immediately appeared on the side of the mountain under a thick mist of glamour. The great stone doorway was nowhere to be seen. Above him, the sky was a pure, pale blue. He was Topside, all right. He approached a hiking trail, thankful that so early in the day, there weren't a whole lot of Topsiders around. Still hidden in the woods, he became a dog and padded away.

He listened for birdsong. Was anything happening he should know about? An overwrought robin was tweeting something, but it was too hard to follow. Something about a hawk counting its toenails? Either that, or a goblin paying his taxes. Neither seemed like something he had time to deal with at the moment.

The first order of business was to get something to eat. He needed to build up his strength. He would need all the magic he could muster.

Half a mile to the bottom of the mountain, then back around to the front of the park. He stopped by the picnic pavilions in hopes of begging a snack from the tourists. The only people there were setting up for some kind of party. No matter how cheerfully he wagged his tail, they just shooed him away.

Plan B was to follow the railroad tracks into the Crossroads area. The closer he got, the more he shivered to be near such a huge expanse of iron, but he was able to dart among the trees and come out near some kind of enclosed stage area. Nobody was in sight. Perfect!

He resumed his normal form, blinked through a hole in the fence, and quickly glamoured himself to pass as a Topsider. Not a teenager this time, though. He took on the appearance of a man in his thirties and blended into the sparse crowd.

He looked this way and that. He needed a good dose of sugar, then he could lie low somewhere and figure out a plan.

The Candy Kitchen grabbed his attention. A large box of chocolate fudge would do the trick.

He snagged a handful of leaves from the nearest tree and headed inside. He set the fudge on the counter. When the cashier told him the price, he magicked the leaves to make them look like paper money.

"Keep the change," he said as he scooped up his purchase and ran outside. The pishogue he put on the leaves wouldn't wear off for several hours, of course, and he didn't intend to hang around there in any case.

He found a bench and dug into his fudge. He kept his eyes open, however. He was sure he wasn't the only fae in the area.

Sure enough, it wasn't long until he spotted a troop of Boy Scouts loitering in front of the 4-D movie theater. There must have been a dozen of them, looking this way and that—way too serious for elementary schoolers on an outing. They were under a really thick glamour, but Danny was sure they were spriggans. Clouds were moving in overhead. A breeze was picking up.

He kept his head down and tried not to draw attention to himself.

He hoped they would say something, give him some kind of clue whether they were with the Summer or the Winter Court. They didn't say a word.

What was he thinking, agreeing to switch out Shanna Hellebore from under the nose of Mrs. Redmane?

If anyone else asked him to do it, he'd have laughed in their face. But Claudia Fountain? He would do anything for her.

She had scried him Wednesday night just before he met Bryn back behind Taylor's house. He hadn't seen or heard from her in years.

"Danny," she said. "I've got a favor to ask, and I'm afraid it's a big one. You know the story about Shanna Hellebore, right?"

"Of course I do," he answered. "Who doesn't?"

"Well, here's the thing: Shanna's been captured by the Summer Court. She's here with me in Dunhoughkey." Danny stood speechless.

"What could Mrs. Redmane be thinking?" he said at last.

"I'm not sure she is thinking. You know as well as I do the Winters aren't going to take this lying down." She paused thoughtfully. "People are going to get hurt—and not just Shanna."

"This is bad."

"This is worse than bad. Mrs. Redmane has crossed a line. I understand you've been on the field for a while so you might not realize it, but things have gotten pretty tense the past few months. At first I thought she only wanted to humiliate the Winters, maybe make them grovel a little and then let them have Shanna back. But it's gone beyond that. I don't know why."

Danny took all this in and let Claudia continue.

"Danny...We've got to switch her out. It's the only way to defuse the situation."

"Switch out Shanna Hellebore from under Mrs. Redmane's nose? Are you nuts?"

"It's that or war."

He shivered in the growing dark. If it had been anybody but Claudia Fountain.... But—curse it all!—Claudia believed in him. That's what made her so dangerous.

"I'm heading that way tomorrow on some other business," he said at last. "I hate doing a rush job...."

"I can give you all the inside information you need," Claudia said with a smile. "And I already know a place where you can work. I can't tell you how much this means to me, Danny. How much it means for all Our Kind."

"Yeah, yeah," Danny said. "I'm a regular hero."

"Oh, I wouldn't go that far," Claudia teased. "But if there's a way to pull off this switch-out, Danny," she continued, serious, "you're the one to find it."

And if he played his cards right, then by oak, ash, and thorn, he could save Taylor as well.

The spriggans split up, some heading toward the miniature golf and the rest drifting back toward the park entrance.

Danny let them get out of sight before moving again. He had finished off his fudge in record time, but he had a long day ahead of him. He bought an extra-large sugary soft drink at a nearby stand and headed off to find the reflecting pool, not sure where exactly to go.

He wandered up a gentle incline, past the Dippin' Dots. Then he saw it: a discarded park map lying beside a trashcan. He grabbed it and opened it up. He got his bearings and figured out which direction he needed to go. There was a path behind the row of buildings that included the Candy Kitchen that led right to an immense lawn in front of the reflecting pool—and beyond that, a wall of solid granite rising hundreds of feet into the cloudy sky.

Everything was going fine until he reached the Funnel Cake Gourmet. Just his luck—he had to cross an open space to reach the edge of the lawn, and that open space was currently filled with half a dozen hungry Boy Scouts.

Danny inched toward the edge of the building. He strained to hear what they were saying.

"...So then the goatherd says, 'Don't look at me; he was like that when I got here.'" The Boy Scout burst out laughing. He may have looked like a ten-year-old, but he had the deep, gravelly voice of somebody who probably smoked too much.

"I don't get it," his buddy said.

"Pasco, you are so dense. Look, there's this goatherd, see? And a Gentryman with a trampoline..."

Danny felt a gentle tingling from inside his shoulder bag. A scry was coming in on his seeing stone. He pulled out the stone and peered into its hole. His surroundings shimmered. A ghostly form materialized in front of him.

"Danny, what's up?" It was Bryn.

The pooka sighed. Not now! It was all he could do keeping Shanna and Taylor safe. He didn't need to worry about how to keep Bryn out of this. He scrambled across the path into a patch of trees where he could keep an eye on things.

"What's the situation there?" he whispered. "Any problems?"

"No problems. But the spriggans left a few hours ago. You don't know where they might have gone, do you?"

I might have a few guesses.... "What about Taylor's parents? They still don't suspect you, do they?"

"I don't think so—but why aren't you answering my questions? What's going on? Where are you?"

He wanted to say *I'm trying to keep you out of this, and I'd appreciate a little cooperation!* Instead, he said, "Well, we made it to Dunhoughkey.... It's kind of hard to explain, actually. There's been some complications."

"Complications? What kind of—?"

"Listen, Bryn, now ain't really a good time."

The Boy Scouts started to fan out, funnel cakes in hand. Pasco and his joke-telling partner ambled toward the lawn, looking this way and that.

"Just keep on being Taylor," Danny said. "I'm gonna bring her home as soon as I can, all right?"

"But what about the party tonight? Is she going to be home in time?"

Bryn, there are more important things going on right now than a stupid party! "I-I wouldn't count on it. You go. Have a good time."

"Really? But I thought—"

"Bryn, this seriously ain't a great time to talk. I'll check in soon, okay? Bye!" He signed off before Bryn could ask him anything else.

Now he needed to find that secret entrance the dwarves told him about. But how? With spriggans roaming the park, he would have to be extra careful. He wondered if the spriggans were alone. How many of the Topsider tourists were really changelings in disguise? How many redcaps might be lurking in the woods? How many water cannibals in the reflecting pool?

He thought about becoming a dog. No, a dog with no owners in sight might draw too much attention. He just had to trust his glamour would keep his true nature concealed even from the spriggans.

He took a deep breath, pulled the veil of magical mist more tightly over himself, and stepped out of the trees, across the path, and onto the lawn.

Nope, nothing out of the ordinary here, folks. Just Danny Underhill, ordinary Topsider from Pekin, Indiana, here to enjoy the park.

To his right was the massive granite mountain. Halfway up its face was an enormous carving of three bearded Topsiders on horseback, riding off to the left. No wonder the Summers pretty much abandoned the place, Danny thought. As if the years of quarrying weren't bad enough, having somebody deface your property like that must have been the final straw.

"Them Jacks sure did a number on 'em, didn't they?" someone said.

"Yeah, I was just—" Then it hit him. Danny whipped around to see who was talking to him. It was a short man dressed as a scout leader.

Immediately he tensed. His glamour had failed.

"Why don't you just come along with us," the scout leader said. Half a dozen Boy Scouts closed in from every direction. Danny peered through the glamour just enough to see their blazing red eyes.

Beyond them, several dozen park-goers were tossing Frisbees or walking about.

Danny cursed. The spriggans drew nearer.

Hoping his glamour was thick enough, he blinked away to just outside the encroaching circle of spriggans. As soon as he reappeared, he became a dog and bounded back into the trees.

"Get him!" the scout leader called. They all took off at a run. Thunder rumbled.

Danny used his canine agility for all it was worth, shifting direction and bolting away at top speed whenever a spriggan got close. There was a larger wooded area opposite the way he came in; if he could get to it, maybe he could lose them.

He spun to his left, barely missing a spriggan's outstretched hands.

He nearly bowled another one over as he charged between his legs. That was too close! If they ever caught him, he knew it was over.

Finally, he saw a straight shot toward the woods. He took off like a flash.

"Do something!" the leader screamed.

Danny felt a sharp pain in his haunches; a magical blast that stung like a stone thrown by the world's strongest man. He tumbled forward in a daze. Blasted! Danny struggled to see straight as the spriggans circled around him. His mind became a blur.

"Mom, why did that boy throw something at the dog?" a little boy asked.

Owwww... Oh.... You don't want to...ugh...know, kid, Danny thought. He shook his head. Where was he, again? He pulled himself up and tried to shake off the effects of the blast, but it was too late. He couldn't keep his balance. His brain was fuzzy. As if that weren't bad enough, in an instant he was once again surrounded.

A spriggan hauled him up into a wrestling hold. "Come along, puppy," he said.

He may have been the size of a fourth-grader, but the spriggan still had gigantic strength. There was no point resisting. Danny allowed himself to be hauled into the woods like a sack of packing peanuts.

They reached their destination and dumped him on the ground. He resumed his normal form.

"Where's the girl?" the leader said. The spriggans had allowed their glamour to dissipate. Half a dozen hideous monsters in tan shirts with bolo ties hovered over Danny.

"Girrrl? ...What girl?" he said. His speech was still slurred from the blast. His tongue felt like it was twice the size it should have been.

The spriggan leader kicked him hard in the gut.

"The sídhe girl we have orders to snatch. The one who's travelling with a pooka, heading toward Dunhoughkey. Does that ring any bells?"

"Pooka? Me? Y-y-you've got the wrong guy...." Danny tried to focus. He pointed to his beaded Indian bag and his buckskin trousers. "I'm a...a m-manitou, not a pooka."

The spriggan leader traded glances with a comrade, probably his second in command. "What do you think, Dewy?"

"If he's a manitou then I'm Crom Cornstack."

"My thoughts exactly," the leader said, cracking his knuckles.

"No, seriously!" Danny stalled. "You're m-m-making heap-big mistake, Kemosabe!"

The rest of the morning was mostly a blur. Two or three of the spriggans took turns blasting and beating the stuffing out of Danny in between further attempts to find out where Taylor was. He could barely stay conscious, let alone tell the spriggans what they wanted to know. Eventually, his body couldn't take any more, and he collapsed in a heap.

He wished he would have just passed out, but he didn't. He was wide awake when his captors tied him hand and foot and foot and left him beneath a tree. That meant they were through beating him up, at least for a while.

The leader offered him a sip of something to dull the pain. It wasn't enough.

Hours passed. Spriggans came and went from the clearing where they kept him. The captain kicked him in the ribs a time or two and threatened additional bodily insults, but his heart didn't seem in it. Danny figured he was a soldier, not an interrogator. He tried not to think about what would happen if somebody got hold of him who knew what he was doing.

As the sun began to set, most of them were gone on other assignments. Only three spriggans were in sight: the leader and two of his subordinates.

"Let me know if he decides to talk," the leader said. "I'll be back as soon as I check the perimeter."

"Sure thing, Cap'n."

The leader faded into the wood.

Danny struggled. The ropes were so tight his hands were throbbing.

"Don't go trying anything!" one of his guards said. "And don't even think about bringing back the puppy. Those ropes are magic, see. They'll shrink to fit even if you change your shape."

"You still don't believe I'm not the guy you're looking for?"

"Not for a second," the other guard said. "Where's the girl? Already at the rath?"

Danny said nothing.

"I don't see why you're hanging around. You got a friend in there?"

"You might say that."

"Must be more than a friend to risk all you've been through."

"You never forget the girl who turned you into a turnip.... Never mind, long story."

"Eh," the second guard said. "You hungry, Bill? What do you say we grab a bite to eat?"

"Good idea, Pasco. Hand me one of them baloney sandwiches and I'll watch the path. You keep your eye on the puke."

Bill collected his supper and took up a position about twenty feet away. Pasco dug into a cooler for his own sandwich and a can of soda.

Danny studied the sky. It shimmered unnaturally, as if a curtain of tiny sparkles was spread over the whole spriggan camp. They must have been under a deep glamour to keep them hidden from any Topsiders who might come strolling through the woods.

He pulled at his ropes, but it did no good. His eyes swept from Bill to Pasco and back. He was running out of time.

An idea came to him. It wasn't terribly clever or original—beneath his dignity, really. But we were talking about spriggans, after all, so it just might work. He summoned up all his anger and frustration—at the Summer Court, at his own stupidity in getting caught, and at the spriggans now charging at him. He stared at the ground.

"Hey, Pasco," Danny said. He tried to keep his voice even, even jovial, though he was starting to seethe inside. "Want to hear a joke? See, there's this Gentryman, and he's taking a trampoline back to his rath. The nearest ring is in the middle of this big pumpkin patch, see, and when he gets there, he runs into a goatherd..."

"I heard this one," Pasco said. "It ain't funny."

"It would be if you weren't so stupid."

"Shut up, Bill!" Pasco said.

"What?" Bill said.

"Then the goatherd says, 'Say there, mister, what can I give you for that trampoline?'.... Hey, by the way, is there any chance I could get one of those sandwiches?"

Pasco gave Danny a suspicious look. He reached behind him for the cooler.

"So the Gentryman says, 'Are you kidding? What does a goatherd need with a trampoline?'"

"I told you, I already heard this one," Pasco said.

"Forget him, puke, he's an elfin moron."

"Hey!" Pasco said.

"What's your problem?" Bill said. "Just keep an eye on the puke, all right?"

"Jerk."

"You better watch it, Pasco!" Thunder began to rumble. Danny glanced from one spriggan to the other. He tried to brace his back against the tree trunk. He didn't dare hope for more than a few seconds.

"Idiot."

"Jack-lover."

"Dwarf-kisser."

"You take that back!" both spriggans yelled at once. "No, *you* take that back!" they hollered.

There was a blinding flash of light. A second later, both spriggans were flat on their backs: they had blasted each other. Danny smiled. The old magical ventriloquism trick rarely worked so perfectly.

Bill groaned.

Danny had to act fast. He became a goat. Just as the spriggan had warned, the ropes around his wrists and ankles tightened as his joints contracted into their new form. But Danny wasn't worried about the ropes as long as he had his teeth.

He chomped into the rope around his forehooves. It could have used a little hot sauce, but this was no time to be picky.

"The puke!" Bill called as he stumbled to his feet.

The ropes fell loose, and Danny resumed his two-legged form and blasted Pasco, the nearest of his captors, with an animalistic grunt. His eyes blazed with yellow fire.

He didn't have enough juice left to blast Bill, so he did the next best thing. He hit him with his best stunning spell—a brilliant flash of light and noise that sent the spriggan to his knees. Danny reached for his shoulder bag. He found his knife and cut through the ropes around his ankles.

"Get him," Pasco yelled, groggy.

Danny was a light-headed, but he grabbed a sandwich and blinked away. Lightning flashed. The rain began as a trickle but quickly swelled to a downpour.

The crevice in the rock was well hidden. It took Danny another half hour to find it, which wasn't easy in the pouring rain, with a couple of cracked ribs, and with the threat of spriggans recapturing him any minute. But eventually, he found the opening and slipped inside.

He leaned against the rough granite wall to catch his breath. He winced in pain from the effort. Then he ducked his head and crept down the narrow tunnel to the ancient door at the other end.

With another deep breath, he whispered the password. The door opened outward. He pulled his glamour as thick as he could and stepped through.

The passage continued. With every step Danny felt himself descending deeper into the Wonder. It was cold and musty; the Gentry must not have used this passage in a hundred years—if ever. At the other end, there was a door. Danny pushed it open, right into the promised supply closet.

The door was hidden behind a built-in shelving unit, now mostly empty except for a couple of small wooden boxes and some metal implements, all covered in cobwebs. He stepped over some broken wooden furniture and out into the hallway beyond.

He was deep in the dungeons, that much was obvious. The doors of every cell were reinforced with thick bands of iron. Danny began to shiver just thinking about them. But somewhere down here was Shanna Hellebore. Almost as important, somewhere down here was Claudia Fountain—and she might know where to find Taylor.

But he felt miserable. The working-over the spriggans gave him had nearly done him in. He decided to retreat to the supply closet and see if he could do anything about the damage they had done to him.

He rummaged through his shoulder bag. He didn't have the ingredients for a proper healing potion, but he scraped some herbs together and steeped them in his whiskey flask by holding it over a warm fire he conjured in the palm of his hand. The concoction at least restored some of his strength and helped him shake off the lingering effects of the blasting he had been given. He had a black eye, a cut lip, and a gut that felt like spriggans had been using it for a punching bag.

He pulled the rest of his equipment from his bag. He was behind schedule. He had to get started. He mixed up an assortment of potions and set them aside one by one in little stoppered vials for when they would be needed.

He found his chalk and traced a circle on the floor big enough to conjure in. He sealed the circle by pouring a little bit of magic into it. Then he got down to business. He worked most of the afternoon, singing and chanting to himself as quietly as possible. Every time he heard a noise, he stopped everything and turned a pointed ear to the door.

At last, he heard the voice he had been waiting for. He jammed everything back into his bag, broke his circle by smudging it with his thumb, and cracked the door.

There was light up ahead; the corridor opened into a room with a staircase leading up just across the way, partially blocked by a statue of a disapproving sídhe matron. Danny peered around the corner. A woman stood at the far end of this chamber, talking with a guard.

"We're to escort Miss Hellebore to the dining room," she said. "Find Bob and meet me here in ten minutes."

Danny sprang back. He listened as the guard plodded up the stairs.

He produced an orb of faery fire in his hand and immediately let it go out. Thankfully, Claudia noticed.

"Who's there?" she called. She didn't sound scared by the sudden flash of light. She knew to expect Danny, even though he was running late.

"Danny!" she said, rounding the corner. She yanked him away toward an open cell, shoved him inside, and followed him.

"It's nearly sunset! What kept you? Not another squirrel, I hope!"

"That only happened once!"

"Well, never mind. You're here now. Are you ready?"

"Maybe. Do you know where Taylor is? The girl I brought in?"

"She's in Shanna's quarters. I'm hoping you've been working on a way to get her out, too."

Danny sighed. "Let me worry about one catastrophe at a time, if you don't mind. I've got a lot of work to do, and I'm behind schedule."

"Of course, Danny."

"You don't know what Mrs. Redmane has planned for Taylor, do you?"

"No, but it can't be good. Best we get her out tonight."

"Yeah. But I gotta tell you, Claudia, right now I don't know how we're gonna do it without blowing your cover."

Claudia was tight-lipped. "We'll do what we have to do. I hear there's Winters swarming all over the place Topside. Is that right?"

Danny nodded. "I don't think they're ready to move just yet," he said. "But they're securing their position. It won't be much longer."

"One more reason to move now." She pulled a silver key off the ring she kept on her belt. "You can work in here. It's a low-security cell; the only iron is on the door itself. Shanna is in the high-security wing. She's the only prisoner down here, though, and there's usually only one guard at the foot of the stairs. A changeling named Sam. Finish as fast as you can and meet me outside Shanna's quarters—second door to the left down the long hallway."

"Long hallway, second door on the left. Got it."

"I've got to take the girl to Mrs. Redmane now. With any luck, we'll be back in a couple of hours."

"I'll meet you as soon as I can."

"One more thing." Claudia leaned forward and brushed her lips across Danny's cheek, but only for a second. "Thanks. Again."

Danny winced, then forced himself to smile. "All in a day's work, ma'am."

Claudia pulled the door closed behind her, and Danny got right to work. He pulled his equipment from his bag and laid it out on the floor. He rummaged once again for his chalk. A couple of hours? He didn't see how it was possible, but he had to try.

It was hard to concentrate. Even after his restorative potion, his face hurt. Heck, his whole body hurt, but he couldn't worry about that. Claudia was counting on him. Taylor was counting on him. He nicked a finger on his chisel and nearly shouted out loud. He had to try the most delicate part or the procedure three times because he was getting so shaky. Two hours passed, and Danny was near the end of his magic. He really should have bought a second box of fudge that morning!

He stood up to look at his work. It wasn't great, but it would have to do. He wrapped it in the bed sheet and stuck it back in his beadwork bag. Then he finished off one remaining apple from the food Moe Fountain had given him.

He cracked open the cell door. Sam the changeling guard sat in a wooden chair beside the stairwell, reading the latest issue of *Better Gnomes and Gargoyles*. His shotgun leaned against the wall where he could grab it in a second.

Danny wasn't sure he could summon enough glamour to slip past the guard. If he was better at imitating Claudia's voice, he might have tried ventriloquism again.

Maybe he could still produce a passable sleep spell.

Danny closed his eyes and took several deep breaths. *You only get one chance*, he told himself. *Mess up now, and the whole operation is a bust.*

Once again, he cracked open the door. He whispered the words of an old Gaelic lullaby in a slow, steady breath. He pushed the spell toward its target with a gentle hand motion. Then he stood back and waited.

A minute passed.

Sam yawned. A sly smile spread across Danny's face.

Danny tried the spell again. This time, the effects were more immediate. Within another few minutes, Sam had slumped backward, his magazine draped across his chest.

Danny slipped past him as fast as he could. The statue of Uasal Redmane glared disapprovingly down the length of the long corridor at the far end of the chamber. Danny skirted past the first door on the left and quietly knocked at the second.

He could hear women's voices inside.

"Could be, Mrs. Hellebore," he heard Claudia say.

There was a click, and the door glided open. Claudia's eyes met Danny's with a look that said, *What kept you?* "Leastwise," she continued, looking back into the room, "if anybody can get the two of you out of here, he's the one to do it."

He stepped inside and pulled the door closed.

Chapter 23

Knowing Who You Are

"You!" Taylor gasped.

She stalked toward Danny in her frilly pink monstrosity of a dress, her fists raised. If Claudia hadn't stopped her, she'd have torn into him then and there.

"What are you doing here? You left me with that...that terrible woman! You left me to die here, you—"

With Claudia's arm across her chest holding her back, Taylor told Danny what she thought of him for a good three or four minutes. The pooka just stood there with his head bowed and took it.

When Taylor had expended her energy—and her vocabulary—she let out a frustrated growl and finally relaxed her muscles.

"Are you finished?" Claudia asked.

"I still want to know what he's doing here."

"He's here because I sent for him," Claudia said. She let Taylor go. Rather than lunging at Danny, she turned slowly to face Claudia. Shanna slipped between Taylor and Danny.

"What do you mean?"

"I asked him to come switch out your mother."

Fear and confusion started to settle in Taylor's gut. "You mean...you planned this all along? To trade me for her?"

"Not at all," Claudia said.

"No way," Danny added. "We didn't even know you were Shanna's daughter. By the way, pleased to meet you, Mrs. Hellebore. I'm Danny."

Shanna's eyes fixed on the pooka.

"Er, likewise," she said. "Call me Shanna. But...I don't understand."

"This vendetta of your mother-in-law's is threatening to start a war between her family and yours," Claudia explained. "She might not see it, but everybody else can. A civil war in Arradherry is the last thing Our Kind needs. Last time that happened, it dragged in other chiefdoms from as far away as New Avalon and even Windhame—not to mention the nunnehi and half the other Indian kindreds."

"That's why Claudia called me," Danny said. "She figured if you're not the Redmanes' prisoner, there's no reason for your two families to fight."

"There's always a reason for our families to fight," Shanna scoffed. "Just ask my dad."

"Even so," Claudia continued, "I thought it was worth a shot...and so did my superiors."

Taylor furrowed her brow. "Your superiors?"

"I work for the Redmanes, Taylor, but my loyalty lies elsewhere. I'd rather not say more."

"I still don't see how I fit into this."

"Neither did we, at first," Danny said. "I worked for the Redmanes, too, but only to pay off an old debt. They had me for ninety-nine switch-outs and then I could go free. It just so happened you were number ninety-nine."

"Danny had no idea you were Shanna's daughter," Claudia said. "At least, not until the two of you talked with my father."

"Your—"

"My father is Moe Fountain," she said. "Poppy suspected you had been captured, Mrs. Hellebore. He has ways of knowing things. So there didn't seem to be any point trying to deceive him when he asked me about it. And it's a good thing, too. It looks like he helped Selena—Taylor—put two and two together."

"But now, we've got a problem," Danny said.

"Only one?" Taylor said.

"Only one big one. We've got to get you out, too. Otherwise, the situation hasn't really changed. The Redmanes would still have a Hellebore hostage. There could still be war."

"But the Hellebores abandoned me when I was born!"

"It doesn't matter," Danny said. "It would still be an insult to their family honor. Honor is a big deal for Our Kind. Really big."

"So I've heard."

"Taylor," Danny said. He looked at the ground for a long time before finally meeting her glance. Taylor finally realized he looked like he'd been through a meat grinder. She wondered what he had been up to since that morning. "I'm sorry about... before. Our Kind keep our promises. We have to. It's not really something we have any control over."

"I'm not going to pretend I understand that."

"Fair enough. But the point is, we've got to get both of you out. Tonight."

"That's not going to happen," Claudia said.

All eyes turned to her. She explained to Danny about Taylor's interview with Mrs. Redmane and about the spell her grandmother used to compel her decide whether to stay and be killed or leave and let Shanna die.

"Okay," Danny said when she had finished. "Taylor has to show up tomorrow at dawn to give her answer. Then, somebody probably dies ten minutes later. That's what we're up against. Good to know."

"It's hopeless, isn't it?" Taylor said.

"No," Danny said. "Maybe. No! There's got to be a way."

The four sat down together, Taylor and Shanna on a sofa, Claudia and Danny in chairs. Taylor kicked off her pink flats. She scrunched and then relaxed her toes. She rubbed the bridge of her nose.

She replayed her encounter with Mrs. Redmane in her memory.

"Our Kind keep our promises," she muttered.

"What's that?" Claudia said.

"I said, 'Our Kind keep our promises.'" As she said it out loud, something clicked in the back of Taylor's mind. It tickled her memory and slipped through her mind's fingers like an eel.

"Taylor, what—?"

She threw up her hand to quiet Shanna's question. She shut her eyes tight.

When she opened her eyes, she turned to face Danny.

"Are you sure you can get Shanna out safely? I mean absolutely sure?"

"Not and save you, too," he said.

"I'm not talking about me. Can you do it?"

"Sure," Danny said. "But as soon as they take you to Mrs. Redmane in the morning—"

"You're positive?"

"Yeah. I can do it."

"Then I think we can both get out of here alive." She asked a couple of questions. Danny, Claudia, and Shanna answered as best they could, and she suddenly felt confident, even hopeful. Then she explained what she had in mind.

The three adult fae stared at her, open-mouthed.

"I think it might work," Claudia said.

"Of course it'll work," Danny said. "It's brilliant!"

"But timing will be everything," Taylor said. "That's one of your rules, isn't it?"

"You don't worry about that," Danny said, suddenly energized. He grabbed his bag and pulled out the project he had been working on since he got there. He set it proudly on the floor.

Taylor frowned.

"You really think *that's* going to work?"

"It's not quite finished yet," Danny said. "Another few hours, tops. It'll work."

She looked him in the eyes.

"Then there's just one problem." She looked at Danny, Shanna, and Claudia in turn. "How the heck am I ever going to stand my ground against Mrs. Redmane?"

The three looked back at her.

"She is kind of...intimidating," Danny said.

"Kind of?" Taylor retorted. "It was all I could do at supper to keep from kissing her feet! She could have spit in my face and I'd have thanked her for it. She's like a force of nature or something."

"You don't get to Mrs. Redmane's position without a powerful presence," Claudia admitted.

"So we're still sunk?" Taylor said.

"Maybe not," Shanna said. "I think Danny's going to need me for a minute, am I right? As soon as I'm done, I'll meet you in the dining room."

Claudia excused herself. Danny toted his project into the bedroom with Shanna close behind. Taylor sat at the dining room table.

A few minutes later, a servant appeared—on orders from Claudia, no doubt. She was tall and blonde like Bryn, with the same pointed ears, but older looking and rosy-cheeked. She brought in a huge tray of cookies, cupcakes, and other treats. Sweet snacks. Somebody was about to lay down some serious magic.

Shanna and Danny appeared in the doorway. Danny went immediately for the snacks. He jammed a pink-frosted cupcake in his mouth and started to fill his beadwork bag with chocolate-chip muffins, sugar cookies, and lemon squares.

"Do you need anything else, Danny?" Shanna asked.

Danny shook his head. With his mouth still full, he winked at Taylor and ducked away.

Shanna helped herself to a macaroon. She gestured for Taylor to eat up as well.

"There's usually a party," Shanna said. "I'm sorry, but we just don't have that kind of time."

"What are you talking about?"

"Your naming ceremony. Which should have happened years ago. It's traditional for all your closest friends and relatives to throw you a party afterward. I guess I'll have to owe you."

Taylor finished her bite of chocolate-chip cookie. "You said you named me Selena."

"Yes, I did." Shanna touched Taylor's arm. "But that's not the only name I gave you when you were born."

The wheels started turning. "My true name?" Taylor said.

Shanna nodded. "I don't know how much you understand about true names, Taylor, but they're very powerful. After I escaped my parents, I used your true name to search for you. If Mrs. Redmane hadn't captured me first, it would have led me right to you."

"Danny told me it makes a fae's magic stronger."

"He's right. A true name is like a piece of concentrated Wonder you hold deep inside you. It's a kind of good luck charm that nobody can take away, because it's you. It's who you are."

Who I am. Taylor thought about all the times the other kids in school made fun of her because she was so frail, or so smart, or because of the odd way she looked at things. She thought of all the times she fantasized about finding her real parents and getting the answers she craved: Why did they give her up? Where is she really from? Who are they—and who is she?

"If you know who you are...," she said, struggling to find the words, "you can finally be yourself."

Shanna smiled. "I think Claudia would say that is an apt summary."

Taylor looked into her mother's pale blue eyes. They weren't washed-out and weak. They were clear and bright with confidence and power.

Just like hers.

"What do I have to do?" she asked.

"Just listen," Shanna said. "Close your eyes if you want." She stood behind Taylor and gently massaged her shoulders.

She began to sing. She didn't seem to pronounce distinct words; it was more like a hum or an extended "la" or "loo" that went on for several serene minutes, low and murmuring like the sea.

Something stirred deep inside Taylor's body, as if the sound of Shanna's voice set up a vibration at the core of her being. She gradually realized that her mother's wordless vocalizations had become a gentle, mellifluous blessing:

May the blessing of the seven elements be upon you:
The quiet earth, soft under your feet.
The splashing water, cleansing and clear.
The whispering wind, strong yet gentle.
The crackling fire, welcoming friend and stranger.
The morning light, the hope of the world.
Long life, always growing.
True love, always returning.
And may all that is bless you, dear child,
And may your name be called *Neunhirri*.

At the final word, there was utter silence. Taylor wasn't even sure Shanna had pronounced the word out loud. Taylor imagined the word drifting from her mother's lips into her ears and down into her heart, like an echo in the deepest part of her. She was overcome with emotions she couldn't even name.

She sat, eyes still closed, and took several long, deep breaths. She felt a single tear running down her cheek.

"How do you feel," Shanna asked. She returned to her chair.

Taylor didn't know what to say. She gave Shanna a smile. She didn't want to ruin the experience by talking. The silence itself was as warm and comforting as a blanket on a cold winter's night.

"You don't have to say anything," Shanna said. "And you don't ever have to say the name. Just hold it in your heart. It is the greatest secret you'll ever possess. You've got to treat it with respect."

Taylor looked up at her.

"It comes from Esrana, the language Our Kind spoke long, long ago. It means 'Laughter in Winter.'"

"Oh."

"When you need to use magic, focus on the name. Let it draw the Wonder up into you so you can release it."

"I...don't understand."

"You will—with practice."

Danny knocked on the door frame.

"So soon?" Shanna said. Danny nodded.

"Time for you to get some sleep, Taylor. You've got a very big day ahead of you."

Chapter 24

The Gentryman and the Ogre

Long ago when the world was young, a fair and noble Gentryman ruled a chiefdom that spanned as far as the eye could see.

It so happened that one day, the Gentryman was hunting dragons deep in his deepest forest, when a fierce ogre fell upon him, scattered his guards, and frightened his horses, leaving him alone and at the mercy of the hideous brute.

Now, this ogre was very shrewd as ogres go, and he quickly realized that his captive was a fae of both power and means. Therefore, even though he was frightfully hungry and would have gobbled up the Gentryman for lunch in an instant, he saw there was more to be had from his good fortune than merely a bellyful of meat.

"What will you give me in exchange for your life?" the ogre demanded.

"I am a fae of both power and means," the Gentryman said— for although he was fair and noble, he was also rather foolish. "If you spare me, you must but name your reward."

The ogre licked his lips at the thought of all he might demand from the Gentryman in exchange for his life. But he knew that fae are clever, and can be trusted to slip out of any trouble before an ogre would even know it. And so he said, "Do you swear it by your own true name?"

"I so swear," the Gentryman said, for all he could think of was the ogre's ravenous teeth and massive jaws, and what was even his chiefdom worth to him if he didn't live to see another sunrise?

"Then I demand three rewards: one for your life, one for your liberty, and one for my lunch, which I now must find somewhere else," the ogre said. "In three day's time, I shall visit you at your rath and claim my first reward."

So the Gentryman went home to his rath and waited in anguish for the ogre to appear.

Sure enough, on the third day, the ogre walked up to the gate and demanded an audience with the Gentryman who ruled the chiefdom. Though the guards were frightened beyond consolation, they had been told that such an ogre was bound to come, and that they must do as he says. And as soon as the ogre entered the Gentryman's council chamber, he made his first demand.

"Make me a prince in your chiefdom," he said, "and I will forgive you taking away my lunch."

The Gentryman was saddened that this was the ogre's demand, but he had no choice, as he had sworn an oath by his own true name. He decked the ogre in the finest robes and set a golden circlet on his head. He appointed for the ogre a rath on the far edge of his chiefdom and named him Prince of the Northern Forest. The ogre was quite satisfied, and promised he would be back next year to claim his second reward.

In the days that followed, the Gentryman and his wife, the Chief Matron, had many pained conversations about the ogre and what could be done with him. But they were unable to reach any conclusions. They both hoped the ogre would simply forget about the Gentryman's rash oath, but this was not to be.

The ogre, as you might expect, made a horrible prince. He terrorized the Gentryman's subjects, raided their cattle, and kidnapped more than a few sprites, changelings, and little folk to serve as his slaves and, it was sometimes said, his supper.

Then, at the end of the year, the ogre returned to the Gentryman's rath to claim his second reward.

"Give me an axe that can never be bested," he said, "and I will cancel the debt you owe me for your liberty."

The Gentryman was saddened that this was the ogre's demand, but he had no choice, as he had sworn an oath by his own true name. Now, it so happened that there was a village of cunning dwarves in the southern mountains of the chiefdom. The Gentryman bargained with them for a magical axe, the greatest they had ever made, and six months later, the ogre was presented his prize. The ogre was quite satisfied, and promised he would be back in six month's time to claim his third reward.

Now, however, things got even worse for the chiefdom. The ogre's raids were more frequent and more brutal, and when the Gentryman's subjects moved away from the Northern Forest, the ogre waged war against the fae of the wild lands beyond. The Gentryman's name fell into disrepute for allowing such a monster free rein over his lands.

Then, at the end of the second year, the ogre returned to the Gentryman's rath to claim his third reward.

"Give me your daughter to be my wife," he said, "and I will cancel the debt you owe me for your life."

The Gentryman was saddened that this was the ogre's demand, for he had but one daughter, whom he loved very much. But even more than that, if the ogre married his daughter, he would one day rule the entire chiefdom—and that would be disastrous! But still, what could he do? For he had sworn an oath by his own true name.

So he called his daughter to his council chamber, along with his wife the Chief Matron. And hugging them both and weeping bitterly, he turned to the ogre and said, "No."

"No?" the ogre said, and his murderous rage grew fierce. "But you have sworn an oath by your own true name!"

"I revoke my oath," the Gentryman said. "Now leave my wife's chiefdom!" He said it this way for he knew what a grave thing it was to revoke a solemn promise. And as soon as the words had left his mouth, he breathed his last.

The Chief Matron called on her guards, and they drove the ogre out of the rath and into the public square, where it was beaten without mercy in return for all the evil it had brought upon the chiefdom.

And though the Gentryman was forever after publicly despised as an oath-breaker, in private his former subjects forgave him, for the latter sin they judged far lighter than the former sin of making a foolish oath in the first place.

For her part, the Gentryman's daughter never forgot how her father spared her the horror of marriage to a detestable monster. And though she and her mother spent the rest of their lives in obscurity, they lived proud and happy lives and helped rebuild all that the ogre had destroyed.

Chapter 25

Being Yourself

Taylor set down the storybook. By the light of the oil lamp, she looked at the clock on the wall. It was four-thirty in the morning. If she had slept at all, she hadn't noticed.

Dawn was ninety minutes away.

She curled up on the sofa in the sitting room and pulled her covers tight around her shoulders. Shanna had offered to share her bedroom, but Taylor preferred her privacy.

Twenty minutes passed. There was no point trying to get to sleep now, so Taylor got up and began her morning routine. She showered and put on the clothes she had laid out the night before: the jeans and tennis shoes she wore yesterday, plus a black tee shirt and leather jacket Shanna let her borrow. She pulled her hair back into a simple ponytail held in place by a black and silver barrette. She slipped the silver hellebore necklace around her neck.

She was pleased to see the kitchen staff had brought her breakfast while she was in the bathroom. She helped herself to a bowl of oatmeal, a banana, and a glass of orange juice. Then, for good measure, she gobbled up the last two macaroons from last night's snack tray.

At five-twenty, Claudia appeared at the cell door with her changeling guards.

"It's time," she said.

"I know. Just let me get my bag." Taylor slung her beaded leather purse over her shoulder.

Taylor, Claudia, and the two guards wove through the stairways and corridors of the rath. It was darker and colder than she remembered.

When they arrived in the dining room, no one else was there. Claudia set her at the same table where she ate the night before. She stood at her side while the changelings stood guard at the door. The air was cool but not uncomfortable. Beyond the great windows, birds sang their morning songs. A butterfly lit at her elbow but quickly flitted away.

From the opposite end of the chamber, the members of the Triad appeared. Anya Redmane led the way, her fiery hair blowing on an unfelt breeze. Nuala, Anya's blonde cousin, came next. Dubessa Fairchild, the black-haired Matron, took up the rear. The three Matrons took their seats facing Taylor.

Taylor had to do two things. First, she had to somehow stand her ground against her imposing grandmother. Second, she had to stall as long as possible.

She hoped knowledge of her true name would help with the first task. That was the only way she could succeed at the second. The only clock in the room was on a shelf directly behind her. She didn't feel like turning around to check it—her teachers never appreciated that maneuver in their classrooms. But she really wished she knew how long she might hope to drag things out. Then again, she was fairly sure Mrs. Redmane would tell her very clearly when her time was up.

Anya Redmane looked her in the eye. She produced the clay figure she had fashioned the night before and laid it on the table in front of her.

Taylor resisted the urge to look away. She concentrated on her true name. *Neunhirri. I am Neunhirri, Laughter in Winter.*

Energy seemed to roll through her in gentle waves. She was getting used to the feeling of glamour settling over her, but this was different. While glamour gave the sensation of something from the outside circling around her, dwelling on her true name felt more like heat or light radiating outward from somewhere deep inside.

Her confidence began to rise.

"Selena Hellebore," Mrs. Redmane began, "have you reached a decision?"

She took a deep breath.

"What you ask is very difficult, Chief Matron," she said. She felt much more in control of herself than she was last night. She addressed her grandmother by her proper title only because she wanted to, not because she felt compelled to grovel in front of her.

Here goes!

"As I understand it, Chief Matron, you want me to decide my fate—and right now. Will I live as a Topsider, or will I die as a fae. Would you say that's an accurate description of my options?"

"Yes, of course," Mrs. Redmane said. "I would have thought that much was clear last night."

"Indeed it was," Taylor said. She purposely left off the "ma'am" or "Chief Matron." Part of her wanted to say it, but she held herself back. She smiled a subtle smile.

I am Laughter in Winter, she thought, *and I'm laughing at you, you old biddy!*

"Of course, the tricky part is, can I live with myself if I choose to leave here safely. What would that say about my concern—or, I should say, my lack of concern—for the fate of my birth mother. You say it's hardly my concern what happens to her if I just decide to go home to the parents who raised me. But that's the point, isn't it? You wanted me to care about her. That's why you put me in the same cell with her. You wanted this decision to be a struggle for me. And I've got to hand it to you: for the longest time, it was."

"It's nearly dawn," Dubessa said in a tone of utter boredom. "Are you going to keep jabbering much longer?"

"No, she's not," Mrs. Redmane said. "It is time for your decision, child."

"Not quite yet," Taylor said. "It's only *almost* dawn. You gave me until dawn to decide. I've still got a few minutes."

"A few minutes that will not make a whit of difference," Mrs. Redmane said.

"Yes, ma'am." Taylor bit her tongue—there was that "ma'am" again. She clutched her purse on her lap and brought her true name up into her consciousness once more.

Neunhirri. Neunhirri.

What Mrs. Redmane didn't know was that timing was everything. Every second mattered.

"Try to put yourself in my shoes," Taylor continued. "It's Sunday morning. This time last Thursday, I didn't have a clue about any of this." She gestured at the room around her, the tapestries, the glowing orbs of light, the butterflies. "That's a lot to think about in just three days. There's probably a million things I still don't know about Our Kind."

"Is this little story going anywhere, or are you just wasting our time?" Mrs. Redmane said.

"I'm only trying to obey your instructions, Chief Matron. You wanted my decision at dawn. And that's when you'll have it."

"Ah, then at last I'm in luck!" Mrs. Redmane said, gesturing toward the clock on the wall behind Taylor's head. "It's five fifty-seven exactly. The sun is rising as we speak, and I will hear your answer. Now."

Taylor's heart pounded.

"Well?"

She swallowed. She squeezed her purse tight in her lap.

Neunhirri. Neunhirri. Neunhirri.

"Miss Hellebore, we're waiting."

"I choose to leave!" Her words reverberated on the granite walls. "I will never again set foot in any rath of Arradherry."

"Do you swear it by your own true name?"

Taylor started. She studied the unflinching eyes of her grandmother. She bit her lips then nodded her assent. "I swear," she whispered.

"And what about your mother?" Mrs. Redmane said in a silky purr. She could barely keep herself from grinning ear to ear.

"You said it yourself, Chief Matron. What concern is that to me?"

"Very well," Mrs. Redmane said. "You are free to go—as soon as you say goodbye to your mother." She gestured to one of the guards, who bowed and left the room.

"Wait a minute!" Taylor said. "You never said anything about saying goodbye."

"I would have thought that was implied."

"Y-you only said I could leave if I wanted to. That what happened to my mother after that was none of my concern!"

"Indeed, it isn't," Mrs. Redmane said. "And I believe your dear mother should be informed that this is your decision."

Taylor's heart pounded. She was supposed to stall as long as she could, but it wasn't going to be enough.

"What if I wrote her a note?"

"News like this should be delivered in person, don't you think?" Mrs. Redmane was relishing every moment of Taylor's discomfort. She absentmindedly invited her cat up into her lap and began scratching its head.

"I was just thinking... A note would be a lot more... impersonal, don't you think?"

This got Mrs. Redmane thinking.

"It does seem more heartless, doesn't it?" she said with a grin.

"And she has a point," Dubessa added. "You didn't say anything about a personal goodbye, after all."

Taylor tried to read the body language between the two Matrons. They obviously hated each other. She wasn't sure she wanted her grandmother's enemy siding with her right now. The Chief Matron shifted in her seat.

"*I* will make the decisions around here," she said. "And I for one would like to see how Shanna Hellebore reacts when she learns her own flesh and blood has abandoned her."

Nuala raised her hand. "Cousin, don't you think—?"

"My decision stands," Mrs. Redmane said. "Ah, here she is now."

Taylor whipped around. Claudia stood at attention by the door. A changeling guard entered the room and hustled to the Triad's table. He whispered something in the Chief Matron's ear.

"What?" she said, suddenly alarmed. "Show me!"

The guard gestured to his comrade. This second guard opened the door once again and ushered in Shanna Hellebore.

Only it wasn't her.

She had the right size and shape and wore the right clothes, but the face was wrong: the ears were a bit too small and the eyes a bit too close together. As she walked forward, Taylor could see spots on her face where a wood grain pattern was barely visible.

"A fetch?" Nuala said.

"And not a very convincing one," Dubessa judged.

The floating orbs of fire brightened, just as Anya Redmane's face flushed pink. She rose from her seat, sending her cat to the floor. She gestured toward the stand-in that was meant to look like Shanna, and it burst into flames on the spot. It cracked open from the top of its head down to the middle of its torso and crumpled to the ground like a pile of kindling.

"Don't just stand there, you idiot! Find her!" The guard bowed and lumbered away. He and his partner left the room. Taylor tensed. She pulled her purse strap up on her shoulder.

"Who dares?" the Chief Matron thundered. "Who dares steal my prize?" She glared at Taylor, who lowered her eyes and concentrated on her true name.

"Surely you don't suspect the child, Anya," Dubessa said. "She's magically incompetent, stunted by years Topside with her pathetic deathling parents. Even producing a crude fetch like that one would take years of practice."

"We'll see how incompetent she is," Mrs. Redmane said. "Take her to the dungeons!"

"No!" Taylor said.

Mrs. Redmane furrowed her brow. Nuala clapped her hand over her mouth. Dubessa's eyes sparkled with wonder.

232

"You were very clear last night at dinner, Chief Matron. I could choose to stay or leave. Well, as I already told you...I choose to leave."

"Miss Hellebore, I hardly see how I can be expected to—"

"Of course you can't, Chief Matron, because the truth is, you don't care about family honor. You only care about revenge." Waves of presence emanated from the Chief Matron: strength, nobility, an almost irresistible magnetism. Taylor folded her hands in front of her on the table and concentrated on her true name as deeply as she could. She chose her words carefully.

"That's why you brought me here in the first place, ma'am" (There was that "ma'am" again!) "How does it restore your family's honor to kidnap an innocent human being...and make her pay for the sins of her parents—as if they even did anything wrong?"

Dubessa grinned so wide everybody in the room could see it.

Taylor saw it, and pressed on with renewed confidence. *I'm Laugher in Winter, Grandma. And before I'm done, you'll be the laughingstock of the whole wide Wonder.*

"Oh, you may say you're doing this for honor," she said aloud. "Heck, you might even think you mean it. But let's face it, Chief Matron, you just want to hurt somebody else as badly as you've been hurt. You made me a promise. You said if I decided to leave, I could go."

"But what about your mother?" Mrs. Redmane growled.

"*You* said that was none of my concern. It looks like somebody has misplaced one of your prisoners. So what? Why should that be any concern of mine?"

"Do you honestly dare to cross me, you little—?"

"I'm only following your exact words, Chief Matron. Now... unless you're going back on your promise..." she looked up to see how the three Matrons would react to those words. She was not disappointed. "I believe I'll be going now."

The two glared at each other for several tense seconds.

"Chief Matron," Dubessa said, "you asked Nuala and me to serve as witnesses to this little family squabble. I for one have seen enough. The child has decided to live as a Topsider." She pulled the clay figure away from in front of Mrs. Redmane and dug Taylor's tooth out of it. "She has fulfilled the terms of your bargain to the letter."

Mrs. Redmane eyed her rival like a wild animal. "Nuala?"

Nuala bowed her blonde head. "It's not the child's fault she was born, cousin. Let her go home."

Mrs. Redmane stood once more. "Fine," she said. "Claudia, see to it." And with that, she stalked from the room. The other Matrons followed close behind.

Taylor leaned back in her chair. She felt like she had just spent the last half hour trapped in an iron coffin. Her legs were shaking. Her whole body shivered.

"Come along, Miss Hellebore," Claudia said. She had come up behind Taylor so quietly she hadn't even noticed. She snatched Taylor's tooth from the other table and slipped it quietly into her pocket.

Still dazed, Taylor rose. Claudia offered an arm to steady her. Together, the two threaded through the rath—this time along a different set of corridors from the ones leading down to the dungeons.

Claudia said nothing, but one time when Taylor was sure they were completely alone, she winked at her.

Once they entered the last great chamber, Taylor recognized where they were. Claudia led her through the huge wooden doors, down the pink marble path, and into the ring of standing stones where she and Danny had first arrived at Dunhoughkey.

"I assume you don't know how to ring-travel?" Claudia asked.

Taylor shook her head.

"Then give me your hand." They clasped hands.

"Hold on to your true name," she said, "but at the same time, imagine where you want to go. Visualize every detail, every sight and sound. Every possible sensation."

Taylor nodded. She closed her eyes and imagined the stone circle outside the palisade at Tsuwatelda. She thought of Ayoka and the songs the nunnehi girl taught her. She salivated as she remembered the taste of sausages and corn chowder. In her mind's eye, she imagined Chief Tewa's compassionate face.

"Ready."

"Then let's not overstay our welcome, shall we?"

Claudia squeezed Taylor's hand. The two traded glances and stepped into the ring together.

Images flashed before Taylor's eyes—pastures and mountains and forests—as she and Claudia seemed to bounce from one ring to the next. She held on tight to Claudia's hand and focused her mind on her goal: the stone circle of Tsuwatelda.

Then there was the sensation of her heart dropping down into her stomach, like she was on an express elevator coming to a sudden stop. She reappeared into a downpour of icy rain. She pulled her leather jacket up over her head even though she was already drenched.

She looked around. There was no stone circle, no wooden palisade. Instead, Taylor found herself standing on top of a single huge boulder covered with strange markings. She had been here before.

She looked around. Four grotesque spriggans in rain ponchos stood guard over the spot, spears at the ready. One of them motioned for Taylor and Claudia to step down from the rock.

"Is there a problem?" Claudia asked. She didn't seem bothered by the rain or the wind.

"State your name," the spriggan commanded.

"I'm Claudia Fountain, and this is—"

"Taylor Smart!" Taylor said. Something told her it would be best not to mention the name "Hellebore."

"Come with me." The spriggans led them squishing across the grassy clearing toward the woods but stopped as soon as they were a good distance away from the rock.

Taylor recognized the place. She had been there Friday morning, after all. This was the rock the two spriggans from the Winter Court had been guarding, and from which she and Danny escaped on their way to Tsuwatelda.

Thunder echoed in the distance.

"I'm afraid I must ask again," Claudia said, "is there some kind of problem?"

"Judaculla Rock is temporarily closed by order of the Winter Court of Arradherry," the spriggan leader said. "We apologize for the inconvenience."

"Closed?" Claudia said. "I don't understand. We have no business with the Winter Court. And at any rate, Judaculla is neutral territory. My friend and I are trying to get to Tsuwatelda, in the Nunnehi Lands. If you would kindly—"

"Ma'am, if you'll just be patient, you can be on your way shortly. But right now...well, we're a little shorthanded. This will all be settled very soon."

"Settled? What will be settled?"

But the spriggan didn't have time to answer. As soon as Claudia asked her question, the sound of shouting erupted from deep in the woods. Angry voices yelled, "Get her!" There were flashes of blue and silver light. Lightning struck not too far away; smoke rose over the treetops, adding to the gloom of the cold, rainy morning.

The frenzied whinny of a horse punctuated the commotion.

Danny?

The spriggans peered into the woods, and so did Taylor and Claudia. Something was approaching: something huge.

Branches parted, and four more spriggans entered the clearing. Each was over ten feet tall, although they quickly shrunk down to their normal size. Only then did Taylor realize they had a prisoner.

"Let go of me, you oaf!" the young woman screamed. She kicked this way and that in her clunky black boots, but it didn't change anything. Her spriggan captor kept one arm around her waist and the other behind her neck. Her wild, black hair whipped around as she struggled. Her dangly silver earrings sparkled in the rain. Her short purple dress and black leather jacket—the twin of the one Taylor was wearing—were sopping wet.

"Shanna!"

Taylor froze with fear. Claudia put a hand on her back.

The spriggan leader turned toward her.

"Young lady," he said, "am I to take it you know this woman?"

Chapter 26

Redmane and Hellebore

The rain began to ease off as soon as the spriggans and their prisoner entered the clearing. The leader sent two of them back into the woods to track down the pooka who had been her traveling companion. Then he stepped away to contact someone on his seeing stone.

Shanna continued to kick and fight, but anyone could see it was hopeless. The spriggans were just too strong. Taylor resisted the urge to hide behind Claudia for safety.

The spriggan leader rejoined the group.

"He's coming himself," he said to his men. "We'll soon get to the bottom of this."

Then to Taylor he said, "I'm still waiting for your answer. Do you know this woman?"

"Sh-she...might be familiar. I *thought* I knew her. Now I'm... not exactly sure."

The spriggan leader scoffed.

"Now listen here, Mr..." Claudia said, a rumble of displeasure in her voice.

"Dingle. *Captain* Dingle, if you please."

"Fine. Whatever. As I explained before, we are on our way to Tsuwatelda. You may not have heard, but Tsuwatelda has no affiliation with any of the sídhe Courts. Do you understand?"

"Oh, I understand fine, lady," Captain Dingle said. "But the one thing doesn't necessarily follow the other. Just because *Tsuwatelda* doesn't have any truck with the sídhe Courts doesn't mean *you two* are neutral parties. Isn't that right, missy?"

He looked over his shoulder toward Shanna.

"Let go of me, you oaf!"

"What do you know about a pooka named Underhill?" Captain Dingle continued.

"That's a fairly common name for pookas, isn't it?" Claudia said. "Right up there with Cornbuck and Goodfellow." She was growing impatient, as Taylor could tell from the barely audible rumble of glamour in her voice, so much like her father. Taylor felt a growing sense of dread washing over her, setting shivers down her spine that had nothing to do with the cold morning wind.

Apparently, Captain Dingle was beginning to feel it, too. He took a half step backward.

Suddenly all eyes were drawn to Judaculla Rock, as a whirlwind of sparkling light fashioned above it.

"Now we'll sort all of this out," Captain Dingle said.

Out of the whirlwind leaped a figure on horseback. He wore a red fur-lined cloak that whipped about in the wind like his long, silvery hair, more white than blond. Above his beard his face was a mosaic of blue and black tattoos.

His horse was the color of the moon, with blazing red eyes. Behind him rode three others: a black-haired woman in flowing gray robes and two others—a man and a woman—in silvery armor and black surcoats. Behind them marched a contingent of musketeers, fair-haired and pointy-eared, with an angry gleam in their eyes.

"Primus!" Captain Dingle said.

The cloaked horseman took in the scene: Taylor and Claudia surrounded by spriggans, Shanna struggling in the arms of another one. The moment Taylor looked into his icy blue eyes, she felt his charismatic aura, just like Anya Redmane's. He must have been a Gentryman.

More than that, she had a pretty strong hunch he was part of the family.

He gazed upon the struggling figure.

"Well done, Captain," he said. "As soon as you and your men wrap up here, you may take the week off. Only, do come dine with my wife and me tonight at Cair Cullen." He nodded toward the woman at his side.

"It's an honor, sir."

The Primus dismounted and approached Shanna.

"You have tested my patience too many times," he said. "What do you have to say for yourself?"

"Let go of me you oaf!" she snarled.

"Children," the Primus said with a shrug. "What of the pooka, Captain? He didn't escape, did he?"

"I've sent two spriggans into the woods looking for him, sir. But he's a pretty slippery sprite."

"So I've been told."

"Begging your pardon, sir, but what do you want us to do with these two?"

The Primus looked at Claudia and then considered Taylor for several uncomfortable seconds. She wasn't sure what was going on behind his icy blue eyes, but it couldn't be good. After all, this was the fae who pulled her away from her own mother's arms when she was a baby.

Taylor looked over his shoulder toward the woman—her other grandmother, Mara Hellebore. She was as beautiful as her daughter, or would have been if not for her cold, murderous expression.

"I'm not of the habit of revisiting past mistakes," the Primus said. "And do not deceive yourself, young lady, you were most definitely a mistake—one for which we all have paid a price. I think it's high time we—"

"Crom Cornstack!"

The voice echoed across the clearing as another group of fae exited the portal.

The Primus swung around, mace in hand. His mounted retainers lowered their lances in the direction of the newcomers.

Anya Redmane and the other members of the Summer Triad strode across the grass in the company of a couple dozen armed guards: changelings, spriggans, and others Taylor didn't recognize: lithe creatures with flame-red hair and slit serpent eyes like a cymbee's.

Claudia put her arm around Taylor. Shanna kicked and screamed. Captain Dingle trained his musket on the approaching Matrons and their retainers. He nodded for his men to do the same, but several gave him worried looks instead. He had to grow four or five inches before he could convince them to comply.

"This is neutral ground, Anya," the Primus said. "Or have you forgotten?"

"You're a fine one to remind me, Crom," Mrs. Redmane said. "Posting guards, delaying travelers here. You'd think the Winter Court owned this portal."

"We're only taking care of our own business here," the Primus said. "This is no concern of yours."

"Yes, I see the sort of business you're up to, kidnapping miserable deathling brats."

"Deathling?" the Primus said with a bemused grin. "Is that what you think of your own granddaughter?"

"You won't pass her off onto me," Mrs. Redmane said. "She has made it abundantly clear she wants nothing more to do with me. Nor is she at liberty to go with you, for she has sworn to leave Arradherry for good. If you know a faraway hole where you can stick her, Crom, you're welcome to take *your* granddaughter—if you wish.

What a warm, loving family, Taylor thought.

"I don't see my counterpart anywhere," the Primus said. "Where is Belas Wakefire?"

"My husband the Summer Primus is attending to Court business," Dubessa Fairchild said. "It's nearly Beltane, after all. There is much to be done before the Summer Assize begins."

"Yes, and we mustn't fail to observe all the expected formalities of court," the Primus said with a sneer. "But what are you even doing here, Anya? Didn't you just say you've no further business with the mistake?"

"Hey, I'm standing right here, people," Taylor said.

"I haven't come for *her*," Mrs. Redmane said. She glanced toward Shanna's struggling figure.

"Ah, I see," the Primus said. "My former daughter somehow escaped your clutches, and you want her back, eh? Not finished tormenting her yet? Frankly, it doesn't surprise me she got away. You Summers never have run a particularly tight ship, have you?"

"I will have satisfaction," Mrs. Redmane said. "My family's honor—"

"Your miserable, washed-up family has no more honor than a pooka's."

Mrs. Redmane seethed. She made a dramatic gesture toward the Primus. A flash of golden light nearly knocked him to the ground, but he seemed to deflect whatever sort of spell she had cast.

Nuala gasped.

The Winter and Summer forces rushed toward each other. The two snake-eyed fae burst into flames. They became flying snakelike whips of fire, skirting overhead and strafing the Winter spriggans.

Claudia put her free arm in front of Taylor and turned her back on the explosion of violence.

Thunder once again began to roll. The rain, which had nearly ceased, became heavy once more. The mounted lancers reared their horses and lunged toward the Summer guards. The fair-haired musketeers shot a volley that filled the clearing with eery green smoke. A handful of Summer warriors fell stunned on the spot.

"Enough of this!" Dubessa cried. A sheet of fire erupted between the two parties. A Winter spriggan pulled away a blistered hand. The air was sick with the smell of melted plastic from his rain poncho.

A changeling howled in fright. The flaming snake-creatures landed beside their comrades and resumed their humanlike form.

"Anya, Crom," Dubessa said. "You're acting like children. Certainly there must be a way to resolve your conflicts like adults. Why not try to compromise?"

"I'll not surrender Shanna," the Primus said. "Snatching her was enough of an insult to *my* family's honor."

"I won't leave here without satisfaction!"

"Then take the brat," Mara Hellebore said, gesturing toward Taylor. "We certainly have no use for her."

"I can't," Mrs. Redmane said through gritted teeth.

"I'm afraid there are oaths involved, Chief Matron," Dubessa explained. "Anya has already sworn to let the mistake, as your husband calls her, go free."

Mara Hellebore began to giggle. "Seriously? That dull-witted little thing? How did she ever manage to pull that off? You really must be losing your touch, Anya."

"Right here," Taylor said. "I'm not invisible."

"I didn't come here to be insulted," Mrs. Redmane said.

You tell 'em, Grandma.

"Then make me an offer," the Primus said. "What would satisfy you, Anya? Anything? Anything at all?"

Mrs. Redmane glanced at the Winter Primus, then at his wife, and finally at Taylor. A smile began to stretch across her face—a fact that made Taylor suddenly very nervous.

"I will withdraw my men," she said, "and you may do as you please with your daughter."

"But?" Mara Hellebore said.

"But first, you must destroy the child. Destroy her, just as you destroyed my Aulberic."

"I see." Crom Cornstack brushed a hand across his beard.

"And I get to watch," Mrs. Redmane continued. "And so must she." She pointed to Shanna.

Taylor gasped. "Hey, we had a—"

"Now, wait just a minute," Claudia began.

"Deal!" the Primus said. He cracked his knuckles as he turned toward Taylor.

It dawned on Taylor that nobody had ever actually told her how Aulberic Redmane met his fate. She certainly wasn't curious to find out.

Okay, Danny, if you've got one more trick up your sleeve, now would be a great time!

Shanna grunted and squirmed in the arms of her spriggan captor.

"Let go of me, you oaf!"

Crom Cornstack was a giant next to Taylor. He looked down on her trembling form, and his icy eyes began to glow with unearthly light.

"Aaaah!"

The Primus spun around. All eyes turned upward as a spriggan soared over their heads into the clearing. Taylor wondered whether spriggans could fly. Her question was answered emphatically as he slammed into the grass face first.

"Ow," he said.

Someone—or something—hurled a second spriggan over the treetops. This one landed on his side and rolled over two or three times before coming to a stop beside Judaculla Rock itself. This one was knocked out cold.

"Put away your weapons!" a voice shouted. At the same time, a lone figure materialized at the edge of the wood: tall, dressed in buckskins and a beribboned cotton shirt dyed black and red, wearing a red headscarf, and armed with a flaming tomahawk.

It was Inali, Red Chief of Tsuwatelda.

"You've no business here, nayehi!" Mrs. Redmane said. "This is a family matter; it doesn't concern you."

"Is that so?" Chief Inali whistled, and suddenly a ring of nunnehi warriors circled the clearing. There must have been at least a hundred of them—maybe two hundred. Each held a bow or a spear or a tomahawk or a war club in his hands. Each had a look of unvarnished hatred on his face. Spriggans, changelings, and fae musketeers spun in every direction, not sure on whom to train their weapons. Each side looked to its own leaders, the Winters to their Primus and the Summers to their Chief Matron.

"Taylor Smart is a guest of the nunnehi of Tsuwatelda," Chief Inali said. "We are here to ensure her safe passage. Let us collect her, and we will be on our way."

"You dare interfere in the affairs of the daoine sídhe?" the Primus growled.

All eyes turned to Chief Inali. His own eyes smoldered with quiet fury.

"Yes," he said.

The standoff seemed to last forever, and Taylor could do nothing but watch. She glanced from Chief Inali to Mrs. Redmane to the Winter Primus and back again.

It was Dubessa who finally broke the silence.

"Chief Matron," she said. "Is this vendetta of yours really worth trouble with the nunnehi? Primus, you have your daughter back. Isn't that enough? Let the natives have the child if they want her so badly."

The Primus shifted uncomfortably. He took another glance at the forces arrayed against them.

"Chief Matron?" Dubessa said.

Mrs. Redmane looked at Taylor with an expression that could have curdled milk. Slowly and deliberately she said, "I withdraw my request. If the misbegotten child wants to go off with the savages, then let her."

Taylor exhaled, but her attention shifted immediately to the Winter Primus.

He glanced at his fighters and gave a subtle nod of the head. He mounted his horse.

"Next time, Anya, I fear you won't have interlopers to protect you from your own hot-headedness."

"Next time, Crom, I will not hesitate to blast you where you stand."

"Until then," he said. He made a clicking noise with his tongue and turned his horse toward Judaculla Rock. The swirling lights arose again out of nowhere, and one by one the members of the Winter Court passed through the portal.

"What a fine job you've done of humiliating yourself today, Anya," Dubessa said. "And not only in front of the Winter Court, but in front of common sprites as well—no offense, dear." She bowed toward Chief Inali. He didn't acknowledge her words or her gesture.

Without another word, Dubessa strolled toward the portal. The spriggans, changelings, and weird fire-snake-creatures followed.

Nuala hesitated, looking first at Mrs. Redmane and then at the procession of fae marching into the magical mist.

"Are you coming, cousin?" she asked.

Mrs. Redmane had not taken her eyes of Taylor since the Winters had left.

"Cousin?"

"Just remember your part of the bargain, Selena Hellebore," Mrs. Redmane said. "If so much as your shadow ever darkens any rath of Arradherry...you will wish your life had ended today. And that, child, is my solemn promise."

The power of Mrs. Redmane's presence nearly overwhelmed her, but as much as she wanted to crumple to the ground, she kept repeating her true name. Its magic steeled her heart.

"Claudia, I expect Miss Hellebore is in good hands. You may come with me."

"Yes, Chief Matron." Claudia flashed Taylor a subtle smile. She shook her hand, quietly passing her a small metal jar. She took off after Mrs. Redmane.

Chief Inali approached.

"Thank you," Taylor said. "But how did you know?"

"Where to find you? Your friend Mr. Underhill called for us."

"Danny? Where is he?"

"Woof!" came the answer. A lanky, black dog loped across the clearing, its sulfurous eyes blazing. In mid-stride, it took on human (well, nearly human) form. Danny opened his arms and Taylor hugged him so tight he had to gasp for air.

"You did it!" she said, grinning from ear to ear. "You really did it!"

"Was there ever any doubt?"

"Actually...YES! But you did it!"

"Miss Smart," Chief Inali said, "I am grateful to see you again. I only wish we could have done more for your mother."

"Oh," Taylor said, her face suddenly serious.

"I will, of course, recommend a rescue mission. We'll find your mother, Miss Smart, and we'll bring her back to you."

"That's very kind of you, Chief Inali," Taylor said. "But there's something you may want to see first."

She reached into her bag.

"I never thought this would work," she said.

"Like I told you," Danny said, "I'm pretty much the best there is at what I do." Danny pulled a knife from his own pack and started to trace a circle in the dirt.

Taylor produced a tiny turnip, no bigger than a purple, splotchy baseball, and handed it to Danny. The pooka set it on the ground at the center of his conjuring circle.

"Yeah, but your fetches need a lot of work."

"Hey, you try making two of them in a single night! I barely had enough magic to make the second one animate at all." He gestured toward the nearest portion of the circle, slowly exhaling.

With a wink, he stooped down and began waving his hands over the turnip. Silver mist began to emanate from his fingertips. He muttered some sort of incantation under his breath.

"Even your first one—the one you supposedly spent half the night on—was a little glitchy," Taylor said. "All she could ever say was 'Let go of me, you oaf!'"

The light began to dawn in Chief Inali's eyes.

"You don't mean..."

"I certainly do!" Taylor exulted.

As if on cue, the turnip at their feet began to glow and expand. It sprouted legs, arms, and a head topped with a wild mop of jet-black hair. At the same time, its color darkened: black high-top tennis shoes, black miniskirt, blood red blouse with a zebra-print pattern, tattoos, studded dog collar, nose stud, and dangly earrings.

Taylor smiled and threw her arms around her birth mother.

Chief Inali stood there with his mouth open.

Chapter 27

Home

There were no further delays on the way to Tsuwatelda. As soon as Taylor, Danny, and Shanna materialized in the stone circle, a welcoming party that must have included half the village swarmed around them, cheering and clapping. Danny threw back his head and laughed into the sky.

We made it!

On the way into the village, Taylor opened the metal jar Claudia had given her. It contained a single tooth, the twin of the one Taylor had lost. Chief Kalahu explained that it was probably the tooth of a panti': a magical creature whose fine teeth made perfect replacements for those of fae and Topsiders alike. He helped her guide it into place. Almost immediately, the new tooth began to take root.

Danny sat with Taylor and Shanna as guests of honor at a luncheon in the home of Chief Tewa. The other Chiefs were there, and many others crowded around the doorways to hear the story of Danny and Taylor's adventures. Danny drank it all in with relish. It wasn't often a pooka got this much praise for playing his tricks.

When they got to the part about both switching out Shanna and freeing Taylor, Danny could barely sit still. He told his side of the story like an old warrior enthralling awestruck recruits with tales of derring-do.

"You see," he said, "Knowledge Is Power. If I didn't have somebody on the inside feeding me information, none of this would have worked. My...associate...kept me in the loop. And at the end...this person...was able to prepare Shanna for what was coming."

"Yes, your associate was—and is—a valuable asset," Chief Kalahu said.

Taylor honed in on the Medicine Chief like a laser beam. "Y-you know about Cl—?"

"It would be best not to mention names," Chief Tewa said. "If we have an agent inside the Summer Court, we must also accept the possibility that they have an agent at Tsuwatelda. But yes, the person of which Danny speaks is a true treasure."

"You can say that again," Danny said. Claudia Fountain always made things interesting, that's for sure.

"But how did you do it?" Chief Tewa asked. "Inali says you used two separate fetches?"

"Yeah," Danny said. "I sort of had to improvise that part. Going in, I figured I'd handle this like any other switch-out: leave a fetch in Shanna's place and sneak out a back way. Shoot, it might have been weeks before anybody realized the real Shanna was gone."

"Unfortunately, Taylor made that impossible," Shanna said.

"Right," Danny said. "As soon as I found out she was Shanna's daughter, I had my doubts. I mean, what good would it do to rescue one Hellebore and leave another one in her place? That's when...my associate...suggested I make two fetches: one for Shanna, one for Taylor."

"But that's not what you did," Chief Inali said.

"No, we had to scrap that plan, too. When Taylor came back from visiting Mrs. Redmane, we found out she was supposed to announce her decision at sunrise the next day. Was she going to stay or go? Well, I had hoped to be long gone by then—with both of them. You see, Timing Is Everything when it comes to a switch out. The more miles I can put between me and the switchee's family before anybody even knows what's going on, the better."

"Mrs. Redmane messed that up big time," Taylor said.

"But then Taylor realized something. Since she knew Shanna would already be safe, she was free to tell Mrs. Redmane that she had decided to leave."

"Right," Taylor jumped in. "Shanna would never be in danger because she wouldn't even be there. She'd be miles away."

"It may not have been dangerous for Shanna, but what about you?" Tewa's daughter—Ayoka's mother—said. She clutched Ayoka tightly. "Wasn't that plan risky for you?"

"Maybe," Taylor agreed. "But I had already learned a thing or two about Our Kind and keeping promises. I held Mrs. Redmane to her exact words. I don't think there was much she could do about that. Plus, there was another member of the Triad that I think was pulling for me. The black-haired one."

"Dubessa Fairchild," Chief Tewa said. "The Fairchilds and the Redmanes have struggled for control of the Summer Court for forty years. It doesn't surprise me the wife of the Primus would try to undermine Mrs. Redmane's standing."

"And the sweet part," Danny continued, "is that Taylor kept Mrs. Redmane's mind on her and off of Shanna. You always want to Create a Diversion on a switch-out."

"Only this time, we had two," Taylor added. "I was the first, but Danny and the other fetch made the second. That part was Danny's idea. He figured we could give them a fake Shanna to chase while I took the real one to Tsuwatelda in my purse!"

"All the time you were sparring with Mrs. Redmane, Shanna was right there with you?" Ayoka said.

"So they tell me," Shanna said. "You can't see or hear anything when you're a turnip."

"It's a very difficult form of transmutation," Chief Kalahu said. "You're fortunate your associate was familiar with the procedure, Mr. Underhill."

"Yeah, but reversing the spell is pretty easy if you know what you're doing."

"And, of course," Taylor said, "that leads us to your fourth rule. Doesn't it, Danny?"

"Y-yeah," Danny said. He was both surprised and perturbed that Taylor would remember there were four rules. "Erm...Eat Lots of Sweets, 'cause...you know...pulling a switch-out burns up a lot of magic.... You gotta be ready for anything."

Taylor smirked and rolled her eyes. She wasn't buying it for a minute.

"Hey, somebody pass the cornbread?"

Somebody asked Taylor a question. Danny thanked his lucky stars the topic of conversation shifted.

A minute later, Taylor spoke again. "I do have one question I hope someone can answer. What's going to happen when Shanna's parents figure out they've taken home a fetch?"

The conversation died down as everyone considered the possibilities.

"They may already know," Chief Inali said, "although if they do, they're not admitting it. No one is tweeting about it, at any rate."

"I doubt they'll ever let on," Chief Tewa said. "Can you imagine how they'd feel if word got out they had been fooled like that?"

"They'd never live it down," Danny said with a grin.

"So it's not likely they'll try to gain revenge," Chief Tewa continued. "Although obviously it wouldn't do for your mother to announce her whereabouts to the world." He turned to face Shanna. "I hope you will accept our offer of sanctuary at Tsuwatelda. We always keep houses built for the next travelers who may come our way. One of them can be yours if you want."

"I would like that very much, Chief Tewa," Shanna said. "And I would also like it if...if Taylor could visit me every once in a while. If she wants to, of course."

"I do," Taylor said.

"It can be arranged," Chief Tewa said.

"But...right now," Taylor said, "I'd really like to go home."

As soon as lunch was over, Taylor did just that. She said her goodbyes to her nunnehi friends and to her birth mother. All three chiefs, Ayoka and her parents, Shanna, Ikegwa and his family, and many others joined the procession to escort her to the stone circle.

Danny smiled as the whirlwind arose. He offered Taylor his arm.

"I got this," she said, waving him off. She filled her mind with thoughts of home: her parents and their comfortable little house beside the woods, Jill Matthews, the street where she lived, the smell of her mom's home cooking, the taste of apples from the tree in her back yard. From deep within her welled up her true name, sliding into and around all of those familiar images, filling her with confidence.

She offered her arm to Danny.

The two of them vanished into the ring. When they came out on the other side, Danny offered her a ride home on horseback. They galloped along under a deep cover of glamour until Taylor suddenly yelled, "Stop!"

She slid off Danny's back as the pooka resumed the shape of a geeky teenager.

"What's the matter?"

"Something I need to check out," she said. They were only a few blocks from Taylor's house. On the corner was a gas station with a convenience store and a fast-food place attached. Without another word, she walked toward the door.

"You can't still be hungry! I'm stuffed!"

Taylor stepped up to the counter and ordered a small fries— the cheapest thing on the menu.

"I'm not hungry at all," she said. "But I have to know...." Her voice cracked a little. "I have to know...if I can go home."

"Oh, because of all the faery food you've been eating," Danny said. "Like that girl you told me about. Per-stephanie?"

"Persephone." Taylor counted out change to pay for the French fries. She clutched the tiny paper sack to her chest as she walked away from the counter.

255

"I-I don't think you need to worry," Danny said. "Like I told you, it's changelings that usually have problems with Topside food. Not Our Kind."

"But you also told me buying in would change me. I just... need to know what I've gotten myself into." She popped a French fry in her mouth. She chewed deliberately—and deliberatively. How would her body react to the Topside food?

"Well?"

"This place always uses too much salt," she said. "But the fries are still pretty good!" She smiled and ate another one.

"That's great, Taylor," Danny said. "Let's get you home."

They turned toward the door just as a family was entering: pleasant, round faced mom; tall, athletic-looking dad; two kids, a boy and a girl both about Taylor's age.

Taylor's jaw nearly hit the floor.

"Jill?"

The girl gasped. "Taylor! I didn't expect to see you here." She eyed Danny with suspicion and pulled Taylor off to one side while her mom and brother found a table and her dad stepped up to the counter.

"Since when do you hang out with Danny Underhill?" Jill whispered.

"It's kind of a long story." Taylor glanced over at William and Mrs. Matthews. William gave her a stupid grin and a weak little wave.

"Well, maybe you better tell me," Jill said. "Something's going on. I'm your best friend; you want to let me in on it?"

"W-what makes you think something's going on?"

"Oh, come on, girl! After the way you were acting at school Friday—not to mention the way you were acting at Jared's party last night. Plus, you've been wearing makeup, being all polite to your teachers, and what have you been doing to your hair?"

"What do you mean?"

"Last night it was almost blonde. Nobody else seemed to notice, but I sure did. But now, it's back to its usual color. What's up with that?"

"You noticed that, huh?" Taylor said. She remembered what Danny had told her about twins and Second Sight. "D-did William notice anything?"

Jill frowned. "Girl, I love you like a sister, but I swear, if you start getting interested in my brother—"

"No!" Taylor said. "It's nothing like that. I-I just wondered... never mind. So...good party, huh?"

Jill grinned a wicked grin. "I wonder what Shelby Crowthers is going to say about those kids she invited to her little get-together that showed up at Jared's instead."

"Y-yeah. That was pretty sweet," Taylor bluffed.

"I can't wait till school tomorrow. Last night is going to send a ripple through the entire Shelbyverse. I guess I can't be too upset about your new look and your new personality and all if at least it ruins Shelby's life."

"I do what I can."

"Jill, I have your milkshake," her dad called.

"Be right there, Dad." She turned back to Taylor. "We are definitely going to talk about this," she said.

"I promise," Taylor said. *As soon as I figure out what to say.* "Enjoy your milkshake. I'll see you tomorrow."

Taylor and Danny walked the rest of the way home. Before she knew it, Taylor was crouching, glamoured, just beyond the fence in her backyard.

Bryn skipped down to meet them. She looked for all the world like Taylor herself, only somehow more sure of herself. Like she was comfortable with who she was.

Taylor held onto her true name. She realized she might not look awfully different from the imposter heading her way.

"Everything turn out all right?" Bryn asked.

"I think so," Taylor said. "It was...educational."

"How'd everything go here?" Danny said.

"Not bad," Bryn said. "Jared's party was awesome. You've got some really cool friends, Taylor. And some cute ones, too!"

"D-don't tell me, I don't want to know!" Taylor said. At least, she would rather hear it from Jill.

"Well, suit yourself... Oh, just so you know: I only gave your cell number to Jared. Don't look at me like that, Danny! I swear I wasn't flirting or anything! We were just making conversation."

Taylor's heart bounced around in her ribcage. "You didn't."

"He's a really sweet boy, by the way. Great sense of humor. You'd make a cute couple. If he ever gets up the nerve to ask you out, I'd take him up on it if I were you."

Taylor felt a headache coming on. "I thought Danny told you..."

"Oh, what does Danny know about these things? Of course, on the other hand, you might want to give William Matthews another chance...."

"What do you mean, 'another' chance? There was never a first chance!"

"Well, whose fault is that?" Bryn said. "He really does like you, by the way. You should have seen the way he kept looking at me—or you, I suppose—while I was talking to Jared and Tom and the other boys."

"Danny, take me back to Tsuwatelda..."

"No can do, Taylor," he said. "You're gonna have to work this out yourself. Come on, Bryn. Let's let Taylor go home where she belongs."

"First let me give her something," Bryn said. She reached in her jeans pocket and pulled out a stone about the size of a pendant, roughly triangular in shape, smooth as ice and black as coal. It had a natural hole straight through the middle. "I worked on it a little this morning."

"It's very nice," Taylor said. Bryn gave her a quick lesson on how to use her seeing stone to call her friends in the Wonder.

"Bryn, can you go on ahead?" Taylor asked. "I need to ask Danny something."

"Sure thing, Taylor. It's been nice meeting you. I hope you have a great life. Bye!"

Bryn let go of the illusion that she was Taylor. In the blink of an eye, she was her normal pointy-eared self. She hopped over the fence and slipped into the woods, her tail swishing happily behind her.

"I've got one more question."

"Shoot."

"Your fourth rule about switch-outs."

Danny stared at her for the longest time.

"You really want to know?"

She nodded.

Danny sighed.

"I've been thinking about that one lately. I ain't sure I trust it no more."

"Yes?"

"It's Nothing Personal."

"What?"

"That's the fourth rule: It's Nothing Personal. The last thing you want to do is start to have feelings for your switchees. It makes you sloppy. It makes you take unnecessary risks. But like I said, I'm gonna have to think about that one some more. 'Cause you gotta treat people like people. If I didn't think I was doing them any good...I never woulda gotten into this business."

"So, make a new rule. Sometimes It's Personal."

"Sometimes it is."

Danny helped Taylor climb over the fence into her backyard.

"What are you going to do now that you don't work for Mrs. Redmane any more?"

"I thought I might go see a little bit of the world. Who knows where I may turn up?" He offered her his hand. "Good bye, Taylor."

"Good bye, Danny."

He gave her one last impish grin as he blinked away in a flash of golden dust.

Taylor walked toward her house. As a smile widened across her face, she started to run.

Made in the USA
Columbia, SC
08 April 2019